THE BOOKSELLER

THE
BOOKSELLER

Matt Cohen

VINTAGE CANADA
A Division of Random House of Canada Limited

FIRST VINTAGE CANADA EDITION, 1997

The author would like to thank Beth Appledoorn
and Susan Sandler, formerly of Longhouse Books, Toronto,
Brian Spence of Abbey Books, Paris, and Stuart Mackinnon of
the University of Waterloo Library for their generous help during
the "research" phase of this novel. The author would also like to
acknowledge the financial assistance of the Canada Council.

Canadian Cataloguing in Publication Data

Cohen, Matt
The bookseller

ISBN 0-676-97096-6

I. Title.

PS8555.O4B66 1997 C813'.54 C97-930638-8
PR9199.3.C63B66 1997

Printed and bound in the United States of America

10 9 8 7 6 5 4 3 2 1

for P. A.

ONE

OCTOBER LIGHT. The long thin knife of memory. October light gets right inside and gives you that little twist. Take an afternoon in late October, an afternoon when the last light of summer is slanting over the fallen leaves, the cold damp green of October grass. Today, for example. This afternoon I drove to the cemetery. At the grave I scraped away the weeds and unwanted crab-grass that had sprung up since my last visit. Inspected the flowers for frost damage. Shed a few tears.

Then I came back to the apartment. By now the store can run itself. Nothing to prevent me parking the car in the garage, climbing the metal fire-stairs to the kitchen door of my apartment. It is October, after all. The last month before the snow begins. By the end of this month I will have planted new bulbs by the headstone, pulled out the withered annuals. Winter is coming, time for the old bones to freeze again, time for the grave to be smooth and sealed over.

October is the anniversary month of the bad things that happened. My month for remembering.

Memory must be in the air for everyone. This morning I came out from the back room to discover Nicko Ross standing beside a remainders table. His face bigger than it used to be, close-scraped jowls red with wind and maybe a few too many drinks. Fake porkpie hat pushed back, wearing a trenchcoat with a dozen little belts and buckles, rolling a toothpick in his big white teeth. "Detective Ross, Special Affairs," Nicko announced, sticking out his big hand as though introducing himself for the first time. "We've been getting some complaints that store owners along Bloor Street are being asked for protection money. Happens all the time. Just thought I'd come by and see if you've had any problems."

"Not until now."

Nicko grabbed my arm and led me to the side where no one could hear him. "You're lucky to be alive, you little shit." His red face turned redder and he started giving my arm the old squeeze treatment. Suddenly he dropped his hand and shrugged. "Just like your brother. More balls than brains." He rolled his toothpick some more, turned his back on me and walked out of the store.

Now I am facing a glowing blue screen. Outside the last light fades over a familiar tangle of trees, the alleyway, cars, bicycles chained to fences. Inside the fan whirs. The screen glows. The microbrain waits. After all these years the silence is broken, or at least collapsed. Perhaps it was seeing Nicko Ross. Or the strange feeling I had, standing over the grave, that those events of which I never speak, those events I thought transformed me from one person to another, have now started to slip away as though they belong to some other life, a life I might soon forget.

Henry, my older brother. I cannot now, any more than I ever could, say what Henry was to me. I cannot even claim to know where it is I end and Henry begins. Better to start with the image I always have of Henry.

Henry fighting out of the crouch, head cocked to one side, blue eyes squinting, licks of blond hair sticking through the holes of his helmet. Our father was Henry's trainer. He started taking us to the gym after my mother left. Male solidarity. Though our father did not have the athletic look. In his store uniform of white shirt and black trousers he was the perfect imitation, as my mother once said, of a soft-boiled egg waiting to be attacked by a spoon.

Henry was twelve years old, starting to fight three-rounders. I was allowed to be in his corner, and between rounds I would put the yellow sponge on my brother's chest and squeeze water down his belly and ribs.

The first fight Henry jabbed his way to victory. Afterwards he jumped up and down in the ring, his skinny arms held high, a cocky bantam rooster's dance. The second fight he got knocked down in the second round. I couldn't believe it. My big brother was lying flat on his back, arms stuck out as though he were crucified. The other fighter turned away from him, waiting for the count to be over. But he didn't know Henry. As soon as he wasn't looking Henry scrambled to his feet yelling *fuckface* in a voice that over the years has changed, in memory, to the gritty smokestained voice of Henry grown up. Then Henry jumped on his opponent's back, pummelling the top of his helmet while they fell to the canvas, where Henry kept pounding him until the referee pulled him off.

Henry was always trying to make me spar with him. "Come on," he'd say, pushing at me and jabbing. "Fight back." But I knew raising my hands would just be an excuse for Henry to knock me down. Not that he needed one. One day, in the kitchen of the apartment, Henry rubbed his hands together and said, "Look, Dungo, we start now." Our father was at the store as usual. We were supposed to be doing our homework.

"Come on," Henry said. He threw his books down and flicked out a jab. Another. I backed away. "Come on." Henry went down into a crouch, pushed back his blond hair. I wished I could scream out *fuckface* and jump my older brother, ride him to the floor. Henry was closer now, his knuckles grazing my jaw. "Crouch," Henry said. "Get those arms out." This time he flicked my cheeks with his fingers. Then he slapped me. I put up my arms. Henry tapped them lightly, dancing. I retreated.

We were in the living room, Henry jabbing, blue eyes squinting. I, reluctantly, had my arms up. I was circling backwards, slowly, round and round the walls of the room. I tried a jab of my own. Another. On the third attempt I got past Henry's arm and my fist encountered Henry's nose. A soft squishing feeling. Henry shook his head. "Fuckface," he said. But as Henry wound up for his Sunday punch I saw an opening. I moved inside to wrap my arms around him. Too late I realized Henry had me in his sights. His left jab caught me in the jaw, knocking me over a chair and into the wall.

By the time our father came home I had washed the dishes from the supper Henry had penitently cooked and had stopped crying. But I hadn't been able to eat. Instead, while Henry was in the bathroom, I threw the food in the garbage. And that whole night I lay in bed, every pulse sending flames through my face and skull.

In the morning I found some aspirins and could open my mouth enough to drink. Twenty years later a dentist asked me if my jaw had ever been dislocated. Even now my jaw sometimes starts slipping in and out of its socket and I have to go a day without eating or talking.

My father trained Henry and Henry trained me. That was the chain of command. I resisted as long as I could, but then, as was always the way with me and Henry, I gave in. My father let Henry take me to the basement of a local school where once a week I and other kids, terrified by their fathers or older brothers, circled each other warily, agreeing without having to speak that we'd go easy on each other. Sometimes someone would hit me so hard I'd be surprised and lash back. "Killer instinct," Henry would congratulate me after. But it was just reflex. Once I was pounded so hard I actually knocked my opponent down. It was a mistake.

"Killer instinct!" Henry pummelled my back gleefully. "We got to get you downtown! Get you some competition! These guys are patsies!"

That was when we were still living at home. "We got to get you downtown" became Henry's chorus. Boxing was Henry's game. He was the coach, I the prize student. But Henry was the one who should have kept fighting. When we showed up at the downtown gym everyone turned to Henry because Henry was the one who looked tough. "Got a guy here," Henry announced. When there was no reaction he found his way to the locker room and after a while he had me out working on the speed bag. Rat-tat-tat. The speed bag was the one place I looked good. Fast hands. I probably could have been a great Ping-Pong player but that wasn't the image Henry was chasing. He wanted to be leaning down, in the corner, a bit of blood—my blood—on his towel—screaming out instructions over the noise of thousands. "Hit 'im, Dungo! Keep it low! Keep it up! Duck! Jab!" Henry would have made a great sports announcer. But instead, there we were, me working the speed bag and Henry watching, his head cocked knowingly to one side, cigarette dangling out of his mouth. Rat-tat-tat, I could make that bag jump, but right then and there, looking at the other fighters, I knew I was out of place. I was going to have to go into the ring with a couple of them, get hurt badly enough that I'd have an excuse to quit. Or else face down Henry, which seemed a lot more dangerous.

My father was relieved to see us spending time together. "Men can trust each other," he would say. That was after my mother left. My mother would never have allowed us to box. Getting into the spirit of things my father would tell us stories about when he was single, single on purpose, the years after the war when he went to university on the veterans' program.

"I had a mixed-blood partner back then," my father used to begin. During that time, among other jobs, he worked for a fishing guide in northern Quebec. "He always told the English customers his name was Dungo Merde. 'Mr. Merde,' they'd say, 'can you bait our hooks for us?' 'My father's name is *Monsieur* Merde,' Dungo would say. 'Just call me Merde. Or Dungo.'"

"Dungo Merde," Henry shouted. "Shit. *Shit.* That's what I'm going to call you, partner. Dungo!"

When I was a child my mother had dark hair, smooth sallow skin, and although she was not so fat as my father, she always seemed slightly heavy, slow moving in a way that was both lazy and somehow selfish. As though her body was announcing itself a ship of state not to be disturbed. My mother did not like to be disturbed. She was always reminding us that as babies we had kept her up at night. She said it in a way that made it clear she hadn't forgiven us.

In the afternoons she baked. Eventually I realized she baked, she ate, she slept because she was unhappy. But at the time I liked the way the kitchen smelled when we came home from school. Often she would be sitting at the table, her sleeves rolled up. I remember the first day I noticed how the fine dark hairs on the backs of her hands and her arms had been dusted white by flour.

She had her own way of eating cookies. Slow and deliberate, not cramming them down the way Henry and I did but thoughtfully chewing each one, she would carefully lick the crumbs from her lips before her heavy arm swung out and her hand dropped to the plate. In those days my father would have to re-size her rings when she put on weight. But she was vain about her hands. Her nails were shaped and smoothly coated with pearl-coloured polish. In my mother's mouth, "chipped nails" was a serious insult. She and the neighbour across the hall did each other's nails. The neighbour worked part-time at a cosmetics counter in a downtown department store, and for two or three years before she left my father, my mother also worked there.

That was where she met Bill. He was down in the city buying Christmas presents and, as he told Henry and me one summer evening, "I bought this scarf from your mother and when she tried it on I thought how much better it looked on her than the place where it was going. She must have thought I had a dozen girlfriends, the way I kept coming round there. Until finally I told her the truth." He would have been certain this declaration of the sincerity of his love for our mother would reassure or appease us. But while my mother emitted the obligatory blushes and giggles, I was left with the picture of my father trudging off to work while my mother painted her face and her nails, gossiped, then took a taxi to her store where she entertained men who pretended to be buying presents for their wives or girlfriends.

After my mother left, my father drank for a year. He drank each evening until he was too drunk to get up from his chair. There he would fall asleep. In the morning, when we got up to get ready for school, Henry and I would find my father awake, still paralysed, sitting in exactly the same position he'd been in when we went to bed the night before.

"Morning, boys," he'd say.

He'd heave himself forward, go to the kitchen and make himself coffee. By the time the percolator had finished he would have shaved and changed. Then he would drop us off at school before going down to the shop to stand behind the counter.

Bill became our stepfather. He used to work at Meaghers' Marina, which was in Pikéville, a small tourist town north of Toronto.

You looked at Bill and you thought "sailor". He was a stocky strong-faced man with a big white smile that showed a gold molar. Around his neck he wore a gold chain with an anchor. His silvery hair had a red sunburned part that grew wider every year. In his most vigorous days he had a supply of white short-sleeved shirts decorated with waves, boats, anchors, seagulls in flight, etc. These showed his tanned arms, complete with tattoos on the biceps, and were unbuttoned enough so that as he ferried customers around the lake in his launch, his shirt billowed out and you could see his big tanned belly.

For two years Henry and I were sent to Pikeville for the summer. My father would take us down to the train station and buy us sandwiches and juice for nourishment on the way. The mother who met us at the other end was not the mother who'd left us behind. She looked like her old pictures, the ones from before she married my father: slim, hair tousled by the wind, smile directed coyly at her man. Our stepfather called us "the boys" or "boys" or, when there was only one of us, "boy". My mother had said he would like us to call him "Bill", the way she and everyone else did; or "Pops", which was, she said, what he had called his father and would have wanted his own children to call him if she had been able to give him any.

When she got to "if I'd been able to give him", she threw us a certain look. Why did you have to be born? she was asking. Making it clear our existence had kept her from running off with Bill years earlier, early enough that she could have had given him a brood of children to call him "Pops".

The summers we went to Pikeville we also worked at Meaghers' Marina. They had a little gas station and repair shop both for cars and for the boats they used and sold. Before he could be assigned any other work, Henry was in the garage, up to his elbows in grease. While Henry made the motors of Pikeville sing sweet songs, I pumped gas, looked at the sky, counted birds.

At the end of the first summer my mother took us to the train and said, "I'll miss you." Then: "Bill asked me to give you this." From her purse she took white envelopes and pressed them into our hands. "Don't open them until you get home." Inside each was a hundred-dollar bill, crisp and fresh, with the slightly off-centre mint smell of Captain Bill's aftershave lotion.

Every night after supper, during that first summer in Pikeville, Henry and I would walk from the house to the main street. "Action," Henry would say. Some evenings we would go into the pool hall. Henry would buy cigarettes, pull his jeans halfway down his hips, do his best to look like a tough kid from Toronto. But at seventeen, he looked barely twelve. That first summer he was so short he was wearing his jeans rolled up. With his smooth cheeks, blond hair, baby blue eyes, he worked his way around the pool table, his shining child's forehead furrowed in concentration, a cigarette drooping comically from his mouth.

After the pool hall we would sometimes go to the movie theatre, but they usually refused us if it was after nine o'clock. "Tin-pot place," Henry would mutter. That year his voice always broke when he didn't want it to.

The second summer, when we came back, Henry had grown. He was still short but he didn't look like a child any more. Captain Bill was with my mother at the station. He hit Henry admiringly on the shoulder—"I should've decked the bastard," Henry told me after—and said that the girls had better watch out.

Eventually Henry turned into the older brother, adult version: a small well-kept man, hair closely trimmed, the skin around his nose and eyes suitably careworn. Only his eyes gave him away: they remained that frightening pale blue, heavy-lidded with fatigue and all the strange and unnameable burdens Henry carried.

But in those early summers Henry was wiry and electric. The

tiny dynamo quarterback who could wobble the ball to targets half a field away. Intense, high-strung, always searching for an excuse to explode.

When Henry asked if he could try for his driver's licence, Bill gave him a couple of lessons, then took him for his test. Somehow Henry passed. That night he asked for the car and off we went, Henry and I, sitting like newly crowned princes in the front seat of Bill's snow white Mercury.

We cruised slowly down the main street. At the edge of town Henry put his foot to the floor. I slammed back into the seat as the car leapt forward, flashing past the used-car lots, the tractor dealership, the fast-food joints. By the time Henry eased up we were on a small blacktop road cutting through the rolling farmland we had seen from the train.

When we came to a crossroads with a gas station, Henry veered off the road and skidded to a stop. "Cigarettes," Henry said.

A girl was standing beside her bicycle, wiping the gravel off her legs and glaring at us.

"Sorry," I said.

"I'm getting smokes," Henry announced, and swaggered into the store, twirling the keys around his finger.

The girl had a knapsack on her back and her face was flushed, but she wasn't saying anything. It was twilight and I was wondering if the light was tinting her cheeks or if she really was angry.

"I'm sorry," I said again. "He's not much of a driver."

"I'll say," said the girl. She had dark blond hair and her eyes shone in the light.

"Live around here?"

"That's right," she said. Then she climbed onto her bicycle and pedalled away.

Henry came out of the store and stood on the steps admiring her. "Some ass," he commented.

We drove back to town slowly. Henry had found the Beach Boys on the radio and was practising smoking. We kept having to stop in order to put out the sparks before they burned holes in the red leather upholstery of Bill's Mercury. When we got home, Henry made me walk around the block with him while he ate a roll of peppermint Lifesavers.

Every night that week we went driving. At first along the concession roads that cross-hatched the farming country. Then we discovered a big field at the edge of town with a long strip of beach where teenagers and tourists gathered around a fire every night.

We would stand at the edge of the crowd, not having the courage to talk and no one talking to us, while in the centre flames from the big driftwood fire shot into the sky and people drank beer and listened to transistor radios.

That Saturday night Captain Bill and my mother took the Mercury.

Henry and I were left at home. The previous summer, carless, we would make our tour of the main street, stop where it ended—a big cement promontory at the lake where there was a war memorial and a little park where parents brought their children to swim—then come back to watch television and maybe Henry would take one of Captain Bill's beers to see if he would say anything. He never did.

On this night, as always, we walked down the main street. A few older couples were strolling hand in hand, talking about the weather and the breeze off the water.

"Dead," Henry said.

"We could shoot a game of pool."

"Not in the mood."

We continued along the waterfront to the marina. It was closed and dark. Beside it was the Kiwanis Club where Bill and my mother were attending a beach barbecue.

"Let's go," Henry said.

"Home?"

"To the barbecue."

Before I could object, Henry was leading the way to the beach, where dozens of couples were standing under the lights, pink drinks in their hands, white tassled loafers dug into the sand.

Bill welcomed us right away, then handed us our first cocktails. Pink gin fizz. Henry discovered where to find them for himself. The night grew egg-shaped, a pink wall between me and the rest of the world. I was beginning to know that I would be sick when I realized I was standing beside my mother, smiling and holding out my hand to a girl I had seen before, the girl on the bicycle at the gas station. "Paul, I would like you to say hello to Jeanine."

"Hello," I mumbled.

"Pleased to meet you." Jeanine extended her hand politely.

She was looking at me carefully, through the pink wall, and I was wondering how exactly I was going to get my hand to hers. She was taller than me. I was Henry's younger brother. I had only been drinking gin fizz to keep him company while he drank more. I looked down to see why she was so much taller than me. I was suspecting high heels made of white leather with tassels. I was correct except for the tassels. I knew this in such detail because once I started to look at her shoes, my head continued ever lower until my body began to follow. Some would call this concentration, others forgetfulness. Just before my face hit her shoes, Henry caught me.

"That's my little brother," I remember him saying. "Please excuse his lack of manners."

"Must go in the family," Jeanine said.

A week later, midnight Saturday night, Henry and I were driving home from Jeanine's. We had been drinking all evening from a bottle of brandy they'd let Henry buy at the liquor store. I felt sick again, the way I had that night with the gin fizz. Henry stopped on a bridge over a small river where we'd once gone fishing.

"I'm going in," Henry said.

"Don't be crazy."

"I want to go swimming."

"I don't."

"Then stay here," Henry said.

He got out of the car, climbed up onto the roof.

"Idiot," I said.

He began throwing his clothes down to the ground.

"Coming?"

"No."

"Chickenshit."

There was a loud splash. I took one of Henry's cigarettes from the dash and lit it. I was twelve years old. I started coughing and got out of the car to escape the smoke. I couldn't hear Henry swimming. I went to the rail and looked into the water. No sign of Henry. I beeped the horn. I ran to the other side of the bridge. "Henry!" I yelled. "Henry!"

Soon I was running back and forth, from one bank to the other, frantically searching in the bushes, hitting the water with sticks, calling Henry's name and crying. My feet were soaked, my clothes ripped. Finally I went back to the car. I would have to somehow drive home, tell my mother what had happened.

I was crying. I wanted to bring up. I opened the door. Henry was lying on the front seat, trying to muffle his giggles.

The town men had a uniform: white shoes, polyester pants with permanent creases, short-sleeved polo shirts with two buttons undone and a pack of cigarettes bulging from the breast pocket.

Henry did not look like the town men, or their sons. He was

shorter, slimmer, had an edge to him. Maybe that was what attracted Jeanine. Whatever it was, I missed it. It must have happened while I was falling on my face. By the time I'd had two Cokes to sober me up, Henry and Jeanine were bending over me, like mother and father. By the time Henry played his trick on me, that night on the bridge, they were already "going steady", kissing each other good-night at the door while I waited in the car. The next week when Henry drove out to see Jeanine I stayed behind. I tried walking along the main street, down to the war memorial at the water, the way I used to with Henry. When I got home I looked around for a magazine to read. When my parents were together there had always been magazines scattered around the house—*Reader's Digest*, various women's magazines from which my mother would clip the recipes and I would read the advice columns, a weekly newsmagazine that my father would sometimes stare at without turning the pages. Bill had television instead. Except in the room Henry and I shared. There, in a small brown bookcase, Bill had a set of Charles Dickens, bound in red-and-gold leather. One night, bored and restless, I cracked open the covers of *Oliver Twist*. For the next two hours, I sank into Dickens's sentimental world of abused orphans and London slums. After *Oliver Twist* it was *A Tale of Two Cities*. As June bugs and moths banged against the windows, I was in eighteenth-century London and Paris, listening to the clamour of revolution, watching prisoners disappear down narrow muddy streets in horse-drawn carts. The next night I went straight from the dinner table to our room. When Henry pulled the Mercury into the driveway at two in the morning, I was still up, rubbing my eyes and trying to get to the end of a chapter.

But though he might throw a rock in the water to make me think he had drowned, Henry never left me behind for long. Three weeks after Henry started going out with Jeanine, Bill complained that the Mercury was getting scratched up on the country roads. The next day at lunchtime, Henry dragged me to a used-car lot and showed me a bargain he'd spotted, an old Ford with four wheels and a price tag we could afford if we pooled all the money we'd made that summer.

That evening we bought it. For the rest of the summer, co-owner of a car my own age, I made the rounds with Henry. But having started reading I couldn't stop. I just had to wait until I'd spent the evening with Henry, Jeanine and her brothers, shooting baskets with them into the hoop nailed to the wall of their barn, or playing the operating-room assistant while Henry fought to keep the car alive.

His plan was to take it back to the city. Going into his last year of high school he was already sure to be captain and quarterback of the football team. Now he would own a car as well. Friday nights he would drive the boys around town, cruising up and down Yonge Street the way they always did, except this time Henry would be behind the wheel. Saturdays he would come to the country, he explained, and visit Jeanine for a little fresh air and tenderness before returning to the city and the school grind.

At the end of that second summer we wanted to go to the annual all-night party at the beach on the other side of the reserve. My mother was worried Henry and Jeanine might "get themselves into trouble". I was delegated to champion their cause, attesting to the purity of their companionship, and even promising to act as their chaperon. Like a truly Dickensian lawyer, I pleaded without regard to time. After it became clear I wouldn't stop speaking for several hours, my mother give me a dubious look then turned to Captain Bill. "Only young once," he shrugged.

The night of the party, the driftwood was piled ten feet high, then doused with kerosene before someone threw a match and the flames leapt up into the twilight, crackling and shooting out in all directions. Henry with his brandy and beer. Jeanine beside him, strangely subdued, holding his hand.

I was trying to act more than my size with a girl I'd met a few times with Henry and Jeanine. She was fifteen years old but short enough that I was as tall as she was, at least when we were sitting down. We drank the bottles of beer Henry kept bringing us. When the music got loud we backed away from the flames. I was surprised to find she was holding my hand as we walked farther into the darkness. Sitting close together in the sand. Not drunk but almost in another world while Becky told me a tractor had rolled over on her brother and every time she thought about it she felt cold. Then sitting closer she said did I want to go for a walk.

Leading me along a series of paths. Stopping to turn. There was nothing for me to do but kiss her. My face pressed to hers; she tasted of beer, warm and soft; my arms circling her, tightening, surprised to feel her so big, willingly pressing into me, breasts, hard belly, knees, exactly matching mine and making my legs want to cave in.

We could see the glow from the fire, hear the singing as it rose from the beach. Then Henry's voice calling, "Dungo. *Dungo!*"

I hesitated. "That's my brother."

"You want to go back?"

"No."

Moving farther away, holding Becky's hand, down a long narrow path to a small cove. Now a small hill was between us and the fire, the music, the voices.

Becky lay down and I lay down beside her. We were in the sand and as we kissed it shaped itself around us.

"You old enough?" Becky whispered.

"Old enough?"

"You know—" Her hand slid down my belly.

"I don't know."

"We'll see."

And then later, hours later because we'd fallen asleep and woken and slept again, we went stumbling back along the paths towards the camp-fire. The air was cool, my legs shaky and full of sweetness. It was still dark, but cars were starting to leave. I could see their headlights flashing through the trees, coded signals from the world to which I had just been admitted.

Henry was sitting on a case of beer, drinking brandy. Jeanine, wearing Henry's coat of honour, his purple-and-gold athletic jacket with his high-school letters sewn onto the new and gleaming satin, was curled on the sand beside him.

Henry looked at me and Becky. We were holding hands, and I wished he hadn't seen us.

"I'll drive you home," he said. He woke Jeanine and we went to the car. Jeanine slumped against the front door, as far as she could be from Henry. Henry was drunk. When he finally got the car into reverse he backed up too quickly, knocking into another car. Then he started forward. I was cuddled in the back with Becky, wondering if I would dare ask her address, when Henry hit the blacktop.

"Not too fast," Jeanine murmured.

"Now you're telling me how to drive," Henry said. He put his foot to the floor, the old Ford shuddered, accelerated. On the first curve a tire blew out. I remember spinning towards the trees, the headlights swinging from trunk to trunk, every circle getting closer, but the impact itself is something I can only imagine. I was the first to hit. Becky must have been thrown over me, right out the door. When I came to, Henry was shining a flashlight in my face and I was spitting blood. Somehow I already knew what had happened to Becky, who was lying a few feet away while Jeanine leaned over her, crying.

After the accident we moved back to Toronto to start the new school year. Henry didn't have his car, but he and Jeanine phoned each other every night. Also, some evenings, the police and insurance company representatives would come to our place to ask Henry questions about the accident. My father would watch over these sessions, his big face creased with worry. When Henry asked to borrow the car to visit Jeanine for the weekend, my father refused him.

Henry cocked his head. My father sat in his armchair, inspecting the light in his beer. Henry shook himself, as though to force himself awake from an unlikely dream, then turned around and went to his room. I was sitting at the kitchen table doing my homework.

I looked up when I heard Henry say, "See you, Dungo." He was standing at the door with his suitcase.

A few days later the phone was ringing when I got home from school. It was Henry. After swearing me to secrecy he told me he had a job pumping gas in a downtown garage and a room in a nearby boarding house.

The next afternoon I met Henry at his gas station. He was wearing a dirty pair of coveralls, his face smudged and tanned. When he saw me he broke into a grin and waved as though his gas island was a Pacific paradise.

After his shift we went to a restaurant where he bought me a sandwich and a Coke. Then we went back to his room. "I'm warning you, this place is a dump. I just need somewhere to squat while I find something decent."

His room was in one of those big downtown houses that have now been turned into offices or boutiques. I could see him eyeing me as I took in the panelled walls, the psychedelic poster on the door, the sagging double bed with its scarlet spread, the chipped sink and hotplate. I felt as though I had walked into a Gordon Lightfoot song, a soft lament about railway stations, missing women, lost homes. "Well?"

"Great," I said. "Really."

Henry grinned and hit me on the shoulder.

Weeks passed before my father broke down and asked where Henry was. When I told him my father paused and then said: "I suppose he's quit school."

"He's got a job."

My father went back to reading his newspaper.

Later I found out from Henry that my father went down to see him twice, begging him to come back home and start school again. But at the time neither Henry nor my father mentioned these visits. My father, it seemed to me, had first watched my mother go, then Henry. I took it for granted that the day I turned sixteen, I would follow.

Meanwhile I went to school, borrowed books from the library, did my homework. Weekends I spent downtown with Henry, when he wasn't in the country with Jeanine. Sometimes my father would ask if I'd seen him. When I said yes, my father would look away from me, then nod his head as though continuing some conversation he had been having with himself.

TWO

THE NOVELS of Charles Dickens were the first books I read for pleasure. That sentimental chaotic world he portrayed, those poor souls scrambling and clamouring to survive—somehow I saw in them the plight of my own ridiculous family. My mother's desperate desire for whatever my father couldn't provide. The sad fate of the man she abandoned, leaving him like a half-butted-out cigarette still smoking in the ashtray. My father's comical, futile attempts to make a household for Henry and me. His dedicated shopkeeper strivings that ended with him slumped to the floor behind the counter of his jewellery store.

Last night I was thinking about Dickens and I took out one of his biographies, the "great man" portrait given him by G. K. Chesterton. It is strange to think of one writer gilding the portrait of another. But perhaps it is just a case of family pride, the way, for example, I am so eager to remember every saving grace of Henry and my own family. Although loyalty is not my motive for setting this down. I admit to beginning cautiously. The painful parts—Becky's death, Henry's defection, the more difficult things to come—have to be approached slowly, with stealth. Until eventually they are fully exposed, like a bedroom scene viewed through a keyhole.

Chesterton said Dickens "climbed towards the lower classes. He panted upwards on weary wings to reach the heaven of the poor."

Innocence, he must have meant. Dickens wanted and panted after innocence. When he made his famous first tour of America he was so full of energy, the desire to swallow the world whole, that he could not bear to spend the whole day sitting in the back of the carriage as the horses slogged along muddy roads. Instead, he insisted on leaping down to walk beside them. He exhausted his wagonmasters, his wife, his hosts, his listeners, his guests.

For dinners at his own house Dickens planned each minute of the evening, taking charge of everything from the menu to the entertainment. The same attention was given to his public readings. He used to rehearse every detail, then arranged the details to provide a mounting rhythm of emotional intensity so that by the time the curtain fell, the audience was in tears and Charles Dickens lay prostrate on the stage. Perhaps that was what it took for him to achieve, even temporarily, the state of innocence he so desired. An innocence only equalled by that of the reluctant young mistress for whom he had so eagerly sacrificed wife and family.

What a perfect minor Dickensian character Henry would have been. Impoverished, without a future, cunning but foolish, stranded by his pride in his downtown exile. The nights of those first months must have been long for Henry. But when I saw him he always had a cocky smile, a few dollars to flash, plans for a movie or a game of pool. Sometimes, on a Saturday afternoon, we would just walk around downtown, looking in store windows while Henry supplied a running commentary on the cars and the girls. Spring afternoons brought an excursion to the racetrack. Henry, playing the expert, would tell me about all the bets I should have made, all the money I could have won. At night we'd go to the Gardens and after the hockey game was well under

way Henry would get us a couple of cheap seats from one of the
scalpers he'd gotten to know. As we stood and stamped our feet
on the concrete, hardly able to see through the smoke, cheering
our team on, Henry would slap my shoulder and yell. A cry of
triumph it always seemed to me, but with a current of sadness
that kept me tied to Henry, kept me trying to give him what he
so badly needed.

When school ended, Jeanine came to live with him. Soon
they moved into an apartment. They chose one big enough to
have a spare room for me and that was where I spent my weekends. Jeanine and I painted the walls of my room white while
drinking a jug of cheap wine and listening to Otis Redding on
their new stereo. Henry bought me a desk and a bookcase. Gradually my time there increased until finally, when I officially
moved from my father's to Henry's, my remaining possessions
hardly filled a suitcase.

My father, or as they called him in the report "Mr. Ralph
Stevens", died two years later, in his store. He was struck down by
a heart attack while standing at his glass-topped counter, preparing to subtract a link from the gold expansion bracelet of a watch
in the possession of a slim-wristed young lady.

Genevieve Wilson was the name of his client. When my
father "sank heavily to the floor" (as she stated in her deposi-
tion), she "thought he must have tripped or something. Then I
looked over the counter. His face was going, like, blue. There was
no way I could get around. He must have been afraid of robbers
or something, and I was afraid if I climbed over the glass it might
break. I ran out onto the street. There was a taxi right there, like
it was waiting. He called the police and I swear you could hear
the siren by the time I got back in the shop." As it turned out, the
courageous Genevieve risked the counter, sliding over it and trying to administer first aid to my father. She had taken a two-hour
course at her office and knew the exact place to hit the breast-

bone with the heel of her hand to start the victim's heart again. Then she moved on to the next step, mouth-to-mouth breathing. She said that at one point she was sure he "hiccupped or something" but by the time the ambulance arrived there were no signs of life, and the hospital later pronounced him DOA, "dead on arrival".

After my father died there was the question of where to put him. The call from the hospital came to Henry's apartment. It turned out my father had written our names and Henry's telephone number on the back of one of his business cards.

Next of Kin:
Henry Stevens and Paul Stevens
(sons)

The writing was shaky. It invited the picture of my father in his easy chair, full of whisky, perhaps massaging his chest and thinking to himself that, all things considered, he might drop dead. So from the breast pocket of one of his white shirts he would have taken the fountain pen he liked to carry, then twisted himself sideways to draw his wallet from his back pocket. The fact that he had Henry's telephone number memorized itself bore contemplation. It was not a number he ever actually dialled. We were the ones who had left home, after all. If we wanted to find him it wasn't so difficult. So he had once informed me. Then, having arranged his wallet on one knee, a card on the other, he had written our names. The way he sometimes, when we still lived at home, would put our report cards on his knee to sign them. "Geometry 53," he once intoned to me. At first I had thought he was going to berate me over my mark, 53 per cent. Then as he repeated the words again and again, "Geometry 53, Geometry 53," I realized he thought this was a particular subject, one marginally different from, say, Geometry 52 or Geometry 54, and was trying, by repeating it, to bring into his mind whatever it might be. In the end he just shook his head and wrote his name in the allocated space.

That is how Henry's telephone number must have appeared to him. A set of numbers to be memorized and repeated but without any particular meaning. Henry 925-3313. They were burned into his brain and could be recited at will. Perhaps he might even have tried to dial them on the telephone he kept under the counter at the jewellery store, then hung up. But I can't imagine my father dialling numbers and then hanging up when people answered. Most likely he was satisfied with the number itself.

When we went down to the hospital to pick up his effects they gave me his clothes and his wallet in a paper bag. He died with four hundred and twelve dollars in his wallet. Henry and I divided it that night. Two hundred and six dollars each. Whenever that number comes up in the cash register, or I am walking down the street and see a house with that number, I'm reminded of the thin wad of my father's legacy. We took his clothes around the corner and put them in a bin for the Salvation Army.

When the ambulance arrived at the hospital a priest had tried to confess him, thinking he might be in some kind of coma rather than dead. After the hospital telephoned he waited there for us. A kind-looking man, Father Mackinnon, with a white beard and a way of peering at us that made Henry call him Father Time when we went home.

Father Mackinnon offered to arrange a church burial. We accepted, and a few days later we—Henry, Jeanine and I—stood and watched while my father was lowered into the ground. Our mother had been, as she said, "unable to make it", although she did show up for the reading of the will.

"I never knew him," Father Mackinnon said. As though this

would come as a surprise to us. Then he added: "Mortal life is short, eternity lasts forever."

When my father was gone, I was all the family Henry had left. Perhaps that was why Henry leaned on me. Or maybe it was because my mother had deserted us at just the wrong moment. Or maybe Henry leaned on me because I was there and he saw no other reason for my existence.

"Dungo," Henry would say, "you're my main man." He would pronounce these words in front of Jeanine, or even strangers. Never, "Dungo is my main man." Always, "Dungo, *you're* my main man." His eyes boring into mine, daring me to break the spell.

Henry always needed someone to be his lifeline to reality. His umbilical cord. His reality processor. Someone who transformed the world into Henry's image.

It's strange, the way people come to need each other. To use each other. To betray each other, sometimes meaning to, sometimes not. It often seemed I was less Henry's younger brother than his child. Less his main man than his main creation. Except, of course, that I eventually broke with him. So in the end I was a failed creation. A trial run that ran out.

"Here your name is Dungo Merde," Henry told me, the first time he took me to a pool hall. "People find out you're my brother they're going to think I'm setting them up or something, right?"

We would go to the back table. Henry, with a cigarette in his mouth, would set up a line of red balls and I would have to try to pot them. "Jesus, Dungo, you got Parkinson's in your elbow, or what?" After I'd missed a couple of dozen shots Henry would guzzle down a Coke, then lay the bottle on the table so I could practise my stroking motion with the cue, trying to slide the tip into the mouth of the bottle.

As with boxing, Henry could think of nothing but preparing me for "the big time". First he took me to a suburban hall where everyone wore white leather shoes. Then he promoted me to a downtown Italian coffee bar. "Get used to the atmosphere," Henry said.

When he decided I was ready, Henry brought me to Diamond Billiards. By then Henry and Jeanine were married and they had moved—me still in tow—to an apartment on top of an electronics store. Diamond Billiards was kitty corner across the street. From Henry's living-room windows you could see the sign, the two crossed cues. At night they lit up.

Sam, the "founder" and owner of Diamond Billiards had chosen the name, he explained to me, because "diamonds have class. Bright. Hard. Makes the place sound tough, you know what I mean? The kind of place where you don't mess around, even if you do have tattoos all over your ass or whatever these people have. Not you and your brother, I know. But you run a place like this and you deal with whoever falls through that door."

When we or any other of the regulars came in, Sam would lift up his arms and spread them wide, as though in the beginning of a hug. Those arms, spread wide, were something to see. Sam wasn't very tall, but his arms were so long that stretched out they made him look like a huge scrawny eagle. Then, as he let them drop to his sides, he'd give you a big beaky grin.

Sam was always there. Behind their thick lenses, rimmed in black plastic, Sam's eyes would be swimming like frogs. He'd give you his big weak smile, his eyes would swim, he'd raise his arms—"Hey, Dungo."

"Hey, Sam." Sam's forehead was pasty pool-hall white, though sometimes, in the summer, he'd spend his free time standing out on Spadina smoking a cigarette and taking in the girls and the bus fumes. Then his skin would get a tinge of pink.

"Snooker balls?" By the time he popped the question his long arms would already be beneath the counter, drawing out the plastic tray. He'd set them on the black Arborite in front of him, then carefully inspect the resin boxes.

I'd play at the back, alone. Games against myself, seeing how many turns it took to clear the table. Or playing against the clock, shooting like crazy. Or only worrying about the cue ball: wetting my finger before each shot and making a little blot on the felt where I predicted the cue ball would end up. Leaning into a shot, letting my chin down, Henry-style, until it grazed the cue, I sought the point of perfect balance, the point where my whole body was poised, effortless, my arm dropping straight down from my shoulder like a smoothly oiled pendulum waiting to move into its predetermined arc.

Up at the front would be Sam's friends, men who owned or managed the cheap clothing shops up and down the street. They had names like Lefty, Myron, Dracheski. They made jokes about the *broads* who worked in each other's places. Jokes like: "Hey Myron, I hear your wife is making you wear a chastity belt since you hired that new *broad* to do the books." "Myron's wife is worried? Is she blind or something?" "She told Miriam she was afraid he'd get a hernia from walking around with a hard-on all day."

Sometimes, smoking a cigarette between games, I'd just stand and look at them. They all wore cloth pants with wide belts, fat wallets bulging out their back pockets. Even in the summer they wore long-sleeved shirts, sometimes ties. A couple had lost too much weight and the skin along their jaws and throats bagged down; the others had pot bellies and big behinds. Where had they come from? I would ask myself. Maybe they'd always been like this and that was why they had ended up their lives selling cheap clothes and telling jokes about the *broads* in their offices; sometimes a *broad* would come in to give a message and these heart-stoppers would turn out to be bow-legged matrons with big red mouths and hair that looked like fat lacquered wigs.

Or maybe they'd once been like me. Leaning over a shot, the whole world suspended, so deep in concentration they could hear the music from cars passing in the street and feel the stale pool-hall breeze trying to force its way into their ears and up their asses. Where did you come from? I thought of asking Myron. I had talked to Myron a couple of times. He had big brown eyes. Sad. He was polite to me but I knew Myron thought I was a punk. Maybe because I often came in with a cheek swollen, a black eye, cuts on my face or arms.

No matter how bad I looked, Sam's froggy eyes never blinked or turned aside. This was a *pool hall* after all. Not a place with a *broad* to do the books where you could die of a hard-on. Though later I found out Sam's pool hall had first been a dress shop. "You know the kind," Sam told me. That was late one night. He'd turned off the lights and we were alone in the hall. Just the sign blinking through the glass door and the glow from the pop machine. "My brother set me up in the dress business. I always hated it. Anyway, who was going to buy dresses from someone like me? I don't even wear dresses. 'So, fuck it,' I said. I bought all these tables from a relative at a wedding, then I had a sale and cleared the store. A week later I had this whole thing set up and I was in business, just like that, the one smart decision I ever made."

Jeremy was born at the end of August, which meant that the worst of Jeanine's pregnancy was in the hottest part of the summer. Sometimes she would go to bed right after supper—their room was the farthest from the street and also missed the afternoon sun. If Henry was working late I'd offer to bring her a cup of tea after it got dark. She'd be lying under a sheet, her swollen stomach sticking straight up into the air. Her belly button had already turned inside out; it made its own little peak that Jeanine would sometimes tap rhythmically, as though the right combination might release Jeremy.

In those days Henry drank beer out of bottles, not cans. While he was drinking he would keep the empty bottles on the table and fill them with flowers he made by twisting strips of newspapers. I wasn't allowed to drink or smoke. I was supposed to be in training. Sometimes Henry would use his flower-filled bottles to stake out a boxing ring. He would stand up cigarettes—boxers, referee, trainers, judges—to dance out their various strategies until they were set up for the big KO. Then, with the tips of his index fingers Henry put them down for the count. "Suckers. Those suckers should have done what I told them." It would be almost midnight and Henry, who had a terrible restlessness the whole time Jeanine was pregnant, would stand up, shrug, yawn as though he were tired, then open the curtains to look across the street to see if the pool hall was still open. If the crossed cues of Diamond Billiards were still lit up, Henry would say, "Might as well shoot a couple of games." Before going out he'd check on Jeanine. I could hear their whispers, picture that big belly swelling higher and higher.

That summer Henry was always wriggling about uncomfortably, as though his skin didn't quite fit. He wanted the baby but Jeanine, pregnant, had become Jeanine involved with someone else more than him. I would see Henry watching Jeanine as she contentedly rubbed her belly and hummed little lullabies to herself. Sometimes even she would start to laugh at the puzzled look that would write itself onto Henry's face. I could just imagine him watching our mother, her belly full of me, thinking, Now why did she go and do that?

When we'd come in Sam would raise his big arms in welcome, then look at Henry and say, "Hey, Pops", just because—I thought—he knew it would bug Henry, maybe even make Henry want to go out and get his ass tattooed. And then, to show me I was right, Sam would turn to me and grin. "You too, Champ," and give me a wink because certain summer mornings when Henry was already at the garage and I was supposed to be doing my roadwork, I'd come into the air-conditioned coolness of the pool hall and shoot a few games while drinking coffee and smoking a few of those cigarettes I was supposed to have given up just so Henry could stand like a big man in the corner giving orders while I got pulverized.

We'd set up the balls, toss for break, then as soon as it was my turn Henry would start looking around to see if there was any action worth watching. Good players, bad players, possible fights, women who had the look Henry liked. Or at least claimed to like. Tight clothes, hard faces, long hair, a bit of extra leather on the belt. That summer any woman who had a big chest and was willing to wear a tight T-shirt tucked in with the aid of a leather belt was bound to get Henry's attention. "Will you look at that?" "What's she trying to prove?" "You telling me she thinks that guy's a stud? Gawd, for her sake I hope he's just her brother. Even that."

Once started, he couldn't stop. "Hey, look at that one bending over the table. You'd think she wants an examination or something. Tell you what, we'll go over to the Coke machine and I'll talk to you saying Doctor this and Doctor that—"

"Sure, Henry. Why don't you try doctoring that ball and give me a bit of a game for a change."

That just came out, one night, a little chain of words I hadn't planned to say, or Henry to hear. Henry straightened up as though he'd been tagged, rotated towards me, hand wrapped around his cue, bouncing its rubber butt on the floor.

A little black hole of silence suddenly opened up between us. This was Henry's game. We'd played it often enough.

"Hey, Dungo," Henry said in his driest, raspiest voice. Now I was supposed to jump into the hole and try to crawl my way out.

I just stood there. Henry was still playing with his cue, rattling it about in his hand. As though if I didn't do what he wanted he was going to beat me over the head with it. With Henry you always knew what movie he was in. I laid my cue on the table, folded my arms in front of me. After a while Henry propped his cue against the wall, took a cigarette from the pack in his shirt pocket, started to light it. As I watched him his cue, not perfectly balanced, began to slide.

"See you," Henry said. He turned and walked out while I lunged forward to catch the cue before it clattered to the floor.

THREE

I SUPPOSE I should have followed him. But I stayed at Diamond Billiards, shooting games alone. When Sam closed down, I went out to the street and looked at Henry's apartment. The lights were on, inviting me back, but my legs wanted to walk. When they finally got sore I went into an all-night diner in the Greek part of town. I ate bacon and eggs with home-fried potatoes cut into thick greasy slabs and sprinkled with herbs. Then I read the paper and drank coffee until it was light.

Instead of going back to the apartment or to the garage I went to the gym to work out. Speed bag, weights, skipping rope, exercycle. I could feel those home fries sweating out of me. Someone offered to set up some sparring but I said I had to go. It was months since I'd been in the ring and, though Henry didn't know it, I had retired. I would never step into the ring again: not for myself, not for Henry, not for any reason I would ever be able to think of. "Then why do you keep training all the time?" I could imagine Henry asking me.

"Sweating" was the only answer I could come up with, even for myself. Looking back at that moment in my life, I can see sweating was the only thing I knew how to do. Take food in, work it off.

When I was finished at the gym, I started back towards the

apartment. I found myself walking along behind a girl who kept stopping and looking around at me, as though I was following her. As though I was Henry, checking out the action. I went into a store.

Dusty windows, cobwebby, dark broken furniture, bookcases jammed against the wall. I thought I had wandered into some crazy person's living room by mistake. Then, at the shadowy end of the store, I saw an old man sitting behind a desk with a cash register. He was wearing a tattered uniform with a chestful of decorations. He nodded to acknowledge my presence, then went back to his book. He was reading aloud to himself in a deep rumbling voice that ran all the words into one long mumble. In the middle of the store was a dirty metal coffee urn with a glowing red light. In front of it were some coffee mugs, including a white one with 5 Cents scrawled on its side. I deposited my nickel, helped myself to some coffee that oozed out of the urn.

Donald Morrison's bookstore had no name. The sign outside appeared to have been bleached clean by rain, wind and sun. "Looks like so much driftwood," he once boasted to me. That was later. By then I knew Donald Morrison was a former Second World War tank commander, the sole survivor of a grenade that exploded inside his tank. By then my eyes were also initiated. They knew how to look at the sign at high noon on a bright winter day in order to sight the ghost of Flo's Fast Food. Flo's Fast Food had gone bankrupt the year I was born, 1954, when coffee was five cents a cup. Two years later it was still bankrupt and uninhabited except for a red For Rent notice in the window. On the day ex-Captain Donald Morrison learned he would be receiving a permanent disability pension, he looked through the sad empty window and saw the barren restaurant counter, its coffee urn, its lonely stools. "Invest in the future," his bank manager advised him when he made arrangements for his pension to be deposited. But ex-Captain Morrison rejected the future and decided to invest in the past. As he said to me: "You never know what's going to happen. The old stuff is all done with." He promoted himself to General. Then he moved several cartons of accumulated war books from his room to Flo's Fast Food. A truckload of volumes he bought from a military historian in Winnipeg forced him to "redecorate" by having the old counter and stools torn out to make room for shelving. Decades passed. The sign turned to driftwood.

All this—and more—I would eventually learn. But on my first visit I was—or so I thought—just deciding whether or not to drink a particular cup of coffee.

"Don't," a female voice advised. I turned. "Professor's wife," Henry would announce, seeing a woman like this. She had blond hair that came down over her shoulders, a vaguely bohemian look, seemed too old to be a student at the university, too well-off to be unemployed, yet was out shopping and without a baby during working hours. Professors' wives, as Henry called them, often brought the family cars in at this time of day, the middle of the morning. They would look about the garage as though they'd suddenly been thrown into a cage full of wild animals. Then Henry, young, clean-shaven, trim, would bounce forward. "Can I help?" he'd offer brightly. My brother's garage was downtown, opposite a police station. He had a coffee machine where cops from the vice squad, who got their cars fixed by Henry, used to hang out. There was a convenient wall phone for the placing of bets, and necessary numbers were scrawled on the wall beside it. Two of my brother's mechanics were ex-cons—sometimes others on probation ran the pumps. The professor's wife, gradually taking in the environment, would fasten on to Henry. And Henry, as though they were not in a greasy cinder-block garage surrounded by cops and ex-cons but standing beside a tropical plant in one of those uptown boutiques where you have to take diet pills just to get through the door, would smile and repeat,

"Can I help?" Then the professor's wife would relax and explain her problem.

So there I was leaning over my coffee cup and looking concerned. I set it down. "Thanks."

"That's okay," she said, moving away, suddenly shy. And maybe because I was so exhausted from working out, or still angry at Henry from the night before, I looked at her and saw not some "professor's wife"—which for Henry were codewords meaning "female parasite leeched onto some useless egghead geek himself a parasite on people like him who got up early in the morning, busted their asses working, then had nothing more to look forward to at night than enough beer to send them into sleep and towards the next day"—but a woman with time on her hands. A woman just a few years older than I was who probably hated her uselessness so much she seldom dared talk to strangers, who probably dared to warn me about the coffee only because after I work out my face is always so flushed I look about twelve years old. Especially in those days when I was living at Henry's, when both my body and mind were still suspended in the outskirts of childhood. Like one of those hitch-hikers you sometimes see stranded at the edge of the city.

"Which war?" she now asked me. As though she'd decided to slow down and open the door.

"Which war?"

"Most people who come here are war freaks. Famous battles, generals' memoirs, books like that."

"What about you?"

"My husband collects books about General Eisenhower. Do you know who he was?"

I was standing in the middle of a strange store, a store I'd gone into for no reason at all, and a strange woman I'd felt sorry for because my brother wouldn't have liked her was giving me a history test. On any other day I would have walked out. Back to my life of being joe-boy at my brother's garage and training for bouts I would never fight. But I was angry at Henry, so I didn't walk out. I stayed. I was having an adventure because for once I was stepping outside Henry's universe. Looking back, I can hardly be proud of the fact that for me, at nineteen years old, adventure was leaving my brother's universe in order to talk about General Eisenhower with a professor's wife. Even one with long blonde hair, a slight stoop, a small heart-shaped face that appeared somehow vulnerable and ready to crumble.

Even after everything that has happened, I can hardly believe I was prepared to make the decisive break in such a way. But when you've been stranded for a whole lifetime, waiting by the highway, you take the first ride. It could have been worse.

"General Eisenhower," I said. "He used to have a crush on my mother. He came to see her every Sunday afternoon."

"Really."

"As soon as the limousine pulled up, my father would rush down the basement to hide. Then General Eisenhower and my mother would have tea in the kitchen. She would spread a war map out on the table and he would take out his toy soldiers and show her how it had all happened. Sometimes he would describe the men he had killed."

"That must have been terrible."

"It was. Afterwards my mother would sometimes cry for days."

"And you? Did you also hide in the basement?"

"No. My brother and I had to dress up as Boy Scouts. We spent every Saturday evening ironing our hats. When the general's limousine arrived we would be standing on the front steps, ready to give him a salute. Sometimes he didn't come and we had to spend the whole day on the front steps, waiting."

"And did you have tea with him?"

"Never. We just played croquet with his bodyguards."

"Amazing."

"Yes."

I was smoking one of her cigarettes.

"You must have become a champion."

"In those days, it wasn't difficult."

"I think I should take you to lunch," the professor's wife said. "My husband would never forgive me if I let you go without finding out everything."

When I got back to Henry's late that afternoon, the apartment was empty. On the kitchen table was a note from Henry saying he was at the hospital with Jeanine, and would call me as soon as there was news.

I have confessed, if confession this is, about my first meeting with Martha. Between our first kiss and our last we shared—

A few afternoons?

A wild passion?

A criminal relationship for which there is no excuse?

A personal encounter, *grosso modo* inner growth and mutual exploration?

A few lies best forgiven?

But perhaps in our case there was nothing to forgive. Narrative was, you might say, our sole and consuming passion. Following our first lunch I began going to see her two or three afternoons a week. During these meetings I would relate to her the continuing adventures of my mother with General Eisenhower.

We are not, incidentally, talking about a JFK–Marilyn Monroe situation. In this story my mother was an attractive woman, her dark hair pulled neatly back, sometimes in a pony-tail and sometimes in a modified bun she wore at her neck. And she made ginger snaps to which General Eisenhower became addicted. But I don't think that even a white sequinned dress, to say nothing of total undress, would have made her look like Marilyn Monroe. Though who knows? Children never think of their mothers as movie stars. But as I described the relationship to Martha, it was primarily intellectual. With my mother's best Royal Doulton china tea service between them, clutching identical copies of Plato's *Republic*, my mother and General Eisenhower would give impassioned readings of the Socratic dialogues. Dickens's evocation of Nancy's death in *Oliver Twist* could have brought on no more tears than did their deeply felt exploration of classical Greek thought. My eye to the keyhole, as I confessed to Martha, I watched and listened mesmerized as … But here state secrets were involved, secrets that could only be extracted from me by means of various erotic enticements.

She tried. The interrogations took place in what she called "my painter's studio", in reality a one-room apartment in a building across from the Wing On Funeral Home, where she was supposedly "finding herself" by painting portraits of various nondescripts she would photograph in places like the one she met me.

One day I used Martha's camera to photograph her. "Do my face," she instructed. She wrapped herself in a sheet and smiled. Through the lens I inspected her features: a small triangular nose, delicate chin, fine-cut lips that made whatever she said seem intelligent and carefully constructed, small high cheekbones that burned easily, big dark eyes with a habit of looking right at you to establish the connection. While Martha struck poses I kept trying to capture her eyes.

When I got the pictures back we taped them to the wall. They were more sheet than eyes, and one day I found she had taken them down and thrown them out.

"Couldn't stand looking at myself," she said, and that was the end of my career as an artist. I went back to lying on her cot, smoking the marijuana she obtained from her university friends and recounting General Eisenhower's adventures. Sometimes it became necessary for us to enact various scenes in order to reassure ourselves they could not possibly have happened. Afterwards we would feel as though we had assassinated history. Given the times, her atelier contained a guitar. Full of remorse I would sing sad songs while she, in mourning for the futility of war, shook her head back and forth, slowly whipping me with her long hair.

This morning I was re-reading *A Sentimental Education*. The scene where Madame Arnoux finally comes to visit Frédéric, where after all those years of courtship and flattery he finally has her alone in his house. Aside from a few moments of exquisite disappointment, nothing happens. After hundreds of pages of long sentences and lofty descriptions, I wanted a final confrontation worthy of the build-up. Instead, Flaubert seemed to be saying that Frédéric and his love had consumed each other until nothing was left but a few tired lines of dialogue. But who had really tired—Frédéric or Flaubert? The puppet or the imagination that had created him?

I wanted to challenge Flaubert on this. How perfect it would have been to make a pilgrimage to visit Flaubert in his castle, that dank bourgeois provincial retreat where he spent most of his life labouring over his sentences. Flaubert, tall and fat, blue eyes red with drink and fatigue, long moustache straggling with last night's dinner, opening his iron gate and extending his huge sweaty palm. In you would have to go. Soon you would be sitting down to eat with him, a gigantic meal washed down by bottle after bottle of table wine, his mother and the servants carrying in endless platters while Flaubert's rant picked up steam. Liqueurs, cigars, then the best part: a trip to the study where you would be seated for a few hours while Flaubert read you his latest. Aloud. In its staggering entirety, even if several nights of reading were required.

That is what Flaubert did for and to his friends. Then his friends would go home and write about it in their diaries and their letters to each other. They would say Flaubert had produced yet another bad book, a book even worse than his last book, which they had also thought to be bad. They would say his breath stank, his food was boiled, his syntax was tortured, his manuscripts too long. But what if those Goncourt brothers, those dried-up clever little men bent over their dried-up clever little desks, had known that one day their diaries would be read only for the light they shed on the big ox for whom they had so much comfortable contempt.

I still have my original copy of *A Sentimental Education*, although it's now dog-eared, and various of the pages are stained by wine and coffee. Martha gave it to me, made me read it. I started during a heat wave, lying naked under the top sheet of her cot in her studio. There was young Frédéric Moreau, on the deck of a steamboat, about to leave Paris. He was my own age, his pockets were empty. His official education was unfinished, his real education had yet to begin.

Martha was in the bathtub. "How are you doing?" she called out to me.

"I don't know," I said.

When she got out of the bath the water made a loud sucking sound. She padded across the room and rolled a joint. She had explained to me that she was using drugs in order to paralyse the thinking half of her brain and thus release her inner creativity.

The boat set off. Soon, along with Frédéric Moreau, I was travelling down the Seine, looking at the summer houses of the Paris rich, their long gardens reaching down to the slowly flowing water, until he discovered the mysterious and beautiful Madame Arnoux, modestly bent over her needlepoint.

I would have loved to hear Flaubert's words in Flaubert's

voice. I would have loved to hear him read that gigantic book to those whom it made so uncomfortable, hear him describe how Frédéric slowly learned how to flatter, to cajole, to draw his gloves on without wrinkles so he could become a useless gentlemen acceptable to the ladies. I would have loved to ask him why, in the end, he couldn't take his gloves off.

Every afternoon for two weeks I came back to Martha's, got into her bed, drifted deeper and deeper into Frédéric's life. I was waiting for him to wake up and realize he was wasting himself on nothing. Instead he only slid further into his dream. "I'm so glad to see you reading that," Martha would say.

In fact, watching Frédéric ruin his life over a woman, I was swearing to myself that I would never do the same. And as Frédéric's flattery grew ever more skilled and less sincere, I grew ever more fascinated. Martha, fresh from the bathtub, would slide in beside me. Her skin cold and clammy from the city water. Lying on top of her, I would imagine I was making love to the so-refined Madame Arnoux. Or to the golden-hearted Rosanette, whom he despised for being a kept woman even though it was she who was keeping him. Or to the elegant and sinister Madame Dambreuse, the rich widow he finally refused to marry so he could go back to the one he really loved, or might have really loved had he been capable of knowing either reality or love.

"What were you thinking?" Martha would ask me.

"Lofty thoughts," I would reply. Though sometimes my brain also had its moments of paralysis. Once, beached on Martha, I suddenly realized I had forgotten the number of women Flaubert's hero had courted. I decided to count. Meanwhile the window was open. Through it came the groans of the buses and trucks on Spadina Avenue. The deep grinding of their gears became the rhythm of our lovemaking and I began to feel that I myself was one of those heavy trucks. Instead of counting to remember the names of Frédéric Moreau's mistresses, I was counting the number of gear changes it took a bus to pull away from the stop beside the Wing On Funeral Home.

Late one September morning, as I was leaving the garage to go up to Martha's, Henry suggested we spend the afternoon at the racetrack.

A few hours later I met him in front of our usual betting wicket. Henry had his face in the racing form and took a moment to register that the woman beside me was in fact with me, not simply a coincidence. His eyes widened and he actually started to whistle. "I can't believe I did this," I whispered, but Martha squeezed my arm and we continued forward. That afternoon, I realized there was much about Martha I had not fully appreciated. She charmed Henry like a kindergarten teacher faced with an unruly child.

"Paul's told me so many good things about you." "It's so amazing, the way you remember so much about these horses." "I don't know how you keep all these numbers in your head." She and Henry smoked each other's cigarettes, she let Henry lose her money for her, she listened to his inside stories about such-and-such a jockey who was known all around the circuit for hitting his women harder than his horses.

Henry grew into the role. He fetched her coffee and poured in rum from the flask he was carrying. He smiled graciously to those around us. He even made a joke about it being good luck to bring beautiful women to the racetrack. Saying this he nodded to a man only a dozen steps away from us—a tall tanned Lothario type with a black moustache. Long-haired, with an open white shirt that showed his gold chain, Henry's friend was with a blonde who looked like an old-fashioned movie star—big bust, red-painted lips, teeth that flashed every time she looked adoringly at her man.

"I don't know where he gets them," Henry said, and for the next hour kept glancing over jealously.

Afterwards I took Martha back to her studio. Family life: that was the closest I ever came to it with Martha. The next day at the garage Henry quizzed me about her, but when I said she was "just someone I knew" he nodded, the way my father used to—as though I had only confirmed something he already knew.

Eventually, by mutual consent, we abandoned our afternoons. An awkward note had crept in. I was not quite desperate, but I was taking. Martha was not quite generous, but she was having to give. A classic case, you might say, of the footloose adolescent and the insecure married woman. Of not quite mistaken identity. Of trying to mistake myself, more innocent than I knew, for a Flaubertian character when in fact I could only find salvation counting the gear changes of buses and trucks.

The parting was uncomfortable. When she kissed me good-bye at her studio door for the last time her lips tasted of cheap Greek wine and incense. My eagerness for that taste had turned. I guiltily ran down the stairs—I couldn't stand in the hall, waiting for the elevator—and even a face full of diesel fumes from a passing bus seemed like fresh air.

Then, after a week, a month, I started to miss her. Sometimes at night I'd walk by her studio, on the far side of the street. If the lights were on I'd imagine myself going up to surprise her. Then I'd tell myself she had probably found some other boy. Not that I had any reason to think so. Not that saying such things, others, worse, made me any less homesick for our afternoon tea parties and the taste of her lousy Greek wine.

I was still working at Henry's garage, where Henry was now the manager, pumping gas. Also, at Martha's insistence, I had started taking night classes at the university. I had also moved out on my own, a couple of months after Jeremy was born. Then

Henry approached me with a proposition: he and Jeanine wanted to buy a house in the Beaches. It had an "in-law" apartment and if I wanted to move in again, the same rent I now paid for my room without kitchen or bathroom would help them with the mortgage....

Somehow this whole change only made me miss Martha more. I would walk across the city, go up and down the streets I used to walk with her. One night I was leaning on a telephone pole, looking at her window, thinking how nice it would be to be lying on her cot, feeling the breeze dry my skin, when I realized she was standing beside me. She was wearing some sort of denim jacket, boutique chic, silver hoop earrings that caught the light from the streetlamp and glistened in her hair.

"Anyone home?"

"I was wondering."

In the old days she would have invited me up. Now she took up a position against a parked car, appraised me, the night, the passing cars—as though we were some sort of scene she had learned to stay outside. As though I'd already become part of one of those forgot-you-in-an-old-café love songs she always liked to play. Across the street was her apartment building, her darkened window. Our side of the street had the Wing On Funeral Home. On its front lawn was an illuminated clock. We used to make jokes about how appropriate it was for a funeral home to have a clock on its front lawn. Why not a statue of Death? Sometimes in the afternoons, when there was a funeral, we would watch the cars lining up, try to guess how many there would be. In a book on quotable quotes about sex I once read that the first person to speak after lovemaking always says something foolish. This seemed the same sort of situation. "Seen any good funerals lately?" "I like your earrings." Nothing possible came to mind. Martha crossed the street. I followed. In the elevator we leaned on opposite walls, not looking at each other. There was something about her new clothes, the way she now wore silver earrings, the darker colour of her mouth, that made it seem she now held the advantage. I found that pleasing. We went into the studio. Through her window the white clock of the Chinese funeral home glowed like a low-flying moon.

"It's good to see you."

"You too."

"Paul, just because we used to be lovers doesn't mean we can't be friends."

"I know," I said. Though I didn't. I disliked her calling me a "lover". It sounded like a word she'd found in the Yellow Pages. As though so-and-so and so-and-so had been her lovers, like so many dogs that had been in and out of her kennel.

"Well, Paul, I guess you'll always be the mystery man." She moved close to me to say that, and when she did I froze. One night she'd knelt above me as I lay on the cot, holding the guitar against her breasts and strumming as she crooned a song to me, "her mystery man"; and after that she'd sometimes snuggle against me and whisper those same words, making me feel that I was someone after all, not just Henry's little brother that he called Dungo, a little shitpile who pumped gas at his brother's garage.

The dusty parquet floor, the cheap oriental carpets and the brightly flowered cushions, the half-finished canvases she stacked in a cupboard so no one could see them, the little cot that used to collapse under the burden of being the stage for the revival of one of the century's great secret romances, all mixed together with the broken lines of old songs we listened to, the Greek wine we used to anoint ourselves, the incense she was always lighting.

FOUR

THIS IS MY DREAM: Martha Fenwick's husband sits by the window. He, too, is greedy for this last October light. He is hunched forward in a wheelchair, head sloped to one side. His hair is white, his face smooth. Free of worries. No earthly cares to drag him down. Although, in fact, gravity has him tightly in its grip. He cannot fly, swim or walk. Sometimes he rolls out of bed and crawls. Towards the bathroom, the nurses say, but I don't believe it. I think at those moments he is trying to escape. In the middle of the dream it changes to night-time, and I am convinced Fenwick has succeeded, is somewhere outside crawling along the sidewalk, feeling for the curb so he won't end up on the road. When the time comes to cross a street he listens for cars; how crafty he is. Then he scuttles quickly across. In the parks he rests. The dewy grass soaks through his pyjamas. He pulls himself up on a bench. Slumped forward, discouraged, nostrils flared, hands pushing at the air heavy with the darkness and the cool wind and all the betrayals that have left him stranded here, wet and cold in the midst of a nowhere he can't see. I dream him down on his knees again, scenting his way home. Dogs mistake him for one of their own. Terrible accidents almost happen. When finally he arrives, his strong hands grip the door as he tries to pull himself up.

The nurses, the doctors, his friends all ask him how he is feeling. We tell him little stories about people he knows. As though all this might be satisfying. We read to him or offer him music. Sometimes he nods, but he will not speak, only listen. Perhaps I even read him what I am writing: this remembrance, this confession. When I wake up I realize I have been telling him what I do not yet know and cannot now remember.

Fenwick's Used and Antiquarian Books was painted in gold letters onto the window of the store. For weeks I had watched the preparations for its opening going on behind the newly painted sign. Then one day I walked in, uninvited and unannounced. Fenwick was arranging some books on a back shelf. Martha had claimed he was big and it was true that Fenwick had size. He was a tall wide man with a creased sympathetic face, fleshy nose, large big-lobed ears. Black hair, curved bushy sideburns that met his moustache. One of those big doggy middle-aged faces that can droop with the misery of the world. When he saw me standing at the door, Fenwick leaned his big face forward and stared at me intently. Then, as his big doggy face began to shift towards a smile, Fenwick hooked his thumbs into his belt. There was always something irresistible about Fenwick with his thumbs in his belt. Maybe the way his knuckles had to push into his belly. And the way the skin on his forehead creased with worried furrows that matched the waves of his receding black hair.

By chance, I was their first customer. Fenwick later confessed to me that he had gone to a palm reader who had predicted that the fate of his new enterprise would depend on the first person who walked through the door.

They started carrying a few best-sellers in one of the windows and offering coffee to the regulars. One afternoon Fenwick told me he was driving to a nearby town to assess the private collection of a retired English professor. I went with him. Fenwick had a big blue Buick station wagon, about ten years old. The old-fashioned ribbed cloth upholstery was permeated with the smell of cigarettes and exhaust. We drove along the edge of the lake, Fenwick smoking and humming to the radio while I was in charge of deciphering the directions. The professor lived in a stone house near the town's main street. First he showed Fenwick the books he wanted to sell, then he brought out his prize, a manuscript purported to be a hand copy of "Kubla Khan" made by the poet himself for a close friend.

The paper was old, discoloured into yellow gold, curled at the edges. The handwriting was a fine but irregular copperplate. It invited you to imagine the author emerging from his opium trance, candle guttering in the dank English night while quill in hand he bent over his masterpiece. Did he speak the words aloud as he wrote them? Were they embedded in his mind like so many jewels studding a collar or was his poem just something that had passed through him, an involuntary word shudder, Mercury on drug-inspired wings.

Fenwick bent over the page and stared. His face first bunched in concentration, then rearranged itself into a mask I felt I shouldn't even be seeing, a combination of desire and greed. His lips were parted, he was taking quick shallow breaths. His eyes were constantly in motion. Not simply reading but absorbing every pore in the paper, every curl, every irregularity. He gave the impression that he would have liked to taste it, to squeeze it between his palms, perhaps even to disrobe and rub himself against it. But he had to content himself with breathing over it, sniffing it, leaning so close to it that his eyelashes brushed against it. Finally he stood up, rubbed his fists into his eyes and looked away as though he'd just had a mildly distasteful encounter with something worthless.

Without even verifying its authenticity, Fenwick then paid out what seemed to me an incredible sum.

"Did you see the way I bargained?" he asked me afterwards on the way home. "I pretended that I didn't want it. That's the only way to get a decent price out of these guys."

A few days later it reappeared in the back room, mounted in a frame. "When I sell this," Fenwick told me, "you'll know I've sold my soul."

When Fenwick offered me a job, I jumped at the chance. Despite all the night courses, I was still living at Henry's, pumping gas and changing spark-plugs to make money, as well as playing babysitter to Jeremy.

Though Martha and I never spoke of our past, we seemed comfortable. That is, we avoided speaking about it even when we were alone in the store. It seemed to have been agreed that this little detour was one to forget. I had other girlfriends, though nothing serious, and Martha took long lunches for which I invented my own explanations.

In the morning, when I arrived, Fenwick would usually disappear into the back room. Sometimes I would see him talking on the old black telephone as he leaned back in his oak swivel rocker. More often, as I passed the open door, he would be intent on a crossword puzzle or working his way through an antiquarian catalogue, laboriously checking items that might be of interest.

He was especially curious about certain Canadian authors. For example, after the Second World War a ruined writer called Frederick Philip Grove had gone to Ottawa to work for a small press. The idea had been to provide him with a comfortable finish to his long and disappointing career. But the press went bankrupt and Grove, at seventy, ended up living north of the city and working in a canning factory to spite himself and everyone who knew him. When he died, his papers became valuable, but because he'd been a prolific writer, both for publication and of letters, the material was widely scattered.

By the time I came to work for Fenwick, Grove had been dead for more than twenty-five years. His reputation had been resurrected, only to plummet when it was discovered that Grove had invented not only his novels but himself. To retrieve Grove's material, Fenwick would advertise in dailies and weeklies all over the province: Napanee, Tamworth, Belleville, Tweed, St. Catharines, Niagara Falls, Madoc, Peterborough, Kingston, Kitchener, Hamilton, Orangeville, Owen Sound, Windsor...

Grove's strange double life was so appealing to Fenwick that he would often take Martha and me to dinner in order to ruminate over why this bizarre man had acted as he did. Fenwick's preferred restaurant was called Le Troubador. It was in a run-down Victorian town house that must once have been the elegant residence of a bourgeois businessman. On the ceiling, plasterwork angels held hands while looking down on the chequered tablecloths and lamps made out of old wine bottles. There were stained-glass transoms over the doors and the hardwood floors had been sanded and covered with liquid plastic. On the front of the menu was a painting of the beret-topped troubador himself carrying a lute in one hand, a bottle in the other. The French cuisine consisted of hearty stews and casseroles, strongly flavoured steaks that required sawtooth knives, big salads served in wooden bowls with layers of oil that shone in the dim light.

From the bookstore it was an easy subway ride and a short walk. But part of our restaurant game, Le Troubador game, was to pretend that we were driving away from our lives deep into the countryside of a nation known only to us. And so, in those days, we would go out the back of the store and pile into Fenwick's big station wagon. The preferred time for these visits was snowy winter evenings. After staying late to finish off the invoices or some other such chore, we would cruise slowly along Bloor Street, fat tires making their snowy hum, waving at our scarved and hatted fellow citizens as though they were spectators lined up to watch our grand parade. Arriving at the restaurant we would stand outside for a moment, looking at the warm lights through the falling snow. Then we would go inside and start with a whisky, neat, a little miracle in a glass to take off the chill. During dinner there were bottles of the red house wine, a vintage best appreciated after a couple of glasses to numb the palate; and then, at the end of the meal, a bottle of Calvados would be brought to the table. At this point Fenwick would lean back, wipe his brow, then say as if for the first time: "Paul, imagine this. A man, a famous writer and translator in his own country, a young man of your age who has already made his mark on German literature, has already met and translated André Gide, of all people, a man of *culture*, finds himself dipping his oar where he shouldn't. To escape the woman he comes to Canada, changes his name, works first as a labourer then a schoolteacher, marries a wife who swallows the whole lie, then starts writing again—this time in English. Writing fiction and autobiographies of his fictional self! And then—the most incredible thing of all—his books are totally boring! Meanwhile, the woman he escaped has herself fled Europe for New York where she becomes a famous lesbian and at night runs naked through the streets of Greenwich Village.

"What does Frederick Philip Grove do? He, the translator who had worked his way through the intestines of dozens of great books? He, the author who invented himself as a boring stiff-necked schoolteacher so poor that, due to his worn-out ribbon, he had to type his manuscripts twice? He, the philanderer who first disgraced himself in Europe, then lived most of his life as a lie? Instead of celebrating his real self, he applauds his bor-

ing self, then does penance in a Lake Simcoe canning factory!
Can you believe it?"

Fenwick, his hands wrapped around his Calvados, would
then look about the restaurant, waiting for a response to his
rhetorical question, as though the answer to his strange hero's
unhappy life would become the answer to his own.

Often, during those first years at the store, I would stop to
admire the strange harmony in which Fenwick, Martha and I
found ourselves. It was an odd Platonic triangle. I thought of us
as equals, distant and serene. We had the store. We had our
dinners. We had our civilized manners. We had our secrets
from each other and the secrets we told each other. Fenwick
often spoke about his years as a high-school history teacher, the
long, fallow period of his life that ended when he fell in love
with Martha and "abandoned", as he put it, his first wife in
order to begin again. Martha, too, had an official past: the only
child of a deserted mother, she had been struggling through
graduate school when she met Fenwick at a lecture. "Charles
Dickens's Britain", it was called. The lecturer was an eminent
professor from Oxford who had met everyone's expectations by
giving his entire speech without removing his pipe from his
mouth. Fenwick had dared to ask a question from the floor and
Martha, working on a paper, approached Fenwick during coffee
break to ask after his bibliography. I, of course, had only my
family for my past. In the non-Martha version I recounted the
whole story of my mother's departure, my first discovery of the
world of books, my father's sad minor-key death, my symbiotic
relationship to Henry, the way I had come to work at the store
to escape the garage. Talk about Dickens. When Fenwick
informed me, gravely, that Henry had come round to the store
on one of my days off—apparently in order to see what manner
of man could have become my employer, he was careful to add

that "a man should never apologize for his family or his wife."

So there we were, a tiny perfect civilization waiting for the barbarians to arrive.

Judith first came into the store on a morning not so different than this, a fall morning when the slanted autumn light gave the store a colour of old wood, leather, ancient paper coded in dark ink, a morning when the store was humming with its millions of strange words and secret messages. Judith was the first through the door. Just inside, she stopped, put her hand to her brow as if a camera might dolly out from behind one of the shelves to shoot the opening scene.

I clapped.

She turned to look at me.

"Perfect," I said, then blushed, unable to believe I'd been such an idiot early in the day.

"It's okay," she said. "Everyone takes me that way."

She had jet black hair that fell straight down, then massed in curls on her shoulders. Skin so white that even from behind the cash register I could see the way freckles sprayed across the bridge of her nose.

"Anyway," she said, "I was looking for, uh, Shakespeare." She was wearing a denim skirt and matching jacket, an ironed white shirt that was too big. Over her shoulder was a leather-strapped canvas knapsack. She looked like a high-school girl bussed in from the suburbs to spend an educational day in the inner city.

We had some fine antiquarian leather editions of the plays, but I pointed her to the drama shelf. There she could find the footnoted edition or crib she was looking for.

She opened up her knapsack and pulled out a cigarette, looked about the store as though her mother might be hiding somewhere. "Got a match?"

I offered her my lighter, the one Martha Fenwick had given to me. Judith lit up. Then, leaving her knapsack on the floor in front of the cash register, she drifted over to the drama shelf. Soon, in a bell-clear voice, she was reading aloud from *Romeo and Juliet*. Fenwick appeared from the back room. Judith picked up steam. Without breaking pace she worked her way across the room to her knapsack, pulled out a bottle of vodka and fuelled herself with a few long gulps. As she pronounced Juliet's final words she slid to the floor, embracing her knapsack.

For the second time that morning I applauded. Fenwick joined me.

Judith stood up. "Well? Do I get the part?"

Fenwick fell for it. "What part?"

"The job. I saw that Help Wanted sign in the window, so I decided to apply."

Fenwick shook his head. "What sign?"

"What are you talking about? The one in the window. You mean I went through all that for nothing? You just put those signs out and people come in here, make a fool of themselves, then you say 'what sign?' Is that the deal?"

"What sign?" Fenwick repeated. He moved towards the window.

"I'll show you," Judith said. She led us out the door and onto the street. There was a Help Wanted sign, in red letters against a black background, in the window of the barbershop next door. Beside it was a second sign advertising that their haircuts were half-price for students, seniors and children.

"Oh," Judith sighed. "I got the wrong store. Anyway, I can't cut hair."

"That's all right," Fenwick said. "You can't act either." He walked back into the bookstore. We followed.

"I was a high-school star. You should have heard me singing in *South Pacific*. My mother cried."

Her knapsack was still in the centre of the floor. She took the stool from behind the cash register, set it up beside her knapsack, stuck a cigarette in the corner of her mouth and waited for me to light it. I did.

"We don't do plays," Fenwick said.

Judith's face began to work.

"I'll do anything," she said to Fenwick, her voice quavering. I handed her a box of Kleenex from behind the counter.

"Free," Judith added. "Absolutely free. Try me out for a week. If I don't make your floor cleaner, your shelves brighter, your store sunnier, you can send me back, no questions asked."

"Sounds like a bargain," I said.

Fenwick gave me the look of scepticism he used when we were out buying and I was playing the bright young enthusiast while he rubbed his pipe and snuffled disparagingly.

Now he just shook his head, mumbled, "She's yours," and turned to walk to the back room.

Judith sprang to her feet and replaced the stool. "Believe me, this will be your lucky day. I hope. I mean, I really *love* books."

So. That had been my lucky day. Judith the first person to walk into the store. *Yours*, as Fenwick had said. Though what I felt for her at first was mostly admiration. She seemed so *certain* about everything. So sure of herself. So enthusiastic.

At first I admired Judith without wanting her. When I began to want her, it was not a desperate need, just a hobby that made going to the bookstore a little more interesting. Then one night we had a particularly enthusiastic dinner. This occasion was a Golden Hole—Judith's translation of Le Troubador—special followed by so much Calvados the owner had offered us a second bottle. Judith and I watched Fenwick's car disappear, then started on our way towards the subway. Just before descending she turned to me and said, "Paul." The way she pronounced my name, that single word, followed by a blank silence, made me think she was in distress. In fact she'd surprised me by drinking so much, and now I expected her to be sick. "I can't face the subway," she said. "Will you, uh—" and she waved towards the bar beside the subway station.

I took her arm and helped her in. The place was dark, half-deserted. A piano player was stumbling his way towards last call.

"Coffee," I said to the waiter, hoping to set a good example. We were in those huge chairs some city bars have, nothing-to-lose bins, Judith once called them, big deep-cushioned semi-wraparounds that make you feel, as soon as you sit down, that you're already in a stupor.

"I'll also have coffee," Judith said.

"Coffee also," said the waiter.

"Also a double brandy," Judith added.

Judith and I were on formal terms. We had never, before this evening, gone out for a drink together. At previous dinners, after seeing the Fenwicks drive off into the snow, we would walk to the subway station together, shake hands, then each depart in our separate directions.

Even before the brandy Judith was sufficiently drunk that her face had changed. Her eyes were not only brighter, but seemed to dart around as if to confirm various presences normally unnoticed. On each cheek a small burning spot had appeared. Her lips were darker, slightly swollen, and they made her mouth look vaguely dissolute. Since dissolution was not what I expected from Judith, the combination of this new mouth, her suspicious glancing about, her sneaky way of ordering more alcohol all made her seem faintly comic.

After another double brandy, we got up to leave. Judith fell forward and I caught her.

Judith on the street was even drunker. First falling against me; then suddenly taking my hand in a Ginger Rogers move leading into a pirouette beneath a lamp as snow drifted scenically through its long cone of light; then falling awkwardly into me again before collapsing to her knees, hands clasped in mock prayer. There were still a few people on the street. In the spell of the mild winter night with its slowly falling snow, everyone laughed as Judith wove her clownish loops about the sidewalk, stumbled into the street, hopped back to safety. All with a catlike grace that made me wonder if she was just putting on another show. Until she came to rest against me, her head on my shoulder, and said, "Take me. Somewhere, I mean. I promise to be a lady."

Before I could decide what to do, she grasped my arm and led me across the street, walking quickly. After a few blocks we made a turn, which brought us in front of an old-fashioned brown brick commercial hotel that must have been built near the beginning of the century for the travelling businesmen of our new country, in the days when the steel of our national railway shone from coast to coast with all the dazzling brilliance of a five-thousand-mile promissory note. The hotel, now dwarfed by nearby office towers, was six storeys high, and its generous double doors were placed squarely in the centre. Now the stone steps were worn hollow by generations of customers and bill collectors. The name of the hotel, barely visible, was carved into the grey stone portico. The Savoy Hotel, read the letters.

The snow was falling thicker. Only the occasional taxi had passed us in the night. Through the ground-floor windows of the hotel came a low amber light made lustrous by the snow.

"There it is," she said, pointing across the street as though at this necessary moment she had conjured the old building out of time. "Do you like it?"

"It's perfect," I said.

"We'll go in. We'll take a room. We'll drink until we die." As she spoke she opened her shoulder bag and showed two bottles of whisky. I raised my arm to stop a taxi but she pulled it down, turned me towards her and looked at me with such fear that I nodded my agreement and we started across the street.

When we arrived in Room 66, Judith locked the door behind us and sighed.

That first time in the Honeymoon Suite, I wasn't thinking honeymoon. I was instead wondering what I was going to do with Judith, what was bothering her, how I would get her to tell me whatever was on her mind, or at least how I could get her sober enough for work the next morning. In sum, I didn't yet know Judith.

She got glasses from the bathroom and filled them with whisky. Then she sat down in the armchair and said: "Thank you, Paul. You don't really have to babysit me. You can go now if you want."

This in a low stagey voice. I turned off the light and opened the curtains. Outside the thick falling snow looked like a movie. The room got smaller and warmer. We started to talk about the store.

For those of us who work in bookstores, the hundreds of thousands of bookstores scattered in their dusty glory over the surface of our planet, this job has a strange romance. We modest bookstore workers are the custodians of all that has been written. The living membrane through which passes the wisdom and the idiocies of the ages. We are the clerks of the hotel of language. It rises out of our collective brains, always available, always dependent on us to keep it smoothly functioning, to welcome new arrivals, to keep the guests moving in and out according to rank and demand, following values carefully constructed over the centuries yet capable of satisfying every need.

And for those of us who live this strange romance, usually planned as something between a one-night stand and a provisional passion on the way to something more suitable, nothing could be less romantic than the job itself. The packing and unpacking. The constant worry about small accounts. The debtors and the creditors. The fact that people never wipe their feet when they come in the door. The way customers lick their thumbs before turning the pages of expensive art books they'll never buy. The way your "best" customers always think you owe them something. And so on. The shopkeeper's litany.

What does a person do to prepare for such an odd life? Some, no doubt, study literature. I pumped gas for five years at the station my brother managed. The morning shift, from seven o'clock until one; or in the afternoons, from one to seven. Either way I had half the day free, and it was outdoors work, as they say. But I got sick of always smelling of gas, of arguing with customers about what they did or didn't owe. Sick of the routine. Sick of the sight of my brother standing at the cash register, it seemed, every time I came in from the snow or the rain, or that raw wind that comes off the lake and gnaws at your skin.

Judith refilled our glasses. We sat silently in the dark, looking out at the falling snow.

"I like working there," Judith said. "I like being surrounded by all that—"

She had her feet folded under her. The darkness was like a blanket we were sharing.

"Although we spend half our time just keeping track of things. Doesn't it drive you crazy? There we are, surrounded by immortality, and all we can do is count."

"Surrounded by immortality," I repeated.

Judith made a funny sound. I leaned forward, concerned, then realized she was laughing. She laughed so hard she made the sound again, a bark. I barked back. That was so hilarious we barked and laughed and rolled on the floor until one of us barked and it started all over again. The next day our stomach muscles were so sore we had to pass a law that no one could say "surrounded by immortality" for at least forty-eight hours.

FIVE

M Y ROOM-MATE'S a little bit weird," Judith told me. That was also the next day, at the store, after we had passed our law. She said it apropos of nothing, during an intermission in customers. Just came up to me and announced it. Of course I knew she wasn't talking about her room-mate. She was telling me there was going to be a second instalment of our relationship, one that would include me coming to her apartment and meeting her "weird" room-mate.

The time was set for Sunday afternoon. It was already Saturday.

Sunday morning I shaved. Jeremy came into the bathroom and watched me. Big round spotlight eyes following my hand. I gave him a glob of shaving cream and he put it on top of his head. For the first time it occurred to me that one day I might have a house or at least an apartment. That my own child might watch me shaving. Glob some cream on his hair.

As I was walking up the stairs to Judith's apartment my palms started to sweat and I had to wipe them off on my pants. I was carrying flowers. An armful of chrysanthemums. Judith answered the door after a long time, squinting into the darkness of the hall as though she didn't recognize me.

She led me in to sit on the couch in her living room. "My

room-mate's couch," Judith explained. It seemed fine to me. "She isn't here."

Then she went to get tea. I wanted to be in a hotel room with her again, drunk if necessary, the lights out and our clothes off.

Judith returned with the tea things on a wooden tray. "Sorry about this stuff. It came with Vivian, too." She knelt down on the floor and began fussing with the tea. She looked up at me. "You look tense," she said solemnly. "Is something wrong?"

I was sitting on the couch. Judith was on the floor, pouring tea, the sun full on her face. Her dark eyes floating in the white winter light. She was wearing a thick ribbed sweater I never saw again, tight jeans that made me wonder if I'd ever really touched her.

Then: "Oh Christ." Pouring the tea her hand had taken a jump and the teapot jerked to one side, knocking off the top and sending a splash of hot tea onto her thigh. "I should have warned you. Sometimes my hands go crazy." She held them out to me. I took them. Her bones danced for a moment, the way all of her had danced under me, then settled into stillness.

I was holding her hands. There had been the months in the store. There had been the night in the hotel room. Now there was this bright chilly winter feeling, the way my hands held hers. Judith's face slowly turned up to mine. Something about the way the winter light slanted off her cheekbones. The settled quiet of her eyes. The way her body was beginning to uncoil.

"It was great you could come," Judith said. She took her hands away and stood up. Our tea was still untouched. She walked over to the chair where I had put my coat when I came in.

I got up and stood beside my coat.

"Well," Judith said. There was a certain doubt in her tone. As though she didn't know how she was going to get rid of me.

"It's all right," I said. I picked up my coat.

"What are you doing?"

"Getting dressed."

"Did you want to leave?"

"Not really. I thought you wanted me to."

Judith took my coat from me. Put it on. It was one of those thick parkas I used to wear pumping gas. The arms were stained with grease.

"I was just cold," she said. "I was going to get something."

"Oh."

Judith laughed. "Oh, he says." She put her hand over her heart. "Something to get warm with. Something to drink."

She put her hands in my pockets. It was two years since I'd worn that coat, but when she came out with an envelope I recognized it right away. Judith held it up. It was blank, but not empty. Inside were two joints Martha had given me long ago, and that I'd forgotten about.

"And I thought you were Mr. Pure," Judith said.

She went into the kitchen and I followed. There she broke the papers open, dumped out the marijuana, then placed it into new papers. Before re-rolling it she took a vial of white powder from the refrigerator and sprinkled it on top. Then she sealed the papers and twisted the ends. "We might as well do this right," she said.

She was still wearing my coat. She reached into the other pocket and found a package of matches. As she was opening the package there came the sound of footsteps on the stairs. Judith grabbed my arm, led me into her bedroom and locked the door. Her finger across my lips. The steps passed, carried on upstairs.

View from Judith's Window, Before Version: Tangled soft maple limbs grey-blue in winter light. Falling-down garage with wood siding, peeling white paint. Green shingle roof bare at the peak, snow along the gutters. Frozen sheets strung between tree and garage, pale panels of white light.

View from Judith's Window, After Version: Shreds of scarlet sky showing through the branches. Snow and sheets pulsing with the moon. Black cat silhouetted on the garage roof. Warm yellow rectangles of light from the windows of other planets repeating themselves into the distance.

Someone has turned up the heat. I have woken with my ear pressed to Judith's belly, filled by Judith's belly. "How are you?" she whispers.

"My left ear."

We twist around. The quilt over my shoulders. Now I remember I was dreaming myself a great-winged bird gliding over the surface of a lake and now the quilt is my wings as I glide into position over Judith who is waiting for me, who opens her legs wide then pulls me into place. I close my eyes. I am in the back seat with Becky, headlights jumping wildly as we crash through the trees.

Waking up, my heart pounding hard. Judith is curled around me, her hand on my chest. I am thinking about that mysterious white powder, the fact we have twice smoked up, the way my heart is thumping loud and fast. A white crippled me is spinning through the bedroom. I can all but see it slipping in and out of the moonlight. The shadows of the bare maple branches that sway stiffly on the wall. Judith's heart in my back, pounding with mine. Bang bang bang. From the floor above us, tinny sounds of a radio, cutlery clanging against plates, a chair scraping.

The white crippled me floats out the window, pirouettes in the night air, dances across the sky with wild cats. The thudding of our hearts mixes with the sound of traffic, the deep cough of an engine opens my veins, when it roars my blood flows faster. In the distance I can hear an ambulance siren weaving through the night. A second siren starts up to counterpoint the first. I see my father lying behind the glass counter. Hear the siren approaching. See Genevieve Wilson pulling open his tie and trying to force air into his lungs.

My heart is still pounding. I am wondering if Judith is monitoring this strange phenomenon, this double pounding that might send us both into our white crippled selves, our dead crippled selves dancing outside forever, our dead crippled feet kicking up little storms of white dust.

This is the first time I have ever thought I might be dying. Judith rolls away. Cold patches of sweat have formed on my back where she was against me, my upper lip, the hollows under my arms. *Die then*, I say to myself. *Die.*

Sirens lace through the night. My heart is still beating too hard, but now I feel beneath it the steady pounding of the city, the thumping current that runs through the pavement, the sewers, the tangles of wires, the steady bass counterpoint to the soprano tinkle of sirens, cutlery, broken voices earnestly telling each other the words I suddenly see in thousands of cartoon balloons floating over thousands of kitchen tables.

I wake up next with my hand on my heart. Judith, dressed, is sitting in a corner. A light perched on a radiator shines over her closed eyes. In one hand she is holding the plastic vial I have come to recognize. Her lips are parted, she is humming softly and swaying to her own music.

I was standing at the kitchen sink, drinking glass after glass of cold water when the apartment door opened, a hall light flashed on and a woman stepped into the kitchen.

"I'm Vivian," she announced. Streaked blond hair, perfectly

coiffed and parted, porcelain features, one of those long suede coats with fur trim that used to be popular.

"Paul," I said. "I'm with Judith."

Vivian's mouth started to open, then she pressed her lips together and smiled. That controlled smile and the fur-suede combination made me think that, like Judith, she came from somewhere with money. Of course I could have asked to see her jewellery: perhaps fearing Henry and I might one day reach above ourselves, our father had taught us how to measure people by what they would be worth in a pawn shop.

Behind Vivian a man appeared. The first impression he gave was of size. He loomed over Vivian and when he came into the kitchen he filled it up. He was wearing a black leather jacket, suitably scuffed. Straight black hair down to his shoulders. A black inverted handlebar moustache. The skin of his cheeks and forehead was red from the cold. "Nicko Ross," he said. He had a strong confident smile and his hand, when it surrounded mine, was hard and muscular. "Man, it's cold out there."

Then he flashed his big white smile again and said warmly, "Paul. So you're the famous Paul Judith has been telling us about." And then—though he gave no sign of recognizing me—I was suddenly sure I had met him before. He was Henry's friend, the one Henry had waved to at the racetrack, the Lothario with the movie star on his arm. Definitely not Vivian. Which was why I didn't say anything—there was something about Vivian that made me cautious, perhaps just the fact that she obviously came from money. Unlike Nicko Ross—you knew right away that his money was in his wallet, not his past. I was still trying to match him with the man I had seen at the racetrack when he put me to work cleaning and chopping vegetables for what Nicko said was his "famous Sunday night stew".

A few minutes later the sounds of electric guitars were wailing from the speakers placed above the cupboards, steam ballooning from the stove. I was drinking coffee, still trying to wake up, while Judith and Nicko sat at the table, sorting seeds and stems from some "home-grown shit", then rolling it into three-paper spliffs that Nicko lined up like so many misshapen baby carrots.

Everything took on a red pulsing glow, as though lit by inner fire. As though the four of us were enclosed in a warm safe cave of our own making. The rich steamy smells of cooking food, the taste of red wine, Judith snuggled next to me as I stood with my back to the counter, the music, Nicko's bright manic smile and the way Vivian kept glancing at Judith and me.

"Paul, you always this quiet? You and Judith, man." Big grin. "You okay, Paul?"

"I'm okay."

Something about the way Nicko's voice filled the room. A magnet that both drew and repelled.

At midnight we went outside. Clouds had settled over the city, and the air had warmed. At sunset the moon had been a hard white crescent. Now it shone softly through skeined breaks in the clouds, and a thawing breeze was making the snowy streets thick with slush.

Nicko and Vivian were walking fast and had gotten ahead. I scooped a handful of snow from a lawn, shaped it into a ball. Judith caught my arm. "Leave them."

Judith's hand trembled in mine. I turned to look at her. A wave of cold seemed to be passing through her, giving her bones a shake they didn't need. She pushed herself against me. Grabbed at my coat.

We returned to the apartment. "I'll make you some tea," I said. As the water heated, I, already an old familiar in this place, got out what I knew to be Judith's favourite cup and the kind of herbal tea she favoured.

When everything was ready I carried it into the bedroom.

Judith was crouched in the corner, inspecting her arm by the light of the reading lamp. Her sleeve was rolled up, a small syringe dangling from the inside of her elbow. Judith's face turned towards me. "I can never quite do this. Help me? Please?"

She showed me what to do, then helped me draw out the needle when I was finished. "That's better," she said. "Once I get started I have to keep going until I fall asleep." She was looking directly at me. Her uncertain smile had changed to that more familiar smile, that cocky smile she'd used on Fenwick and me the day she'd walked into the store and started reading Shakespeare.

Judith turned off the light, then lay down on the bed and pulled the quilt up over herself. From beneath it she threw her clothes out onto the floor. "Thanks for everything. I'm dead. I have to sleep. See you at the store."

For a minute I stood outside her house. A few taxis were driving slowly through the wet streets. I went round the back and looked at the garage I'd stared at earlier that evening. The maple branches. The black sleeping square of Judith's window. I tried to imagine myself going back home to Henry's. Explaining my lateness. Trying to shave the next morning with what would surely be the world's worst hangover while Jeremy put globs of cream on his head.

I was thinking about this while I walked and nothing seemed more natural than my arriving, as if by chance, in front of the Savoy Hotel. The lobby lights were still on. I went inside and approached the desk. I could see the key to Room 66 hanging on its brass hook, warm and waiting. The clerk looked up to me as though nothing could be more normal than the arrival of this particular person at this particular time.

"Would this be Fenwick's Used and Antiquarian Books?"

Almost every day someone, apparently unable to read the sign on the window, would ask that same question.

"This is it."

"Great." Then he stuck out his hand. "I'm Leonard Marks, the publisher."

"Pleased to meet you," I said.

It was not a cold day but Leonard Marks, publisher, was wearing one of those threadbare heavy wool army-surplus over-coats you could get for ten dollars. Also a toque, which he now removed so he could shake out his pony-tail. He reached into his pocket for a package of tobacco and while he stood silently in front of me he began rolling a cigarette. Bits of falling tobacco clung to his coat. When a few makings dropped to the floor he looked down regretfully, then kicked them out of sight.

"Mind if I look around?" he asked.

"Go ahead."

He had a skinny raw-boned look and an American accent. The accent, the toque, the way he peered suspiciously around the store—I knew right away he was one of the draft dodgers or army deserters who came up to Toronto in those years to avoid being sent to Viet Nam. They always looked tougher than the soldiers they hadn't been. Science fiction was what they read.

He finished rolling his cigarette. The ends of his fingers were stained with nicotine, his nails bitten short and raw. Then he took off his coat, folded it and put in on the floor.

At closing time he was sitting in the customer armchair drinking coffee Martha Fenwick had brought him and reading a fat tattered paperback.

"*Madame Bovary*," he offered, when I told him I had to lock up. "Great stuff. This is what happens if you let your wife get bored in the afternoon." Neither of us looked either married or eligible enough for such an exalted station. But I knew what he meant, or at least thought I did.

He bought the book. When I finished locking up he was standing outside under the streetlamp, reading.

The next day was cold and rainy. When he came into the store just after noon his face was wet, his toque soggy. He nodded at me, as though we were old friends, then installed himself in the armchair and began rolling himself a cigarette. Judith looked at him, then went to busy herself at the back of the store. A few coughs managed to attract Martha, who brought him a cup of coffee.

"This is it," he said proudly, handing us copies of his magazine. The front cover featured a drawing of the Wing On Funeral Home.

Martha looked at me. The Wing On Funeral Home and everything associated with it were topics banned from our conversation since I had come to work at the store. Yet the view he had drawn might have been as seen from her studio window. Although, of course, she no longer had that studio.

"That's my house. Very quiet at night."

"Looks great," I said.

Leonard turned to me. "Why don't you give me something I can publish. You must be a writer. Everyone who works in bookstores is secretly a writer. Or are you already famous?"

I shook my head.

"Tell me what you did before. I bet you were an English student."

"I worked at a garage."

"It's true," Martha said.

"Of course it's true. Great experience. A man is his car. Why not write about that? Anyone can write. Don't let them give you that bullshit about an education. The world needs to hear from people like you. All you need is a thousand pieces of paper and a typewriter."

Leonard had wide lips and when he smiled the corners of his

mouth turned down as though to announce he knew everything he'd just said was ridiculous. He supported himself and his magazine working as a printer at a literary press. Recently he'd been switched to the midnight shift, which was why he was free to spend his afternoons drifting around bookstores.

"The pay is shitty but they let me use their machines," he explained to me. Sometimes, after closing, we'd go out for beer. Or we'd buy some cold cuts and a loaf of bread and go back to his apartment where Leonard would read to me from his latest epic.

Under his overcoat he always wore the same uniform: jeans, a plaid shirt, a leather vest with his tobacco and papers sticking out of the pockets. "My Canadian outfit," he explained.

His epics were plays about workers rising up against capitalism. "It's my name. My grandfather changed the spelling but it didn't do any good." His plays featured huge strike scenes with dozens of workers shouting obscenities as they fought on the picket lines. Often there were long speeches about the end of the world as we know it.

"What do you think?" Leonard would ask me. Then he would put down his sheaf of papers and shake his head. While he was reading I would be re-imagining the whole thing as an opera. However, I never said this. Leonard had a strong deep voice, "loud enough to wake the dead," he would growl, though no one, dead or alive, ever came up to see why we were making so much noise.

Despite the drawbacks of his current productions, I was convinced Leonard would become a great writer, a Thomas Wolfe exiled to Canada. When I told him this he pointed to a cardboard box beneath his desk, half-full of yellow typing paper. "It's all there," he pronounced melodramatically. I believed him.

One night Henry asked me what kind of person I thought Judith was. Henry with his head cocked to one side, waiting for my answer as though it was an exam I was about to fail. He had met Judith a couple of times at the store, and then once at the compulsory "let's check her out, Paul" dinner at the house. After which he had remarked on all the wine she'd drunk— as though he himself hadn't put back half a bottle of Scotch.

"What kind of person? What do you mean?"

"You know what I mean," Henry said. "Is she a good person for you to hook up with or is she just some kind of lush?"

"She's not a drinker."

"Drugs," Henry said. "The skin around the eyes always gives it away." He announced this with such authority and conviction I didn't doubt for a moment that he knew every detail of Judith's habits. Her habit. I didn't even ask myself how it was he felt qualified to make such a snap judgement, or how he'd tuned his antenna so finely.

That was the thing about Henry: I always believed he *knew*. That he had a direct vision into the terrain of cunning and conning, a front-row view of a certain region of the human heart, the country of small lies and cover-ups.

Nicko Ross also gave that impression. Of *knowing*. He certainly wanted to find out. He was always asking me questions— unlike Vivian, "the weird room-mate". She was a different case, a case study. Her streaked hair. Her make-up. The virtuoso way she could juggle knives and frying pans and fifteen minutes or three hours later you would be sitting down to one of those meals that Toronto's food writers would be slobbering over in the papers the next week because Vivian-the-weird-room-mate was also a cook, a *chef*, a temperamental anorexic junkie creator of masterpieces who spent her evenings off on the nod in the living room, ears tuned to sitar music, Paul Bowles books piled at her side, eyes fixed on that secret imaginary point the guru she rented twice a week had taught her to find.

If I was in the room, her eyes would occasionally turn to me, look right through me.

"Ever since she started meditating she's gone strange," Judith said, when I asked if Vivian had something special against me.

"Or maybe she's only that way when she's stoned," I offered.

"She's always stoned."

That was true. Judith used drugs but was not an addict. Or so I told myself at the beginning. Vivian was in another category. Sometimes I wondered how she could afford to support her habit, which seemed considerable, and where all the drugs came from. "The restaurant," Judith said, but to me it seemed Nicko's comings and goings were the sun and the moon of Vivian's existence.

Vivian shot up only in her bedroom. Out of sight. Nicko would arrive, go with her to her room. When Vivian came out she made straight for the living room, the record player, that secret place between her eyes.

Eventually Nicko would emerge and come to the kitchen to make coffee. Then suddenly he would turn curious and start with the questions. Whenever I talked about myself he would sit motionless, his eyes sparkling, a half-smile on his face. He seemed a few years older than I was, and not only did he remember everything I told him, but sometimes he would, out of the blue, ask me a question about some loose end. We might be in the kitchen, smoking and drinking coffee, and he would turn to me and say, "Did you read that thing in the paper today about those guys up north? Didn't you used to go up there in the summers?" And before I knew it I would be retelling the story of Henry and Jeanine, adding new details, grabbing a hat and turning my chair around so I could imitate Captain Bill with his shirt unbuttoned, peering out from under the brim of his cap and talking out of the side of his mouth as he roared across the lake in the launch.

Sometimes Nicko would suggest we "step outside". When we went to the pool hall, certain restaurants, even strolling along the street, everyone knew Nicko and Nicko knew everyone. There was always a smile, that little sparkle of curiosity, a clap of his big hand on the shoulder, a "see you later, man." I would imagine Nicko in kitchens and coffee shops all across the city, listening, recording, asking questions, supplying little packages of what it took to stare at the secret space between your eyes.

Some nights at the apartment it was just Vivian. When Nicko failed to arrive she would sit frozen in the living room, and then it would be like sharing the apartment with a corpse. Judith would put on her coat and we would go out. Often as not we would end up at the hotel, in Room 66, the Honeymoon Suite. Our world. Our own. Winter slid into summer, but we were too occupied with each other to worry about how quickly time was passing.

One evening as I was coming out of the bookstore I saw Nicko across the street, arguing with a cop about his car. The cop was giving Nicko a ticket because the meter had expired and Nicko had his face stuck into the cop's, shouting loud enough that I could hear him across the street and the traffic. The cop said something back to Nicko, put his hand up to push him away, and suddenly Nicko's hands flew forward, he grabbed the cop's coat and lifted him in the air, depositing him on the hood of his car. Then Nicko stepped back and roared, "Hey man, what you doing sitting on my car?"

The whole scene was so ludicrous, so many people had gathered, that when Nicko laughed the cop had to laugh with them and then before anything more could develop Nicko had spotted me across the street and had slipped through the traffic to greet me. His arm was around my shoulder; we were walking fast, turning the corner. "Keep moving before the son of a bitch shoots me," Nicko said.

But I couldn't believe Nicko expected to be shot. I couldn't believe Nicko was afraid of anything.

It was the end of August. One of those times of year when the city used to seem so magical to me, suspended in the slowly emptying light of summer. The exact colour of the sun against bricks. The fading green of the leaves. The way August light gradually filled the streets, the spaces between houses, the growing gaps between leaves and blades of grass. The way even people's eyes changed in that light, as though they too were looking at you across what they knew to be the last days of summer, the last days before the season changed, the leaves began to turn, the city accelerated into the rush of autumn.

Nicko had turned into an alleyway. He stopped and from the foldover pocket of one of the khaki shirts he often wore, he pulled out a joint.

My nervousness must have shown on my face.

"Hey, don't worry, I eat cops for breakfast." Nicko's big smile.

"That's what I'm worried about."

Nicko lit up. When we started walking again it was more slowly. I felt dizzy, almost nauseated. We came to a tiny park, not even a real park but just a glorified traffic circle filled with grass and a single bench. I collapsed on it.

"You okay?"

"Sure," I said. The cars going round were making me dizzy. I looked at Nicko. He was fine.

"Man, you're wiped," Nicko said. He slid his arm across the back of the bench towards me.

Here it comes, I thought. What, I didn't know. Somehow I managed to get to my feet before his hand arrived. Even while I was standing up I had decided to get through this by pretending

I was my brother Henry. I pushed back my hair, then cocked my head to one side. "Got a smoke?"

Nicko produced a cigarette. We stood, smoking, in the midst of this tiny island while rush-hour traffic swirled around us. "Shoot a few games?" Nicko asked.

In those days it seemed I was never more than a ten-minute walk from Diamond Billiards. We started across the street. A woman in a car slowed to let us by. She had black hair. Her fingers were tapping on the steering wheel. I wished she were Judith. I wished I could be in a car with Judith, just the two of us, heading out to some highway we'd never driven.

I broke first, a stiff crack I made for the sound of it, for the rush up my spine as the red triangle of snooker balls pushed into each other, nowhere to go, then burst outwards. A red ball fluked into a corner pocket. I followed it with a black, another red giving me shape for a black that I sank while leaving my cue ball on the rail.

"Cowboy," Nicko said. "If I'd known you played like that, I might have given you a spot."

Three games later I had one of Nicko's cigarettes in my mouth and was leaning down low, legs braced wide, chin touching the cue while my eyes fixed on a blue ball, the yellow-white reflection of the lamp, the thick green nap of the felt. Nicko, who had won every game, was leaning against the next table. He called up to Sam for a Coke. Then he broke into a little hum. Why not? He had good eyes, strong arms, a cue that danced around in his hands as though he'd been born in a pool hall. He also knew something about snooker. Had the cue ball on the proverbial string. Hadn't left me a single good shot until now. Homing in on the blue ball, I could see a long run opening out in front of me. I waggled the cue. Nicko's weird humming swam through the dark air. "Don't look ahead," Henry would say to me when I was fighting. "Don't try to be too smart. Just be *there, right now.*"

I was there. I was right now. I was fixed, poised, balanced, waiting.

Pock. One blue. An easy red bank. Another blue. Two pinks. A brown to bring the cue ball back to the last red. *Pock.* Stay downtown for the yellow, green and brown. Moving easily around the table, the pace all mine, screwing the tip into the chalk between shots, can't hear anything but my own muffled footsteps, the slow draw of breath, the high squeak of wood against skin. The blue and pink are on the spots where I left them. *Pock. Pock.*

Only the black ball is left.

It is lying snug against the rail. Lazy. Confident. Come and get me if you can.

Commandment #63. From the book of life as taught to Dungo Merde by his older brother, Henry: Thou shalt not fear the ball along the rail.

Commandment #64: Winners don't worry about losing.

So there it was: the black ball against the rail. In that situation the safe course of action, the cautious choice with no bad consequences, the choice favoured by the odds, is to aim directly at the black ball, banking it off the rail and sending it to the opposite end of the table while leaving the white ball, the cue ball, awkwardly positioned against the cushion where the black ball had been.

But you can't win the game without sinking the black ball. Not sinking the black ball is guaranteed to be a fatal mistake.

Sliding a ball along the rail to the pocket is not so difficult if you have practised it thousands of times with your older brother patiently setting it up, over and over again. "Dungo. *Dungo.* Don't think. Just do it. Like you're on automatic."

I was leaning over the ball. Balanced. Fixing on the reflection of the lamp. All I had to do was empty myself and wait until the automatic pilot took over, put the cue into motion. But there was something uncomfortable about the way my socks were scrunched into the toes of my shoes. Maybe that explained why I was swaying just a tiny bit, swaying from side to side and my feet were trying to grip through my shoes to the floor to stop the swaying, steady everything down. But all this toe gripping was making my feet anxious.

I could hear Henry's voice: "Dungo, if you want to take your shoes off, take them off. It's your turn. Do anything you want."

I straightened up, kicked off my shoes, pulled my socks straight.

"Jesus," Sam said. "I wouldn't do that here. You ever *look* at that floor?" He had come over to watch this great moment.

I leaned over once more. My toes spread. My mind emptied. The cue began to move.

Pock. The black ball slid towards the corner pocket. At the last moment I noticed it had lost contact with the rail. At the pocket it did a brief tango, then stopped obediently at the edge of the hole, waiting for Nicko to put it to sleep.

Commandment #65: Don't lose.

On the way back to the apartment we decided to cut through a back lane of the market. A light glowed through the windows of a parked van. Nicko peered in. And as he did two men emerged from the shadows and jumped him.

Nicko must have heard them coming because he whirled as they got to him. One buckled over as Nicko sank a fist into his belly. The other saw me and attacked. His head in the darkness was like a speed bag suspended in the night. My hands jumped out on their own, then stopped as my attacker turned and ran.

The man on the ground moaned. Nicko looked into the van,

waved me over. Two men were playing cards and listening to the radio.

"Let's go," Nicko said.

"Aren't you going to call the police?"

"Us? You have to be kidding. What have we been doing?" But at the corner he phoned the hospital emergency and told them the location of the van. We were blocks away before we heard the sound of sirens.

"You okay?" Nicko asked. "You really handled yourself well."

"I didn't do anything."

"Go on. If it weren't for you the two of them would have mugged me."

"Sure."

He stopped under a streetlight. "Let's see your hands." I held them out. "They're clean."

"Why not?"

Nicko looked at me strangely. "That guy who came at you. You must have nailed him six times in the head before he even moved."

There was a new tone in Nicko's voice, an admiration I'd never heard before. I was still surging with adrenaline. But I knew those little flyweight taps I'd landed couldn't hurt anybody. Nicko was the heavy hitter. People could jump Nicko, but Nicko was the one who would walk away.

We went into a bar and got a drink. Nicko led me to a table off to the side. "No big deal. From now on we'll watch where we're going in the dark." There were so many things about Nicko, about the way he was with me, that kept reminding me of Henry. The feeling of being known. The older-brother protection. Except that with Nicko, unlike Henry, it was free. He was willing to cheer me on with Judith, supply me with drugs, give me a lesson in the pool hall, protect me from monsters in the dark, but nothing was demanded in return.

Yet instead of making me resent Henry it made me feel sorry for him. These days when I saw him, Henry often seemed tired and washed out. He had his house, he had bought the garage, but the burden of it all seemed to weigh on him too heavily. Everything was so hard for Henry, so easy for Nicko.

SIX

I NEVER INVITED Leonard over to the apartment. He had joked about drugs but I didn't know what he would make of Vivian, Vivian playing corpse in the living room, Vivian who had taken to moaning and babbling to herself while listening to the music.

"I've got to get her out of here."

"Why don't you move?"

"It's my apartment."

"Move anyway."

"It's not like that—"

Winter came early. Vivian had begun to invite friends over. Their bottles of Coke and their containers of take-out Chinese food filled the refrigerator. Often I would find them in the kitchen, asleep with their heads on the table or heating little concoctions in spoons.

To get away we would sometimes walk half the night. Judith, stoned herself, striding briskly through the snow. We would end up at the hotel, exhausted. Cuddle together between the rough white sheets listening to the sounds of the hotel, of cars humming through the snowy streets, of our own slow breathing as we moved into each other. Our bodies, the body our bodies made.

We stayed at the hotel so frequently I sometimes took the Honeymoon Suite for a week at a time.

The hotel was my place. To read, to dream, to wait for Judith when she wasn't there with me. Alone I would buy a bottle of soda water and arm myself with books, papers, magazines. Sometimes the clanking of radiators would be so loud I'd have to put down whatever I was reading to kick them. Then stand at the window and look out at the parking lot and the office towers across the street.

There was something relaxing about the way the Savoy Hotel was slowly crumpling into the ground. The weekly rates were low, the monthly lower yet; perhaps if you promised to stay for a year it was free. Most nights there was hot water, and once I even heard the sound of a vacuum cleaner in the hall.

All that winter and spring the store grew more and more crowded. As Fenwick prospered, the occasional dinners at Le Troubador became more frequent; sometimes there were even two or three in a week.

Those Golden Hole specials. The golden light of the storm candles. The fake plaster angels smiling down at us. Judith trembling beside me, making her trips to the bathroom for chemical refreshment. Sometimes, just before we left in the big car for a trip through the snow, I would have sneaked off with Judith for a quick hit of cocaine, angel dust for the plaster angels, and then leaning back in my chair as Fenwick talked, eyes half closed, white lightning flashes digging through the smoky air, Judith's leg under the table pressed against mine. The chains of the sea. Until we drown.

One evening when I came out of the bookstore Leonard was standing at the sidewalk. The snow was melting but the city air was raw and cold. Leonard had a new issue of the magazine to show me. I happened to glance across the street. Nicko Ross was talking to someone in front of the delicatessen. He nodded at me, I waved back. A few seconds later, Leonard started away from me. I walked after him. "Are we going for a beer?"

Leonard looked at me. "Sure. You buy." He walked into the tavern and I followed. When we were seated in our usual corner, Leonard, with his back against the wall in case the place was stormed by Nazi death squads or whatever his reason was for always facing out, rolled a cigarette, then asked me who I'd been waving to.

"Nicko Ross."

"I know his name," Leonard replied. "But do you know who he is?"

"No," I said, suddenly knowing. My pal and protector, Nicko Ross.

A few days later Vivian moved out.

"It was her idea" was all Judith would say. I wrestled with telling her about Nicko, but I had no proof, and Judith was as suspicious of Leonard as I was of Nicko.

Our bodies were still their own kingdom but Judith was taking more and more drugs. Sometimes we fought about it. Then she made a deal with Fenwick to work Saturday afternoons but leave an hour early during the week. That left me to close up, which I didn't mind, and Judith free to take off on her various errands without having to make explanations to me.

One night Judith stayed late to work with me at the store. When the last customer had left, the blinds had been pulled and the front door locked, we stepped into the back alley for a smoke. Layers of light on the chipped paint of the bricks. A cold hollow wind. Judith close to me for warmth, one hand snuggled into the pocket of my coat. She inhaled sharply, her eyes on mine as she fought to hold the smoke in her lungs. Then: "To work. To work."

Inside the store she made for the cassette player. During the day hidden speakers emit a honeyed stream of bland classical music, soothing harmonies for the refined ears of the clients of Fenwick's Used and Antiquarian Books. Night-time is blues time. Steel strings twisting out their tomcat howls while whisky-pocked voices float through the empty store. We were unpacking some cartons that had been stacked in a corner for weeks. When we were finally done, we threw them out back, then went across the street for beer and chicken wings. After a trip to the bathroom for reinforcements, Judith started feeding the juke box. By the time we got out onto the street again the after-dark crowd had emerged: students on their way home from the library, clusters of skinheads exchanging drugs in the doorways of closed shops, couples arm in arm on their way to and from movies and restaurants. Judith's black pupils open wide to funnel in the night. Her glossy hair. Her taut pale cheeks. Her fingers digging hard into my arm. The slow traffic crawling through her nerves.

We stopped. Judith reached out to the street, opened a taxi door, beckoned me to follow. I slid in beside her. She clung to me, shivering. Her need. When Judith needed, her bones got the jumps. We came to one of those big restaurants with white table-cloths where the staff dress in tuxedos. Judith gave the driver a bill. We got out. Then Judith led me around the side to the kitchen entrance. Overflowing garbage cans propped open the metal door. Inside was a world of steam, noise, cooks and waiters dancing to avoid collision. Vivian Armstrong was in its midst. She looked at me, through me, as though I were an undesirable odour that should be sprayed away. Then she took Judith to one side, not even bothering to conceal what she was doing, gave her a packet from her purse, leaned forward to kiss Judith on the lips.

Outside, the wind was colder. Judith against me as we started walking quickly, not talking. Soon we had crossed out of the district of fancy shops and restaurants, into a no man's land of office buildings, warehouses, fenced-off construction sites. The wind was coming off the lake, blowing old papers and garbage along the pavement, banging it off the hoardings. We stopped for a moment. Above the wind and the distant traffic I could hear the screams of the seagulls wheeling above us. A few minutes later we were in an old part of the city. Some of the century-old buildings had been sandblasted and renovated, others were boarded up.

At the hotel door Judith stopped, took a breath, turned and smiled up at me. "Shall we?" I felt the little jolt that always arrived when Judith somehow exposed herself.

I bowed. "At your service."

"Kind sir." Arm in arm we climbed the steps of the Savoy Hotel. Inside the door we were immediately surrounded by warm air smelling of ancient radiators and musty carpets.

"Home," Judith said.

The desk was at the end of the lobby. Judith leaned against the old varnished counter. "The usual. The Honeymoon Suite." Her cheeks flushed from our walk, her eyes black and shining, Judith could have been the youthful and radiant bride arriving at the most glorious of destinations.

The clerk—a woman with eyes whose whites were a veined and yellow porcelain, a woman who had seen and possibly experienced more than one or two honeymoons in her day—smiled up at Judith and reached behind her to the hook where our key always hung. Key number 66, black numerals stamped into a worn brown wooden oval.

As we went towards the elevator another couple arrived. We were all crowded in together. Judith, strung out and anxious, pressed against me. The man whispered something I didn't catch. "Go fuck yourself with a broom," Judith replied. Thick silence. The man and I glared at each other. His face was scarlet. The elevator door opened. The couple left. The woman turned to look at us, her throat working. The door closed and the elevator jerked upwards.

In our room Judith got a glass from the bathroom. Poured herself a drink. "If mothers are what make men that way," she said, "I never want to be a mother." She sipped at her drink. I was thinking that she was trying to calm herself. Trying to convince herself that she was relaxed, no problem, that everything she was doing was by choice and not necessity.

"Look at the wallpaper. Does it drive you crazy or what? We should take a can of paint to this place."

I looked at the wallpaper. It was the same as always, the Honeymoon Suite special, a mottled mustard background covered with flowering vines.

"It's not getting any better," I said. Although the truth was that I liked the wallpaper, liked everything about this room. I liked this room so much that after our first night here I could have told you its every detail. But by the time this particular night had arrived, we had been in Room 66 many times. Too many for me to remember the exact number, the way I did early on, but not so many I didn't feel a terrible pang every time we left, every time I thought might be the last. One day I will sort them out in my mind, list them carefully one by one and perhaps even mark them on old calendars.

But this evening, although I feared Judith and I might have entered some sort of twilight, I was still prepared to hope that this twilight could endure. I will admit I have always been an optimist about Judith. I can be convinced of anything. I want to be. On the evening in question I was even prepared to believe that the menacing twilight would dissolve into nothing worse than an ordinary night, a night dark and sad but nothing to get hysterical about, just a dark sad night that would eventually give way to the brightness of a new day. Possibly a day that would burn so long and so bright that it would last my whole life. Such ambition may sound ridiculous, but on the evening of which I speak, I wanted nothing more than to spend my life drowned in this love.

Judith put down her drink and stared at me as though, like the wallpaper, I was in need of renovation. This was a new development, Judith turning on me, and that was why I had begun to think in terms of twilight. Judith, it seemed to me, was getting ready to move on. The previous Sunday, for example, she had invited me to her apartment for lunch.

When I arrived at noon Judith was just waking up. Her face swollen as it sometimes is after she has been drinking too much. Fresh from the shower, wearing cut-off denim shorts and a T-shirt that was also doubling as a towel. Another time I could offer a discourse on Judith's body, lithe and whippy, long slim legs that had earned her the three small trophies displayed on the bathroom shelf where she keeps her toothbrush.

But that Sunday I was not intrigued by Judith's past as a cross-country star. Tell me someone is an athlete and it only reminds me of Henry. Left jab snaking up out of nowhere takes your jaw half off its hinge. I was standing in front of Judith's sink, looking at the plastic rack she used to drain her dishes. Not that I am the detective type, but I couldn't help seeing the carefully washed remains of an elaborate meal for two: salad bowls, dessert plates, serving platters, wineglasses, water glasses, little demi-tasse coffee cups she and I had bought together at the market, brandy snifters I had never seen before, big palm-filling snifters with a little stripe of gold around the top.

I picked up one of the snifters and held it to the light. The glass was smudged with fingerprints so large I looked at the tips of my own fingers to confirm that these stranger's traces truly were gigantic. It was not a pleasant feeling, jealously holding a brandy glass to inspect the marks left by the fingers of another man, contemplating the vague wide mark at the top that must have been left by this other unwanted mouth, the mouth that after an elaborate dinner had drunk from the mouth of this glass, the mouth that might have drunk from the mouth of my Judith, who of course was not mine. Ownership was not part of our agreement. And so, when she came into the kitchen and I was still holding the glass, I put it to the tap and filled it with water. "Thirsty," I said. But unable to carry through the mouth to mouth to mouth of it all, I ended up standing in front of the sink, watching the water slide over the shining gold rim.

When I first met Judith I didn't care about her moods, didn't worry about the giants she might be seeing in her spare time. We would come to the hotel and I was happy enough to stand guard while Judith exorcised her demons, drank whisky, ranted and raved until finally some sort of peace settled in, a temporary truce big enough for both of us, a temporary truce that some-how worked its way deep enough inside me that for a few moments, perhaps only the length of a sigh, my own demons were also put to sleep and life was simply itself. The breath I was breathing, the flowered vines patiently climbing through the mustard, the sweet-sour taste of Judith, the babyish way she tumbled into sleep instantly and without warning: in the bath, sitting cross-legged on the floor and talking to her imaginary ant collection, lying on her back reading a magazine.

With a tiny sound I am sure I once heard, her eyelids would come down over her eyes. Like a curtain being dropped in mid-speech. And suddenly Judith would be breathing the way she breathes when she sleeps, a slow child's breathing slowly deepen-ing, her face smooth and neutral, her fingers seeking each other out and twining together as if praying.

After I had injected Judith, I would open the window, lie on the floor, and listen to the sounds of sirens criss-crossing the city. They approached, they faded, they drew emergency maps through the ether. Fire engines, ambulances, police cars making their high-pitched symphony of a city at war with itself. The next day you could read about it in the papers. The shootings. The bombings. The police chases. Or the way a certain Mr. Ralph Stevens, small-time jeweller and watch-repairer, had been struck down by a heart attack while standing at his glass counter, preparing to subtract a link from the gold expansion bracelet of a watch in the possession of a slim-wristed young lady.

"Confess," Judith once insisted, "you're jealous of the needle. O prick of fate, would that you were mine." Maybe she was right. It sometimes seemed to me she was a city that had been captured by the enemy, a city occupied by the absolute authority of her addiction. Within the attractive and well-kept walls of this fortified city, I was welcome to wander—on carnival occasions I was even invited to invade. But in the end, I would never be more than a tourist, while the occupying army remained, implacable and smug.

Or perhaps I *was* jealous, because every time I tried to relapse into some grand explosion of consciousness, I would hear the sirens and think of my father sinking to the floor right before the horrified eyes of poor Genevieve Wilson. How embarrassing the whole event must have been to him. How he must have struggled to keep his face under control. Surely he had planned to die with dignity, in his armchair, drink in hand, Henry's phone number tucked away in his wallet.

We are in the Honeymoon Suite. Room number 66. Judith has finished her drink. It is time to get down to business.

Holding Judith's arm I feel nauseated. The insides of her elbows are pocked with scabs, her veins purple and ropy.

"I don't like this," I say.

Judith, her lips pursed, is staring down at the needle. "It's supposed to be good."

"I don't like doing this."

Judith doesn't reply. Just waits, trembling, her arm outstretched. We both know she can't inject herself. That her current alternative to drugs is drinking herself silly. That if I don't help her I will be betraying her. That eventually, or not so eventually, if I don't help her she will find someone else.

"Last time," she says. She has often claimed she would give up drugs—someday—but this kind of declaration is new and her voice is almost convincing. "Last time for both of us. After this we stop dead. Cold. Together." She looks straight at me and I am sure she believes she is saying the truth.

I push the needle home, filling her veins with the gift of her restaurant friend. Judith's eyes are closed. I want to kiss her eyelids. Instead I watch the riptide of her blood, carefully extract the metal from her flesh, lead her to the chair where she folds her arms across her chest. Then I go into the bathroom where I am supposed to inject myself. The idea that we are doing this together is a fiction invented by Judith. Although I've tried a few times. Maybe more than a few. In fact, it seems that with drugs I am no longer sure when I am lying to Judith, when I am lying to myself. But not this time. Because it is to be the last time, the time after which we will stop dead. Cold. Together. Because I didn't like the way Vivian Armstrong looked right through me. I flush it away, then go back into the room and lie down as always, feeling vaguely expectant because I'd carried out most of the usual routine.

Soon I begin hearing the sirens. And also, as usual, I begin to see the replay of my father's last scene at the jewellery store. That scene gives way to a blankness filled by my own breathing. It is amazing, when you do listen to your own breathing, how loud and complex it can be. On this night I am listening to my breathing. I am lying in my usual place on the floor. I am thinking about Judith, about the way her face must be at this moment, the angelic calm that comes over it. I am remembering other times in the Honeymoon Suite, eyes closed, each in our own little universe but faithfully breathing together. How united with her and content I have often felt listening to the counterpoint of our faithful lungs. Which is when I realize that I am not now hearing that counterpoint. That it is my turn to lean over the still body, feel for the pulse, drive the heel of my hand into the ribcage, contemplate exactly what she meant by her last words as I first turn her over to clear out her throat, then back again to try forcing air into her lungs before I pick up the telephone and get one of the sirens coming my way.

SEVEN

JUNKIE." This word, outmoded, scornful, ringing with all the conviction of a false coin, was once thrown at me. *Junkie.* I was standing across from my mother. Between us was an open grave. Sometimes, on a Sunday or even a weekday afternoon if the weather is warm, I go back. Those who glance my way see a middle-aged man not ashamed to get down on his knees while planting flowers from a wooden box, or tending the plot with the little set of orange metal garden tools I keep in the trunk of my car.

That middle-aged man sometimes sighs as he straightens his back. He wears sombre-hued shirts, often with a tie. He has suits, tweed jackets, flannel pants. Shoes that from time to time he polishes. Lining them up on his kitchen counter the way he once lined up empty beer bottles.

Over the years he has taken on a little weight. His hair is still black, cut slightly longer than is the fashion. He wears gold-rimmed glasses that make his features seem somehow severe. Strained. Something about the way his skin presses uncomfortably against his bones. At least that is what I often think when I see myself in the mirror. My face looks as though I have been under intense pressure for years.

I knelt over Judith, that night in the Honeymoon Suite. "After this we stop dead. Cold. Together." Had she meant she was going to kill herself? That she intended me to die, as well, with the dose she had measured out for me? The dose I flushed down the toilet of the Honeymoon Suite?

That was what I thought as I emptied the air from my lungs into hers. I hadn't yet telephoned for help; I was so frightened and in such a panic, I couldn't decide where to call first. I kept thinking I had to stop working on her long enough to throw out everything that might incriminate. But what if she died while I was trying to save her from being arrested? And how could I save her? When the ambulance came I would have to tell them what had happened, and with the ambulance would be police. Or would I just say I had been having a few drinks with my girl-friend and she'd passed out? "Oh, is that a scab inside her elbow? I never notice such things—I work in a bookstore."

Crude, yes. You think crude thoughts when someone is dying. Especially when it seems to be part of a suicide pact, one in which you turn out to be the silent partner, the partner who never spoke because he was never told.

Judith retched. I pulled her up, hit her on the back. She kept heaving as I dragged her to the bathroom and positioned her head above the toilet. Her face turned colours. I stood beside her while mopping off her mouth with a wet cloth.

An hour later she was sitting in the armchair, her feet twisted up as usual, "perfectly normal", drinking one of the cans of cola I had fetched from the lobby. She was wrapped in towels. Her black hair was wet and clung to her shoulders. The skin of her face seemed to have collapsed, her dark eyes had swollen in their sockets and burned dully, her forehead was sallow and beaded with perspiration that she kept wiping away. When she smiled her mouth twisted slightly.

I too was drinking pop and smoking cigarettes. Of course I was relieved. I had not had to call an ambulance. Judith had survived.

Neither of us was dead or on our way to prison. But I was also angry. "Dead. Cold. Together." Together, yes, I wanted us to be together, but not at the price I had been paying these last few months. A price I had hardly considered until now when suddenly the bill presented itself. Romeo and Juliet? Yes. I could believe that. I had wanted to play Romeo courting Judith's Juliet. But I had never agreed to the death scene. These thoughts, others, worse, welled up. Mixed together. Melted in confusion. I was too angry to speak. Finally I tucked Judith into bed, piling all the extra blankets from the cupboard on top of her. She fell asleep before I was finished. Her mouth was in repose, the soft exhausted mouth of a child. Her long dark eyelashes, lashes that ended in a small perfect curve, lay still and serene. Her breathing was slow and clear. I took one of her hands. Her fingers closed trustingly around my own. The storm had come and gone. Now Judith was happy.

Something inside me rebelled. I ran to the bathroom, thinking it was my turn to crouch in front of the toilet. But nothing happened. I put on my coat. Then I knelt by the bed and kissed Judith's outstretched hand. "Goodbye," I said, not sure what I meant. But aware of the strange sound of my voice in this room where I was speaking only to impress myself.

It was three o'clock in the morning. The streets near the hotel were dead but when I went towards Yonge Street I could see the lights of cars moving up and down the street. A few sex and dirty-movie shops had their lights on, but only a few twenty-four-hour restaurants were open.

I was drinking coffee and reading the review of a movie Judith had said she wanted to see when a man slid into my booth. He had thinning dark hair that came down to his collar. The skin of his forehead was burned and peeling. His face, big-boned, cavernous, was unshaven. His eyes, large and feverish, tried to catch mine. He was breathing hard, as though in the midst of a long climb.

He put his hand out for money. His hand was so filthy that the dirt was crusted into the lines of his palm. When he opened his mouth to speak, he half stood—then he collapsed back into his seat. His head jerked forward and bounced off my newspaper. On the rebound it started to whip back and forth, as though protesting; he was still trying to say something, then someone had an arm around his neck and was forcing a spoon into his mouth.

They were calling an ambulance when I left the restaurant. I ran across the street, turned into an alleyway, then headed for the Wing On Funeral Home. Leonard's lights were out and he didn't answer my knocking.

He worked only a couple of blocks away. The building's brick walls were covered with graffiti and posters. I went round to the back lane. There was a set of double glass doors, wide enough for machines and skids of the giant sheets of glossy paper used for printing the fancy picture books in which they specialized.

Leonard was standing with his back to me, surveying the big Heidelberg press. It was clanking noisily. I pounded on the doors until he finally turned around and saw me.

A few minutes later I was drinking coffee strengthened by a healthy dose of the bourbon he kept in his workbench. "They like me drinking on the job," he explained. "Their last night-shift printer took acid all the time and used to print the pictures upside down."

Leonard and I were the only ones in the building. He shut down the machine. The civilized plucking of classical guitar wafted through the premises. We were surrounded not only by the picture books that the press printed for various of the city's publishers, but by the books of the press itself, post-Joycean "streams-of-unconsciousness" as Fenwick never tired of saying. "Listen to this jawbreaker," he'd call out from the back of the store, and then Judith and I would come to listen as he read out poetry filled with words long enough to occupy entire lines. Or critical mumbo-jumbo that sounded like buckets of pennies being poured down concrete stairs.

"Civilization" was all I could say.

"You look like shit," Leonard offered. "What happened?"

As I spoke, Leonard nodded. He had wrapped a bandana around his hair to avoid disaster with the ink rollers. Recently he had grown a moustache. It was much darker, almost black, and the contrast between it and his hair made his appearance seem more deliberate than it used to. He had also recently acquired a girlfriend with whom he was considering, as he put it, "a live-in situation". This certain Lillian was one of the most advanced of the press's avant-garde, so much so that instead of relying on the printed word, though Leonard had appointed her associate editor of his magazine, she specialized in performances during which she sang and shouted slogans—political, advertising and poetic mixed in an unpredictable rag-bag that was in fact quite entertaining. In her between-poem patter she claimed to have applied to various arts councils for the money to rent billboards, which she considered her true medium, but so far had been, as she pointed out, censored.

Now as Leonard listened to my own story I felt he was present not only as my old friend but as the adjunct of the performance poet, someone who would be able to interpret my own slogans and clichés.

When I was finished Leonard took a card out of his wallet. It was the business card of a bookstore in Kingston. "Nice quiet town," Leonard advised me. "Just the kind of place you need to be. You'll go here. You'll get a job. You'll listen to the radio and read. You'll dry out. When you need me, call or write. Don't come back until I give you permission."

When I started to object he led me to the bathroom and

made me look in the mirror. My face was like a question mark. One eye screwed up tight with tension. My mouth lopsided. My forehead crunched in on itself. "Wired," Leonard pronounced. "You're wired and your wires are crossed."

"Very funny."

"Speaking of crossing, have you run across your friend Nicko Ross lately?"

"Nicko Ross—"

"Constable Nicko Ross, I should say. Don't believe? Take a walk down to D Station. You can find him behind a desk. When he's not out on the street, raking in suckers like you."

The kind of sucker who had fallen so hard for Judith that I had forgotten how to ask questions. The kind of sucker who had exhausted himself trying to bridge the gap between myself and Judith. The kind of sucker who refused to recognize that each person must struggle with his own occupying armies of addiction, no matter how generous his policy towards tourists. Leonard was pouring more coffee and pushing his friend's business card towards me. I was picturing myself with Judith, standing in Vivian Armstrong's restaurant, watching Judith accept, without question, her little packets from a woman whose favourite occupation was staring at the empty space between her eyes.

By sun-up I was at Union Station. Leonard was with me. We had passed by Henry's, tiptoed in and out, and I had thrown together some clothes and a few favourite books in a suitcase.

By the time the train actually left, Leonard had whipped me up into such a state of paranoia I felt like a nineteenth-century revolutionary fleeing Moscow. As the train rocked slowly down the tracks, snow began to fall. Huddled in my thick garage parka I drank coffee and read the newspaper while waiting for the train to be stopped and police to burst in and arrest me.

Leonard's friend and my future employer, Duane Gray, was waiting for me at the Kingston station. He had an impressive dark beard and soft brown eyes that peered out through gold-rimmed glasses with such concern that I didn't dare ask him what Leonard might have said. He took me to lunch at a restaurant called The Library. It had eighteen kinds of imported beer and cheese sandwiches with two choices of cheese. We had beer and a cheese sandwich. Duane reassured me that Leonard had phoned and that "everything" was all right. This I took to mean that Judith was still alive.

It was late March. Toronto's snow was almost gone, but in Kingston there were mounds of it between the sidewalks and the streets, and the small front lawns of the downtown houses were piled high with snow that had been shovelled to clear porches and stairways.

On the way from the restaurant to the store we passed a big stone house with a For Rent sign in the window. Like a father watching his child collect on Hallowe'en, Duane stood on the sidewalk while I rang the bell. A woman whose name I later learned to be Mrs. Weismann answered the door. She had a divided face: one half had a purple-red birthmark that entirely surrounded one eye and part of her nose. The normal skin seemed abnormally smooth and white in comparison.

The house had long ago been chopped up into tiny apartments like the one I was shown. But it was warm and it had a large window that looked out onto a park. The main room had a double bed and a large table on which I eventually committed various literary crimes. No kitchen was immediately visible, but what looked to be a closet door led to a bathroom large enough to hold the refrigerator and stove. The refrigerator was beside the bathtub, which meant that every time I took a bath, the heat from the water would set the motor chugging.

"It's not bad" was Duane's verdict. So I took it, paying the first and last week's rent. I ended up staying for six months.

When I came back to Toronto, I had just turned twenty-five. For some reason this birthday seemed significant to me: a quarter century of my life had now passed—like one of those big square Kingstonian stones dropping into oblivion. Leonard had not, as he demanded, given me permission. The last time I'd phoned him I'd been told his number was disconnected.

I came back because I could no longer stay away. Perhaps it was boredom, lack of Judith, most of all the feeling that I had left something unfinished behind me, things I needed to resolve before my life could be set in motion again. And I was, after all, a quarter of a century old. It was now or never. Over our custom-ary beer and cheese sandwich I told all this to Duane. He lis-tened and nodded as though what I was saying was the most plausible thing in the world, as though he had been waiting for it. I would fade away from his store the same way I had appeared: without explanation. "He left," I could imagine Duane saying softly. Who could ask for more? I sold the books I had accumulated, re-packed my suitcase and Duane drove me to the train station.

If leaving the city I had felt like a fleeing revolutionary, return-ing, I felt old for the first time, suddenly conscious that all those youthful dreams I'd once had, especially those I'd never really formed, were now in the past instead of the future. Like Flaubert's Frédéric, I needed to go back to the capital, but other-wise I was without plans.

I walked from the train station towards the Savoy Hotel. The season was fall and the city's huge oaks and maples, with their giant overhanging spreads of yellow and golden leaves, added to my elegaic mood.

When I got to the hotel I stood in front of it for a moment.

Through the coffee-shop window I could see a few heads bent over the newspapers and coffee. Across one of the front glass doors a wide strip of black tape now made a corner-to-corner diagonal slash. New curtains had been put on the windows of the bottom two floors, which had the "luxury" rooms I had never seen. The dark red cloth billowed out from the occasional opened window. I walked up the steps as though something was going to happen when I opened the door, maybe a voice calling out that I had no right to be here. I opened the door. Nothing happened. Silence. The deep eventless silence of the lobby of the Savoy Hotel. Then the desk clerk, a woman I had never seen before, raised her head. I crossed the lobby. She offered me a room on the second floor, one of the fancy rooms with new curtains. I shook my head. Before I could ask for something cheaper she turned to the board, then swivelled back with my usual key in her hand, number 66, the Honeymoon Suite.

The view from the window was unchanged. Two long white limousines were ranged on the sidewalk across the street. A tinted window came down. A man whose face was the colour of thick cream was looking straight at me. A developer dreaming of the day a wrecking ball would convert the Savoy Hotel into a pile of broken bricks and plaster dust? Downtown you could make more money with a parking lot than a run-down hotel. Until you found the right combination, the exact mixture of grease and oil to unlock city hall and give you a permit to put up a shining new office tower, the ground floor set aside for a few of those fancy boutiques with glass shelves that no one ever goes to. His window was entirely open now. I could see his dark suit, the red leather upholstery of his car. He had a telephone in his hand and was punching in the numbers. Maybe he was just one of the pimps who used this place for certain customers. Late at night you would often see them pacing around outside, conspicuously inconspicuous, anxiously smoking cigarettes while they pretended to boast to each other.

In the morning it had been sunny and the light through the leaves had been vaguely exhilarating. Now the sky had a thin shell of cloud and the leaves seemed dimmer. I walked slowly north, zig-zagging my way through streets and alleys I knew by heart, then turned west onto Bloor Street. As I walked along Bloor the clouds began to thin. Then the fierce yellow eye of the sun burst out with such a piercing light that people on the street suddenly stopped, averted their faces or shook their heads.

I had been moving slowly, enjoying the feeling of strolling past familiar storefronts. When I arrived at Fenwick's I paused outside the window. With my new white shirt, the longish hair I'd trimmed the night before with nail scissors, my dark glasses, my reflection looked the way it always had, as though my former self had stayed behind and was now anxiously watching me through the window.

I went inside the store. Fenwick was behind the cash register. Fenwick of Fenwick's Used and Antiquarian Books. The owner. The *patron*. The boss. He looked unchanged except that his black hair had receded farther and the long bushy sideburns that angled out to meet his moustache had started to turn grey.

When Fenwick offered his hand it was with the impression that he had hesitated. So I waited a moment before responding. Then his big hand had swallowed mine and I felt suddenly relieved.

"Well, it's about time," Fenwick said. He was big, not just tall and wide, but expansive, almost charismatic, with large-sized gestures in all respects and an unshakeable belief that everything revolved around him. At least that is how I saw him. His size made him look indestructible, and the way he leaned towards the world, his big face thrust forward and his thumbs hooked into his belt, made him seem like a shaggy throwback challenging the present to prove it could stand up to him. Then Fenwick beamed out his big smile and I tried to smile back. It was a peculiar feeling, trying to smile, but it must have worked since Fenwick stretched his wide moustache even wider.

"I'm sorry," I said. Meaning—well—there was more than one thing to apologize for.

Fenwick just nodded. As though either he forgave me or my worst sins were still unknown to him. He was leaning forward the way he used to, and such was his power over me, and my concentration on him, that even before he spoke I could feel his heart rearranging itself to give me back my old place.

"We missed you," Fenwick said.

Judith appeared. I hadn't seen her approach but now she was standing beside me, smiling that almost insolent smile she sometimes has where the eyetooth on her right side, at a slightly irregular angle and even whiter than her other teeth, seems to be kicking out slightly, like an overeager leg in the chorus line. She was smiling and she was standing close. The last time I had seen her, she was sleeping under a pile of blankets in the Honeymoon Suite. I had kissed her fingers thinking this would be the last time I would ever touch her, then I had left. Now she touched me. She reached up and put her fingers on my cheek. A totally unexpected act of possession. I had to fight the urge to jump away.

"Paul," Judith said. Her hand dropped. "I never thought I'd see you again." She spoke in a voice tinged with just enough sarcasm to raise the question of how to take it.

Fenwick had not moved.

"You're back?" Judith asked. "Or just visiting?"

"I hope he's back," Fenwick said. "I was just going to ask him if he could start again tomorrow morning."

"Good," Judith said. One of Fenwick's favourite string quartets was sawing away in the background, a tide of velvety sound rolling through the store. Judith was now so close to me that it seemed nothing was left but for me to put my arms around her. The telephone started to ring. There were customers in the store. Judith moved closer yet. We touched because there was no space left between us. Then suddenly she was at the counter, talking on the phone, and I was left awkwardly turning to Fenwick to resume our broken conversation.

I returned a few minutes before seven, closing time. Fenwick, unhooking his thumbs from his belt and rubbing his palms together the way he always did on such occasions, had proposed that "a small celebration would be in order." Now I had time to notice the changes in the store itself. The number of shelves and tables devoted to new books had increased. During my absence everything in the city had apparently added a layer of prosperity. The clothes people wore were flashy and bright, calculated layers of signs I was no longer able to decipher. But what they had done to themselves, to each other, was inscribed into the curves of their spines, their guarded eyes, something closed and resentful in their faces. Or perhaps none of this was new—perhaps because of my absence I was now seeing for the first time how it was people survived Toronto.

Judith and Fenwick had both put on weight. Fenwick's addition only increased the amount of space he took up, but Judith's had been puzzling me all afternoon. Something about the way she'd touched me, the way she'd been, the way she'd grown from one person into another. Maybe because she was the one person in my life over whom I'd had some sort of power, though at the time I hadn't seen it that way.

I went to the back room. Framed and in its usual place on the wall was the page Fenwick pretended to believe was an original of Coleridge's poem. So, I was to take it, his soul had remained intact.

On top of the worktable were neatly stacked piles of invoices. There was also the ledger of purchases made. The notations on the invoices and the ledger inscriptions were all in Judith's hand. When she came to work with us I'd been surprised by her handwriting; the firm, clearly formed letters might have been set down by a schoolmaster intent on creating an orderly universe. Judith seemed aware of this contrast. She liked leaving concise logical memos in her readable hand. They made an impression on paper that she couldn't make in person. Or hadn't then, I should say, because by the time I came back to the bookstore on the evening of my return to Toronto, I became convinced that she, too, had changed. Her face and figure seemed fuller, but more than that, it seemed she was radiating outwards instead of shrinking in. For example, the way she'd made a point of reaching up to touch my cheek now reminded me of the way she used to underline key words and numbers. That is the problem with first impressions: you see someone, even someone you know well, and then something changed about them strikes you. Later you find out that in a hidden chamber of their life there has been a revolution: they are mortally ill, or have fallen in love, or now eat only root vegetables. Meanwhile nothing is betrayed but the fact of change, a small surface ripple you could easily miss.

I could hear Fenwick working on the front-door locks. I wondered where Judith was. I thought I heard her voice through the back door. She hadn't been in the store when I came in. Perhaps she had gone to run some errand, then planned to meet us in the lane where Fenwick always kept his car. I unlatched the door, turned towards Fenwick.

"Ready?" he asked. "Where's Judith?"

"Out back."

Fenwick turned out the light. As he did I opened the door, still looking at Fenwick and not outside. I thought I was hearing footsteps on the gravel. As I turned I had the sudden idea that

Judith was going to spring at me. Once, when we'd been drinking together at the hotel, she'd hidden while I was in the bathroom. When I came out I found the room empty. There was a moment of panic, then Judith leapt out of the closet.

But when we stepped into the alley, Judith wasn't there.

"She must have gone around," Fenwick said.

He hadn't yet locked the back, so I went through the store to look for Judith out the front windows. When I returned Fenwick was standing at the pine table, writing her a note explaining we had gone to the restaurant and would meet her there. "Now I remember, she had a doctor's appointment," Fenwick said. "You never know how long they're going to keep you waiting."

As always we went to Le Troubador, the famous Golden Hole, but the night of my return was not to be one of our most sparkling. For one thing, my alcohol consumption was, as the literary critics say, under erasure. Erased, or at least whitewashed. Worse, although Martha came to join us, Judith did not show up.

I had spent the whole afternoon walking the sections of the city I once knew with Judith. On a street not far from her place was one of those big chestnut trees that flower in the spring. Beside it was a streetlamp. One spring night Judith and I had stood under that lamp. The scent of blossoms. The cool air filled with the promise of a sweet fragrant future just waiting to carry us away on a cloud of blossoms and birdsong. Judith scooped some fallen petals from the grass, held them out to me. "What could I give you that would be perfect?" Then she tossed the blossoms in the air and they fluttered down on us. In the morning I noticed one of those pale pink petals caught in a tendril of her dark hair. I reached for it. At the same time she bent forward and it floated down into her coffee, lay like a small exotic raft on the black liquid. We both stared at it. "This must mean something," Judith had said.

Like her touch in the store. I was sure it must mean something, but what? In the sobering company of Martha and Fenwick, the obvious occurred. By her touch Judith had been signalling me that while I was away she had not only changed her drug situation—that had been clear from the moment I saw her—but had also found a replacement for me. Perhaps just as I'd seen her as the person I needed to escape in order to accomplish some basic hygiene and clean out my bloodstream, she'd seen me the same way. In my absence a new order had been established: one with her on the inside, like the sun; me on the outside, like a circling planet dependent on its light.

As always Fenwick ate slowly, big shoulders hunched forward, knife and fork laboriously working until his plate was absolutely clean. Between courses he gossiped about various people we knew. Clients. Suppliers. A "scout" who had once specialized in buying science-fiction books for us at garage sales and now supplemented his income by selling cellular phones he obtained from mysterious sources.

Martha ate what gaunt-cheeked women eat: salad, bread, fish, lots of water. She was more than ten years younger than Fenwick, and unlike him she was still trying to look like a youthful version of herself. When I first met her, she was thin but lush and the combination of her features, her eyes, her shoulder-length dyed blonde hair made her look too glamorous for the bookstore. Or me. Or Fenwick. Fenwick, I had always presumed, was the alternative to glamour. A choice she had made because Fenwick offered her, as he offered Judith and me, the kind of shelter we were unable to find for ourselves.

Now her face looked tired. She had always made a habit of seeming weary when Fenwick talked, but her skin seemed thinner, lined. As always, she smoked during the meal. And she was drinking fast—red wine, which I kept pouring into her glass as she gave me searching looks as though to invite me to quit stalling, put down my cutlery, make the full confession. But, like Fenwick, she didn't ask me where I had gone or why.

When the bill had been paid and we were standing outside, Fenwick turned to me and said, "I suppose Judith told you she was starting her holidays tomorrow."

"No."

"I thought she must have talked to you this afternoon before she went to the doctor." Fenwick shifted uncomfortably. "So. I was hoping you could start again in the morning. Or wait a couple of days to get set up if you want to."

Martha, as though the whole conversation wasn't happening, had put her hands on my shoulders and was giving me kisses on each cheek. Then they were off. Fenwick shambling, his arm looped protectively over Martha while she gave her hips a little extra accent and turned grinning to wave to me—"Velcome to Budapest"—all this in reference to one drunken Christmas Eve when the four of us had played movie-star charades and Martha had cracked us all up by using Fenwick's pipe as a cigarette holder and doing Zsa Zsa Gabor.

It was still only nine o'clock. I called Judith from a phonebooth. There was no answer. I looked up her number in the book to be sure it hadn't changed, then dialled it again. It seemed strange, now, that she would not have shown up. I telephoned the hotel to ask for messages. There were none, the receptionist said, and I recognized the dry voice of the woman who'd checked me in. When I didn't reply, she added that there had been a call just before seven, a woman.

I began walking across town. The evening was breezy, warmed by the southwest wind Toronto sometimes gets in the fall. Overhead the leaves clacked together, drifted down through the light of the streetlamps. Couples were strolling arm in arm. As I got near the university I could see the library rising up in the sky, a gigantic grey monolith. Fort Book, we had called it then;

Fenwick was never able to drive by without pointing at it and spluttering something.

Judith lived on a back street not far from the university. But the lights of Judith's living room were out, and when I walked round the back of the house I saw that her bedroom window was also dark.

EIGHT

WHEN I RETURNED to the hotel, it was midnight. I was half expecting to find Judith waiting for me, sitting in her usual chair. But the room was empty and when I called her apartment again there was no answer.

I lay down in the dark. Gradually the sounds of the elevator, steps in the corridor, voices from other rooms stitched themselves into my nerves. Through the angled slats of the venetian blinds came the lights of passing cars—they played across the ceiling like an out-of-tune blues piano. My tuneless Judith blues. A tuneless ragtag counterpoint so clear I could almost see the piano keys dancing.

I woke up at four in the morning. My stomach was crawling with need for Judith. I dialled her number again. Again there was no answer. Sometimes when she was drunk she unplugged the phone. Or there was the boyfriend theory. But surely Fenwick would have said something to me. I had to see her before she left.

I went to the sink and splashed water onto my face. The hotel had fallen into that strange hollow silence I'd forgotten while I was away, that brief middle-of-the-night intermission when every single person in the whole building was cruising—asleep, exhausted, contented—whatever it took to stretch them out on the bridge to the next drink, the next orgasm, the next needle. The temporary absence of desire.

When I went outside, I took the talisman I'd carried the whole time I was away, my key to Judith's apartment. Having someone else's key can give rise to strange feelings. A peculiar kind of ownership. You are walking along the street without enough money to buy a newspaper, you put your hand in your pocket and find this small bit of metal that is your pass into someone else's universe. An act of trust waiting to be betrayed.

"You'd better have this," Judith had said to me one night when we were drinking. And fished into her purse for the key she'd had made. The most common of keys. An ordinary shiny brass key with a round top and a hole for threading onto a key chain. That night, when I saw her home, she said, "Try your key. Let's be sure it works." I used it first on her front door, then on the door to her apartment. We shook hands in the grave mock-political way we had developed; in the same vein we murmured "Good night, comrade." I went downstairs while she waited as she always did, not wanting to close her door behind me until I was on the street.

Judith's apartment was on the second floor. There was a huge beech tree in her front yard; its yellowing leaves glowed in the light of the nearby streetlamp.

The key she had given me two years before still worked the lock on the common entrance. I took off my shoes and carried them upstairs. I listened outside her door for a moment. Nothing. I slid the key carefully into the lock, turned it, went in.

I closed the door carefully, easing the lock back into place. You might ask me how I could justify using Judith's key under these circumstances. How I could allow myself to barge into her private life this way. I had done it only once before. That was during the period when she had apparently made me guardian angel of her soul, after Vivian Armstrong moved out. On the night in question Judith's connection had failed to produce the particular smoke she had come to favour, an opium-soaked hashish that would set me looking out her window to the glow of those receding planets, then let me close my eyes and hear space music bouncing through the city darkness. But at that time I was also beginning to be able to actually *feel* my nervous system, and sometimes when I drank coffee in the mornings that nervous system was beginning to feel like the corroded and greasy wires Henry and I would pull out of old cars—the insulation burned through, the copper coming apart in your hands. So I suggested to Judith we might be better off giving it a rest than chasing all over Toronto. We'd been walking along Yonge and were standing in front of a liquor store. Judith gave me her mustard-wallpaper look. "When did you get a job as my social worker?" She walked into the liquor store and came out with two bottles of whisky. Then she hopped into a cab and slammed the door in my face.

Perhaps I *had* become her social worker. Convinced she would be trying to drink herself to death, I went back to her apartment in the middle of the night. Walked in my stocking feet up the stairs. Eased the door open and closed, listened.

She was breathing loudly, long rasping intakes, each one followed by a strangely wistful sigh. I went into her bedroom to check on her. She was lying on the bed, uncovered, wearing the comical donkey-patterned pyjamas she put on whenever she was depressed.

Now I had no excuse except the mystery of the footsteps on the gravel. A touch I had interpreted a dozen different ways. I listened for Judith but could hear only the refrigerator. After a while it shuddered to a stop. I checked the bedrooms. They were empty. I walked slowly into the living room. The curtains were drawn back and the room was covered in the jagged silhouettes of beech leaves.

Opposite the window was a low-slung couch Judith and I had bought one afternoon. Fenwick had sent us to the Queen Street strip to check out various items in the second-hand bookstores there. Instead we ended up drinking draft beer at the Cameron House. Then back into the blinding sunlight of the street where, a few seconds later, Judith stumbled against the sofa and fell across it. The owner of the store came out and stood beside me while Judith pretended to sleep. "Ten dollars," he said. We carried it on our heads all the way to her apartment. Various stops were necessary. Also, the legs were jettisoned because Judith claimed that seagulls were perching on them and making fun of us. "For Christ's sake, listen to them," she kept insisting, even after we'd unscrewed the legs and put them in a big round-chested red mailbox.

I stood up from the sofa. Then I saw a suitcase in the corner, under the small drop-leaf table she used for her record player. I went closer. The suitcase was shut—possibly packed for her vacation. I knelt down and unsnapped the latches. A hand came over my eyes and there was a sharp explosion at my right temple. I was trying to turn to face whoever had done this to me when I was yanked up, my head smashing into the table. The fist struck again, this time burying itself in my stomach. While black waves of nausea swirled through me, I was shoved out the door and hustled down the stairs, sent face first onto the lawn.

When my eyes opened it was light. A dog was standing over me, a rangy tan Doberman, looking at me quizzically and poking at me with its muzzle. I could feel its spit on my neck, but my first reaction wasn't disgust but relief that I wasn't completely paralysed. I tried to move my legs, then my upper body. Everything ached. As I stood up the dog sprang away, then trotted down the street. I wiped my hand across my face. No blood. I was half-crouched over the pain in my right side. My skull was throbbing. On the ground beside me were my shoes, neatly side by side. There was something unsettling about finding them that way. I couldn't help imagining the hands that had arranged them.

A car drove by. A woman in high heels walked past on the other side of the street. My watch said 7:04.

I started walking. The pain in my ribs was working itself out, but the side of my head was swollen and pulsed with every step. I stopped at a milk store to buy aspirins and a bag of ice. At the hotel the night clerk was drinking coffee and reading the newspaper. He handed me my key without looking up.

When I woke up there was just time for me to shave and take a taxi to the store. I had used the ice as a pillow and though my head was still pounding, the swelling had gone down and I was able to brush my hair over it.

I arrived as Fenwick was opening the door. He glanced at me curiously, then waved me towards the cash register as he himself retreated to the back room.

As in the old days after one of our dinners, Fenwick had prepared me a huge mug of black coffee. I sipped at it for a few moments, sitting on the stool and looking about me.

On the shelf below the counter was a pile of publishers' catalogues, copies of *Books in Print* for Canada, the United States and England, recent literary magazines. Also a telephone. In my absence a new system had been installed. Before, there had been one line to the front of the store for customer inquiries. That line had an extension to the back room. Also in the back room had been a second telephone, a separate line from which Fenwick could call out or to which Martha could call in.

Now the telephone in front of me had a row of buttons, indicating three separate lines. I picked it up, pressed number one which was clear, dialled Judith's. After three rings a machine came on. Judith's voice recited the correct date, then invited the caller to leave a message at the sound of the tone. I hung up and considered the fact that at some point since four in the morning, Judith had switched on her answering machine and recorded a new message. This meant I didn't need to worry about going back to look under the beds or in the cupboards. The other implications would require a clearer head to consider. I redialled and told the machine that I hoped I hadn't missed her, and that I was at the store. "For the record," I told myself, as I hung up a second time.

My head throbbed and my ribs hurt every time I breathed too deeply, and as they had all morning various gory images of what might have happened to Judith floated through my mind. Yet both bedrooms had been empty and I had no reason to believe anything other than the obvious: Judith had taken up with some sort of jealous gorilla who hid in the dark waiting for people like me. When you're hanging on to a counter, trying not to pass out, ridiculous ideas seem perfectly normal. My main task of the moment, I kept telling myself, was to keep drinking coffee and eating aspirins.

Meanwhile I stood at the cash register and looked through the window. I had returned to my old job, my old city, my old compulsion for Judith. And I couldn't help thinking that what had happened to me was an instant punishment for falling back into that old need.

Now the door opened. Swinging through it came a burly dark-haired man with a thick neck and a face that looked fed on a diet of organ meats. The effect was heightened by a fringe of beard. The collar of his white shirt had curled up over the lapel of his suit. He stopped in front of me, staring. The swelling on my head pulsed. The way, when you've gotten food poisoning, your stomach gives a twinge when you think of the particular food that was responsible.

"Can I help you?" I asked. The adrenaline had started. I had the absurd idea he was going to come after me now. I wanted him to. In the light. I began to edge out from behind the counter. Perhaps he just needed to be encouraged.

"Fenwick," he said. "Is he here?" His voice was soft and with a twinge of British accent. Definitely not a gorilla voice. When he talked his round eyes opened wide. They were a strange colour, more grey than brown, and they seemed to be pleading for understanding, trying to explain it was no fault of their own that they and the soft voice that accompanied them were trapped in the body of this short burly red-faced man who had his fists jammed in his pockets and leaned aggressively forward while waiting for my answer.

I was looking down, trying to figure out how to use the new phone system to alert Fenwick, when Fenwick himself appeared. He moved quickly forward, put his arm around the visitor and led him to the back. "I think I have what you're looking for," I heard him say. Then came the sound of running water as Fenwick filled the coffee machine. I remembered the way Judith and I would estimate the buying power of the customer by whether Fenwick made fresh coffee for a client.

The store grew busier. Students with bags and briefcases full of books to sell. The professional scouts went to the back entrance where Fenwick appraised their wares. The front-door offerings were mine to deal with. To some I offered cash, others only credit. Then came two shipments of new books, along with a delivery of cartons of instant remainders—the kind of books customers see displayed on tables in bookshops at half to a tenth of "original" prices. What the public doesn't realize is that many of these books were published with the sale tables as their known destination. Or maybe, in some way, they do realize it since the sale of hardcover books at full price is only a tiny fraction of the whole business. "Raw books," Fenwick used to sniff. "No person who respects books would go to the kind of store that specializes in that kind of meat. Here, you buy a book that has passed the test of time, not the instant garbage people put out thanks to government grants and the best-seller lists."

Just before noon, a woman I recognized from the old days arrived. She was a poet, one of the "weirdo downtown word slaves" as Judith called local writers. She also had a reputation as a book scout specializing in Canadiana. Scrounging from her friends, her publishers, shamelessly calling at magazines and newspapers that received unwanted books for review, she had a constant supply of first editions and literary arcana. These she carried to us in plastic Dominion Store shopping bags, the handles neatly tied together for strength. As always she had used magic marker to initial them in big letters: MTS. Later the books would be evaluated by Fenwick, and on Friday afternoon, just as though she were a regular employee, he would give her a small brown pay envelope with cash for the week's take. After setting her bulging shopping bags beside the counter, she went to see which of her own books were in the poetry section.

In an ordinary trade bookstore, she would also have gone in search of her own. If the books weren't there, she would have anxiously accosted the clerk, or put some friend up to calling and requesting them. If, on the other hand, her new book *was* on display, all the worse. What is more discouraging than the sight of unsold wares? They could be mere minutes or, at best, days away from being re-packed and sent back to the publisher for credit to be used on some newer flashier trendier work by some newer flashier trendier more politically correct word zombie, possibly even a zombie from another, trendier town. The anxiety. The hate. The envy. The wasted sweat.

In our bookstore, such anxiety is unnecessary. "These aren't used books," Fenwick would insist, "they're chosen books." That is the beauty of stores such as ours. Once a book has survived its first owner and been sold for the price of a cup of coffee ten years ago, it passes from the nervous realm of commerce into a permanent golden age. There it finds true calm. And there it can listen to the sound of eternity—the slow turning of pages in the comfortable customer armchairs of Fenwick's Used and Antiquarian Books. The Sunset Inn. Literature's very own palliative care café.

The name of the poet was Meribel T. Simmons. MTS. Her friends, who sometimes accompany her, call her Mary. Mary is also the name she uses. The title pages of her books that we have here often bear the dedication: "To my dear——, from Mary". In one case, for a man we knew had been her lover, she signed herself "Mary, Queen of Words". When I pointed this out to Judith, her face turned the way it does before she cries. I had always thought the only pathetic thing about the dedication was that it showed that even going to bed with someone won't stop them from selling your book for ten cents. Seeing Judith's tears I realized Meribel T. Simmons had actually been in love with this person, that the sale of the book had signalled not just routine greed, but the death of love. That's what Judith was mourning, the fact that people could outlive love the way they outlived everything else.

"You weren't here last week."

"No."

The poet was standing in front of me. She was holding a book of her own poetry. *Love, & other tragedies.* Her face was grey and seamed, a bit collapsed on itself, as though she hadn't been eating properly.

"I was thinking of getting this," she said, holding her book towards me. I took it from her hands. I looked carefully at the outside, wiped away some imaginary dust, opened it slowly. This one wasn't signed to anyone in particular. It just had her name written in ink: *Meribel T. Simmons.* Inside the back cover was a paper case meant to contain library cards. The case was unstamped, which indicated it had never been borrowed. I remembered buying this and several hundred other books from the Port Hope Public Library. They had been clearing the shelves. The total cost to us had been seventy-six dollars. Of course, as the librarian pointed out, the fact that some of the books had never been borrowed did not mean they had no value. Also, much of their trade was in people who preferred to do their reading on the premises, usually on days when it was raining or snowing. These readers, according to the librarian, were among the city's most discriminating.

"It's a good book," I said.

"Is it?"

"One of her best."

She nodded her head. I didn't remember her hair being so grey. She was wearing jeans, sandals without socks, a flannel shirt and jacket that must have once been intended for a man much larger than she was. She smelled of beer, or maybe it was just her clothes.

"So you think I should buy it?"

"It's good," I said.

"Someone else might want it?"

"Absolutely," I said. "When you buy a book, you have it for your own. On the other hand, you also deprive other people."

"It's a difficult decision," said Meribel T. Simmons. She looked at me closely. "I'm sure I've asked you your name."

I nodded.

"I knew it."

I had set the book down carefully, behind the counter, where she wouldn't have to pick it up again.

"There's a girl works here too."

"She's on holiday."

"I like her."

"So do I," I said. I wanted to take Meribel T. Simmons by the arm, lead her to the cheap restaurant across the street, order a litre of house wine and tell her the whole sad story. Then to take her with me to Judith's apartment where together we would sort through the clues.

"Did she give you that bump on the head?"

"No. I don't know who gave it to me." I put my hand up self-consciously, pushed some hair over the swelling.

"Whoever it was, I don't like him."

"Neither do I."

Meribel smiled. She was getting old, she smelled, her stringy grey hair hung below her shoulders, but she still had a sweet smile. "I remember you," she said. "You're the one who never lets me buy those books."

"That's me."

"God bless."

She dipped her head submissively, the way she always did when she left the store. As she lowered her head, her hair parted on one side and I saw her left ear. The lobe, an angry red, sagged with the weight of a heavy golden hoop.

Judith was the first to notice the abused earlobes of the poet. Not usually visible, they had been exposed one day when she came into the store with her long greying hair pulled back into a pony-tail showing her ears and some long beaded earrings.

"Beautiful!" Judith had exclaimed, going up to Meribel and actually taking one of the earrings in her hands before Meribel could jump away. "Did you get those from the boy selling them on the sidewalk in front of Holt's? I've always liked his things."

After that, every time Meribel came into the store, Judith would ask to see her earrings and Meribel would push back her hair to show them.

Meribel's swollen ear, pierced and dragged down by its golden burden, reminded me of my own swelling. As the door closed behind her I touched it again. It felt strange, as though Meribel's comment had given it a life of its own. I massaged it carefully. Beneath my fingers it was bristly and hot. I'd been swallowing aspirins all day and my headache had receded to a dull pulsing. But I kept remembering the feeling of those strong hands on my neck and shoulders, the easy way they'd hauled me out from under Judith's table and hustled me down the stairs.

Another customer edged forward and put a small stack of mysteries on the counter. I tapped the prices into the adding machine. The buyer was a middle-aged man, stocky and reserved looking; tweed jacket and creaseless grey pants told as surely as the clock that here was a civil servant out buying his mysteries during the lunch hour.

The mystery shelves at Fenwick's turned over so fast that it seemed half the population must be lonely insomniacs spending their nights reading about murders committed, murders solved, macabre murders, cold-blooded murders, death by everything from poison to poison pen.

For another hour or so there was a flurry of customers. Suddenly the store was empty. It was early afternoon. I was just thinking I was hungry when Martha sailed in, a bottle of juice in one hand, a sandwich in the other. It was wrapped in white paper, the way the fancy delicatessen down the street did their sandwiches. At that moment one of the red lights on the telephone began to flash. I pressed the button and picked up the receiver. There was a silence and I almost hung up.

"Dungo." The raw edge of my brother's voice. Dry, quiet but somehow aggressive. Over the telephone it had a sandpapery sound. Grit? Why not. Henry was well supplied. It made his voice abrasive, pushy. "I like pushing people," he once told me in his quiet sandpaper voice. Henry always kept his voice quiet. It was part of his image, like the way he insisted on wearing white shirts to work. Open at the neck, sleeves rolled up. Or the way his blond hair, cut close to his neck, thick and tufted, always looked as if it belonged to an eight-year-old kid.

"You there, Dungo?"

"Yes." Martha was still standing at the counter, holding out the sandwich like a hand waiting to be shaken.

"So you're back," Henry said. "When are we going to see you?"

"I'll come down tonight."

"All right." Pronounced deadpan, followed by a long line of dialtone.

At dinner I had avoided Martha's eyes. Now they were locked on mine, questioning. "Henry," I said.

Once Henry, my fear of Henry, my need to escape Henry, had been the bridge that led me to Martha.

"Are you all right?" Now that I was coming out of the whirlpool of Henry, I could feel the funny way my face must have fallen, talking to him, thinking about him. As though all the skin and muscle had decided to give in to gravity.

"Thanks."

Martha's hands on the counter were long and bony. When she was seventy, the bumpy blue veins would twine around from her wrists and the backs of her hands, twist themselves about her knuckles and fingers. "Hard to be back?" Martha asked. "Or are you just afraid of me?"

"Not afraid," I said. I realized that my voice had automatically slid into the dry sound I'd learned from my brother, Henry. I raised my eyes to Martha. "Not afraid of you. Just picking up the beat."

Now I put my hands over hers. She gave what might have been a smile, turned away. She was back, holding a baseball cap. She placed it gently over my head, her fingers grazing the swelling.

NINE

W HEN Martha left I was alone in the store. But in a bookstore there is always too much to do. Especially when there are no customers. You are standing in the middle of the store. Adjusting shelves, sorting out a couple of cartons of newly received books. Your hands are working. You are thinking official thoughts. All of human history and evolution have been required to lead up to this incredible triumph of efficiency. Meanwhile you're not there. Without planning or wanting it you've dropped into another universe.

So it was that first afternoon back. I was rearranging books in the drama section; in bookstores the alphabet is always under stress. But though I was officially occupied, the smell of the books was reminding me—as it always had—of the inexplicable slightly musty odour that rose from Judith's skin.

Now, standing at the drama shelf, I was bathing in the memory of Judith's skin. Its odour, the way her bones made their vulnerable way to its surface, its long silky racecourses, the places where it thickened, the sharply defined tan lines across her upper arms and the way, north of the tanline above her breasts, a few freckles dotted her sternum like tiny lost islands from summer. I can remember everything about Judith's body except how it actually felt to be inside it. The voluptuous mutual discovery of constant need, fear, satisfaction.

Desire: a sharp prolonged sensation brought on by the lack of Judith.

Desire: the need to complete myself by losing myself in Judith.

Desire: the secret glue of memory.

Desire: the desire for Judith had led me strange places. It even led me, I will admit, to a completely different desire—one common to many bookstore employees surrounded by great shifting seas of text. This came to me in Kingston. On the one hand, I was without Judith and missing her. On the other, I was surrounded by novels, poems, discourses on subjects real and imaginary, centuries of travel books to countries that no longer exist. The most modest set of covers contains twenty thousand words. And that is a very slim volume. Even a Harlequin Romance is longer. To say nothing of the multi-hundred-thousand-word barn-burners that dominate the best-seller list. And yet—a few words in the right place. Judith hypnotized by Juliet's romantic lament. Judith, yes. In my case, she was the decisive factor. Judith that first day, her too-white skin and bell-like voice cracking open the store like a time-line from the future. Where more whiteness would be displayed. Skin, snow, the glowing emptiness of the night. The hum of tires, the scraping of shovels, the long white limousines of the pimps with their windows, their slamming doors, one man turning to the other in the middle of the night and saying "that hot bitch".

To ease the burden of that desire. To take that desire and put it outside the room of my mind. To turn that desire into an inspired little trickster doing its tricks on a page instead of in my blood. Surrounded all day by centuries worth of the fool's gold of love transformed into the unstable currency of words, how could I not be tempted to try the same? Nothing more natural than to lay down a few choice lines, let history be the judge. Sit in my stone fortress typing discreetly into the night. Send poems off in the mail with a terse autobiographical note consisting only of the date of birth, the name androgynously foreshortened by initials.

I started off with the intention of writing a thousand poems in a thousand nights. I ended up with nineteen poems in fifty-three nights. I sent them all out. Most came back but a few were printed in literary magazines whose proprietors depend on stores like this to distribute their product. One experience of seeing my own words in print was enough to cure me. Now I've come to think that publishing a few bad poems is, for someone in my position, a necessary minor disfigurement. Like the gold tooth of a candy-store owner, the butcher's missing fingertip.

After the store closed, I walked down towards the lake and my brother's garage. The glass service station door was locked, but the back entrance was open. Henry was bent double over the engine of one of those long white limousines. I went to stand beside him. He was happily grunting away, the way he had ever since he was thirteen years old and had figured out how to get under the hood of the old man's car.

"Is it going to die?"

"These fuckwagons never die. They just get turned into taxis." Henry stood up, wiped his palms on his jeans, turned towards me and extended a greasy hand.

Henry. Seeing Henry again was a jolt. A literal jolt that made my whole body go off balance as his callused hand slammed into mine. "So, hey," Henry said. "Here you are again. The original Dungo Merde."

"His ghost."

"Now he's starting on that Hamlet shit. Whatever."

"Whatever."

"Whatever. Back in town. Back at work. Back at the hotel. Dungo, you are one hell of a triple threat."

"They phone you from the hotel?"

"Judith. She called looking for you. Now that you're back, everyone wants a piece."

Henry retreated a little half-step, went into a crouch, flicked out his left arm. His knuckles grazed my cheek the way they used to, except for certain times, lifetimes ago, when Henry tried to use that jab to nail me to the canvas or put me through a wall.

But this wasn't then. This was now. So I stood still for Henry's little tapdance, forced myself to smile, watched while he went into the next inevitable number, which was reaching into the breast pocket of his perpetual baggy blue overalls for one of those filtered menthol cigarettes he'd been smoking for almost as long as he'd been poking into cars.

"You want?

"Still quit."

"You in shape?"

"No way."

Henry lit up, peered at me through the smoke like a boxing manager in a black-and-white movie.

"What happened to your head?"

"Bumped it against a table."

"Want to see a doctor?"

"I'm okay."

He came towards me and I bowed my head for him to inspect. He parted my hair carefully, ran his fingers gently around the swelling, whistled. "What happened? Your hands get stuck in their pockets?" He let me go. Big brother Henry. Ready to take on the world. "You in trouble?"

"No. Not that I know."

"You wouldn't."

We drove from the garage to Henry's place. Jeanine was sitting on the steps, reading the paper and waiting for us. There was something heavy about the way she stood up, pushing against her knees.

Now Jeremy was big enough to own a racing bicycle. He had it turned upside down in the yard and was straightening his wheels with a spoke wrench.

"You saying hello, or what?"

Henry standing cockily on his back deck, cigarette dangling from his lips, hand wrapped around a can of beer; King Henry surveying the flat green kingdom of his lawn. Jeremy looking around at me, unable to resist the beginning of a smile, then turning importantly back to his work, the last light fading quickly now, the houses opposite a long row of illuminated windows.

Amazing to think that Henry, of all people, had somehow pulled it off: family life, life in the centre lane. Amazing that Henry, of all people, could open the newspaper and read stories about families like his own, people like himself, turn to the "leisure" section for a few ideas on how to decorate the rec room, check out the TV guide for suitable family entertainment, read the police column to see if there had been any drug busts at his kids' schools.

By midnight, Henry had a few crushed beer cans clustered together on the kitchen counter but was drinking coffee. As I told Henry about my first visit to the store, the dinner at the restaurant, what had happened at Judith's apartment, he took cigarettes out of his package, set them standing on their filters like little toy soldiers, knocked them down then set them up again.

Almost impossible, at this moment, to unravel all that happened between that night in the pool hall and the night I finally saw Henry after my return to Toronto. Years of ruptures, healings, scars, reconciliations ending in relations ever more distant and yet somehow liable, at any moment, to revert.

Revert to what? I never know how to talk about Henry. I never did. There was always something symbiotic about us. Something about us that made it impossible for me to know where I ended and he began. Even after I started working at the store, even when I had fallen under the magic spell of words, howling night-time blues, cheap cocaine flashes—I would look out into the darkness and the world I saw was Henry's world.

Though in Henry's eyes our worlds didn't touch. He was the hard-working citizen. Living real life. Having children. Getting his hands dirty. I was just a clerk. A parasite. A man who couldn't do anything useful with his hands. One of those "jerk-off intellectuals who think they know how to run the world and can't even fix their own car".

And Henry to me? Also less than perfect. Especially when it seemed his big thrill in life was putting his thumb down on me or Jeanine. But as the years went on it seemed Henry, whatever he'd once done to me, had become a good father, a reliable husband, a steady presence at the garage. One of those solid citizens who make the world go round.

Henry, finally. Henry at his kitchen table. Henry standing up and reaching into the cupboard above the stove for the Scotch. Putting it on the table between us. Henry, the solid citizen, pouring his measure into his glass. A sudden clatter of raindrops outside, cold air sluicing through the open window.

He knocked over one of his cigarettes.

"So you're at the apartment of your true love and this guy drills you."

"That's it."

"Tell me about it," Henry said. Meaning he'd heard enough. Meaning that he thought I was, as usual, a fool. Meaning there'd been enough talk because between Henry and me, not much was ever said.

What might Henry have told me if, at various times, Henry

had chosen to speak? What disturbing prospects might Henry have been considering those dozens of nights I had sat with him in this kitchen, or in the kitchen of his apartment across from Diamond Billiards, and watched the Scotch line travelling up and down the side of his glass. He's swallowing it, I always said to myself when Henry drank. Not only the whisky but whatever else in his life had to be swallowed so he could continue undisturbed, keep living the life of the solid citizen, keep living the life of a man who will never be a jerk-off intellectual, a rat-bag con, a fat-assed cop-out, a fairy with wings on his ass. All those things Henry had to keep down in order to keep being Henry, pure and simple.

All this is so easy for me to see now, now that I realize Henry was living not only the small lies I knew about, but larger impossible contradictions that already had him in their grasp. I only noticed that Henry was drinking hard.

"You going to stay at the store?"

"I think so."

"You could come to the garage."

"Thanks. But I said I'd start again at the store in the morning."

"You want to move back here? Jeanine started to use your room to do accounts but she doesn't need to."

"The hotel gave me a rate for a couple of weeks. Then I'm going to find an apartment."

Henry nodded, looked down at his glass. He still had thick tufted hair and a wiry bantam-weight body, but in the harsh light of the midnight kitchen Henry looked as though he had skipped a generation since I had last looked at him carefully. His fingers, wrapped around the glass, had developed a fine tremble. The first touches of grey had started at his temples and around his eyes, the lines you only used to see after the first day of strong sun had settled in. In a way it looked good on him. A certain maturity. A certain possible flowering. As if all those years of fighting himself, refining himself, denying himself had actually done what he'd intended, had in fact purified something inside him, was actually making some part of him as tough and resilient as he'd always wanted to be.

"Well," said Henry, "things here are pretty much the same." I nodded.

"And Judith? Her shitty little world. She'd kill you for another hit."

"I don't believe that. Neither do you."

Henry laughed. "Really, Dungo. You and your women. You spend your whole life chasing after them but it doesn't do a lot for you, does it?"

Suddenly his hand pounced on mine. "Hey, little brother, what are you doing?" The whole weight of Henry on my hand now. I'd forgotten how strong Henry was, the heavy iron feel of Henry's strength. "You promised me, Dungo. Remember?"

"I remember." After leaving Toronto I'd phoned Henry and told him about the overdose scene. Henry had volunteered that he would "kill" either me or Judith if ever I touched "that stuff" again. "Don't worry. My blood is pure."

"Thanks," Henry said. He squeezed my hand, hard, then let go. The cigarette I'd been holding was now so much torn paper and tobacco. I took a new cigarette and lit it. Henry renewed his Scotch.

So that was it. My first time back at Henry's. Another cup of coffee for me, another Scotch for Henry, a handshake, me walking out the door with a borrowed umbrella and Henry's old high-school windbreaker. Me looking back at Henry framed in the light, watching me.

The rain came down on my brother's umbrella with a taut hollow sound. Every now and then the wind would lift it up and back, and a spray of water would wash across my face. The wind, too, made the wet falling leaves flap together. The sound of dead hands clapping. I was thinking I'd had Henry wrong the whole time, that while I'd been watching him swallow whatever he'd been swallowing, Henry had actually been turning himself into someone, a man with a place, a family—a man of property. While I, as he explained over that last cup of coffee, "just seemed to be drifting. You know what I mean, Dungo? To tell the truth, I sometimes look at you and I wonder where you are."

The rain slowed to a drizzle. I rolled up the umbrella, breathed in the cool night air. Things had happened. Time had passed. But a person could still go for a walk in the rain, breathe in the wet air, hear the voices of others like oneself, insinuating, cajoling, humming wild little tunes that broke off into a cough, a fit of laughter, a shout directed at a taxi.

I was on Queen Street, directly across from the bookstore where I had first met Martha Fenwick.

"Evil days," a voice offered. I looked up and saw the General himself. He towered above me. "Evil days require strange disguises." He touched my baseball cap, then rocked back and forth until he lost his balance and had to place his hands on my shoulders to steady himself. His face came down towards mine, stinking of beer. He pushed my cap to look at me more closely. "Evil days bring the destruction of the planet. Peace, brother." The rain had started again and the General's moustache was streaming water. "Never mind. I'm working on something great." He took my arm and led me across the street. "Don't move." He unlocked the door, pushed me inside. "Let down your umbrella, brother. We are in occupied territories. Here we have nothing to fear but friendly fire and the violence we have done to others." He led me through the crowded aisles to the corner where he had his desk. There was a cracked leather armchair beside it. "Wait here," he ordered, and stumbled towards the back.

A few minutes later the General had still not reappeared. I went back to see what he was doing.

Weeping, it turned out. Kneeling in front of a cardboard carton full of file folders and weeping.

"General," I said.

He turned to me. I might have been a stranger, a dog, a passing hallucination. For a few moments I stood waiting. He stared at me, then finally shook his head and went back to his papers.

By the time I got back to the hotel it was almost two in the morning. I set my alarm clock, then laid my clothes out to dry. When I'd finished and turned out the lights, I opened the blinds to see what was happening on the street. As always, a few white limousines and taxis were keeping their vigil. I got into bed. The feeling of the sheets against my skin made me think of Judith. From here and there throughout the hotel, various sounds could be heard. Sounds of commerce linking hotel beds to limousines, hotel toilets to hotel kitchens, pumping hearts to cupboards full of dark green plants blooming under artificial suns.

The rain was still falling, a steady soothing rain that washed everything else away. I was just drifting off to sleep when I heard voices in the corridor. "The important thing," said a man's voice, a deep familiar voice, "is never betray your inner self."

"Sshh. Quiet." Judith.

"Your inner self is all that counts," the male voice went on. "'To thine own self be true,' Polonius said and although of course I am no camp follower of Uncle Polonius, I believe Shakespeare gave him a special insight—"

The voice and the footsteps had stopped in front of my door. I slid as carefully as possible from under the covers, gathered my clothes in my arms, edged towards the closet. Often, when Judith and I had played house here, we would put a chair in the closet as part of various games. Now the voice recommenced. "I know this is an incredibly awkward way for me to express my feelings for you—" I opened the closet and carefully closed myself in.

A key worked its way loudly into the lock. Then the door swung open and the light came on.

"I don't see him. Perhaps he jumped. Poor boy, I knew him well." The rich, self-satisfied tones filled the Honeymoon Suite. *Poor boy, I knew him well.* Now, finally, I recognized the voice. How could I have missed it in the store this morning? The red face. The self-satisfied expression you sometimes saw in the literary sections of newspapers and magazines. The voice. The contented purr with which that familiar voice had rolled out, hour after hour, on the national airwaves. The man who'd given me the once-over in the bookstore that morning was none other than Norman Swardlow, literary man about town, wit and wag extraordinaire. Now followed the little chuckle that made it sound as though Swardlow had, in his furry roly-poly genuine warmth and intimacy, foamed right out of the speaker to sit beside you in your car or living room. "Forgive me. I come to find Stevens, not to bury him. I'll look in the bathroom." A pause. "Someone's things are here."

There was a silence. Then Judith's voice. "Maybe I'll wait for him."

"Why don't you just leave him a note and come back to my place?"

I peered through the keyhole. Judith was standing with her back to the dresser. Swardlow was close beside her. His dark hair and fringe of beard made a perfect circle. Since I'd last seen him he had promoted himself to a midnight blue suit and one of those striped ties whose stripes are meant to hint at something distinguished. He looked round and sleek. Judith too was dressed to impress. As always, when she wore high heels, she was bent slightly forward. It made her look eager and attentive. They made quite a couple: the old literary lion, slightly foolish but still sufficiently alive to be unpredictable. The unknown, attractive, obviously willing young prey. Perhaps they had been making this couple ever since I had left. Perhaps that was why Fenwick had been so evasive about Judith the other night.

I had my eye pressed to the keyhole. In movies this works out well but in real life, or at least in the Honeymoon Suite, it's not so easy. The main problem was that the keyhole was not exactly where my eye would be if I were standing, sitting, or even kneeling comfortably. This meant I was crouched over, my neck uncomfortably bent. Also I had to keep changing positions, not only because of my neck but for the sake of my knees, which were getting sore.

As Swardlow made his move, my foot tangled in a wire hanger at the back of the closet; it rattled. I froze, then pulled myself forward again. Swardlow now had one hand posed, with the utmost familiarity, on Judith's shoulder, and as he leaned towards her it seemed that hand, unconcerned, was sliding down.

Swardlow's face had arranged itself into a slightly quizzical expression, the one you see in magazines when he is featured for one of his anthologies of nature poetry with which, as I now remembered him saying once, "I keep whole-grain bread on the table."

"A bed, a pillow, the sound of wild geese—what more can a Canadian writer ask when confronted with his muse?" He was holding her against him and she wasn't struggling.

"I don't hear the wild geese." Judith broke away.

"I was being metaphorical. Has anyone ever told you that people who work in bookstores are idiots? Especially when it comes to books?"

"Yes," Judith said.

"Take your friend," Swardlow said. "Paul Stevens." He spoke

my name slowly and clearly, rolling it in his mouth as though it were an after-dinner candy he was about to spit onto the sidewalk. Then: "You know, I didn't recognize him in the store this morning. But, like you, well, not exactly like you, I have always been one of his admirers. Perhaps that is why I did not recognize him. His poetry has, if you don't mind my saying so, its own true face. Like all real literature, written from the heart." Pause for effect. "Believe me, I'm a true fan. If you were going to waste your life with someone before you met me, why not Paul Stevens? Why not Mortimer Snerd? Of course I'm terribly jealous." As he said this he stepped back from Judith, gracing me with a full frontal view, and smiled. Swardlow had the kind of smile certain "personalities" in our city seem to favour: they stare into the eyes of the intended object, then suddenly pull back their lips for a full disclosure of teeth, gums, tongue, the way in other circumstances someone else might whip open their dress or drop their pants. Having thus exposed the full force of his or her naked humanity, the personality then nervously shifts his or her eyes around the room.

Crouched in the closet, I found myself trying to draw my own lips back.

Swardlow kept smiling. Judith was getting not merely the ten seconds of universal sincerity but the full half-minute celebrity treatment.

"Judith. You really *are* special to me." Now his voice had the slightly nasal mid-Atlantic accent so familiar from his radio program. *Good evening. This is Norman Swardlow and tonight we will be talking to some of my favourite people about some of their favourite books. Pull up your chair. Turn down your lights. Open your mind. And before I introduce our first guest let me say I hope you will find this evening's edition of "Swardlow's World of Words" a memorable one....*

"Thank you," Judith said.

Swardlow chuckled. "*Thank you*, the maiden says drily. But who cares. I love you, anyway. You make me feel like a drooling old man in pursuit of a wild nymph."

"I know," Judith said. Now she allowed Norman to nuzzle her cheek.

I decided that I had to get my pants on. I was sitting on the closet floor, frantically pulling them up, when I heard the hotel-room door open again. The sound of whispers in the hall, then Judith's sigh as she returned to the room, kicked off her high heels and sat down in the chair.

I stepped out of the closet. "Behold the wild goose."

"I should have know you'd be in there."

"This is my room."

She had drawn her feet up onto the chair. Our first night in the Honeymoon Suite she had curled up into herself this way, her dress pulled down over her knees.

"Last time I was at your apartment you weren't there. Unless you were hiding. And one of your gorilla friends tried to turn me into hamburger. Or was that Swardlow, in his Mighty Mouse incarnation?"

Judith's face turned red. "No, I was with Swardlow that night."

"I won't even ask what you were doing with Swardlow—"

"Generous of you. Do you also have a list of questions I can't ask you? All things considered, you're lucky I showed up. Even with Norman Swardlow."

From somewhere faraway in the hotel came the sound of breaking glass. A little rush of treble notes, the piano starting up again.

Here we were again: same chair, same look, same whatever it was about Judith when she got like this, something that made it impossible for me to do anything that might hurt her because I knew, for at least this moment, she felt the same way about me.

And so, cast back into this state with Judith, this state of non-attrition, this state of grace.

She moved forward.

"Does it hurt?"

At first I thought Judith was asking if I was jealous of Norman Swardlow. Then I realized she meant my head. I put my hand to the swelling. It was now smaller and harder than it had been. Instead of aching all around it now gave off a sharp pain from the centre.

"It did hurt. I picked it up at your apartment."

"Martha told me."

"And?"

"I swear, Paul. I don't know who did it. I wish I did."

"When did you go back there?"

"It was the middle of the night. I was out with Norman."

"I was lying on your front lawn. Didn't you notice me?"

"I didn't notice anything. I went in, I put on the answering machine, I went to sleep. It was afternoon when I woke up. Martha called and told me what happened. So I decided to come here to see you. Norman insisted on coming with me. Just to make sure I'd be all right."

"Generous of him. But what about the other night? No one waiting for you when you got home?"

"No. No one."

"Giving out a lot of keys to your apartment these days?"

There was an instant of hesitation. So I thought. "I'm getting the locks changed tomorrow," Judith said.

"Who was it?"

"I don't know."

"You don't have any idea?"

"I don't know. I don't know anything. I don't even know what you were doing in my apartment."

"I wanted to see you before you left."

"Here I am."

Looking back, thinking of this scene, I imagine different things I could have done at this point. *Here I am.* I could have jumped up from the window ledge where I was sitting, crossed over to Judith's armchair and demanded she roll up her sleeves to prove she had changed her ways. I could have pursued that brief hesitation she had had when I asked her about giving keys out to her apartment. I could have asked her to leave.

But my skin was starting to react to Judith; it felt uncomfortable inside my clothes the way it used to be when I was with Judith, wanting her.

"So," Judith said. "I went to Kingston once to see your house. Nice big stones. I hope they were strong enough to keep out the forces of evil."

"And then?"

"And then what? Was I supposed to come to the door and beg? I just wanted to drive by. See where you were. Just because I never quite knew whether or not I was supposed to be waiting for you to come back. Or did you ask yourself what it must have been like for me waking up the next morning? Wondering where you were. Finally getting your clever little postcard saying, 'I've left town. Henry will pick my stuff up from the hotel.' I liked that 'left town'. Like you're in some old 1930s baseball movie and the camera follows you down to the bus station and you chew a bit of gum before deciding which bus to take. Bye-bye, town."

Judith's legs were crossed under her. She was sitting ramrod stiff. Her eyes sparking, her face gone dead white. "You thought I was trying to kill you, didn't you. That's how crazy you are."

"I am that crazy. I'll admit that. But I never really believed you were trying to kill me. Maybe I just thought you couldn't tell the difference any more."

"I'm not that crazy. I was never that crazy."

"Dead. Cold. Together. After this we stop dead. Cold. Together. Do you remember telling me that?"

"No. I remember that I always wanted to stop."

That was true. Judith was always saying she wanted to stop. She would talk about it and I would listen and encourage. Although I liked being stoned with Judith. I liked being with her in the Honeymoon Suite. The wild confused ways our bodies melted together. Of course I knew it was dangerous. But being with Judith was like that. Danger. Fusion. Necessity.

Now Judith was wearing that vulnerable look again.

"You're afraid of something," I said.

"I'm afraid to lose you. I'm afraid to be with you."

And then suddenly her coat was on and she was gone while I sat on the window ledge, unable to move, unable to do anything but listen to her footsteps going down the hall. Eventually I turned to look outside. I saw her go into the street. A taxi appeared miraculously from the darkness. Judith raised her arm to flag it. A small triangle of light shone onto the street when she opened the door. Then the door closed and I watched the red tail-lights disappear down the street and around the corner.

TEN

"HE'S MOANING," Henry would say whenever our father managed to get out something of what he felt for our departed mother. Later, when we'd see him asleep in the chair, whisky glass still in hand, I'd tiptoe in to turn off the light that was shining in his face. Our father would grunt in his sleep. "He's moaning," Henry would say. "They all sound the same when they moan."

Certainly the moans I used to hear while walking the halls to and from the Honeymoon Suite were hard to distinguish. Though there was an exception: Eileen, a woman who worked for one of the cowboys in the white stretch limousines. She had thick red hair that bounced against her shoulders, a permanently tanned face, a huge paste diamond ring. When I first saw her there was still a faint cloud of teenage moisture in the skin around her eyes. Green eyes, Irish eyes. Looking at her flowing hair, her emerald eyes, I would think that a long shower would surely wash away the past two years and she could start again, re-emerge as someone's beautiful pampered daughter, go to school, study French.

She would sometimes be in the hotel coffee shop something to eat between customers. Once when the booth next to hers, she recognized me as a fellow regular and asked me for a match. Then she brought her coffee over and sat across from me. She was feeling bad, she said. Her "guy" owed. He had taken on "two new girls. Janice and her sister. You wouldn't see them here yet. They're too fancy for a joint like this. They got mink pussies or something." On this day Eileen was wearing sunglasses. She took them off to show me the bruise beneath one eye. "He doesn't even want to fuck me any more. He fucks the minks and gives me this instead." She was eating white toast slathered with butter and strawberry jam. On her plate were stacked four of the plastic jam packets that are brought into Toronto by the truckload for all the speed freaks having glucose breakdowns.

Eileen was not normally given to moaning and groaning, at least not with her customers. Instead she produced a series of high cheeping sounds, long ever-mounting treble cries that could be heard from the moment you got out of the elevator, all the way down the hall, and even, or perhaps it was only their disturbing echo, after you closed the rusted fire door and started up the stairs. Sometimes I would pause outside her room to listen to those cries. Calls for help, cries of abandonment, the sounds of some poor fragment of humanity being destroyed. Finally one morning in the coffee shop, I said that while passing a room in the hotel I had heard someone in pain. "That must have been me," Eileen said. She looked down at her toast, blushed beneath her tan. "Whenever one of them touches me, it just starts. I can't help it. Even Janice, the other night, she got me going. Only my guy. With him it's like—I don't know—" she raised her face and looked at me, flushed, full of love, the face of a young girl enthralled by her idol "—different. You know what I mean?"

I nodded.

"I guess I'm just a love slave," Eileen said. She had picked up the sugar bowl and was pouring it into her coffee. "That's what my guy says. He says I'm the slave type of person."

That night after Judith left, I dreamed about Eileen. In my dream she was an old crone out of a Bergman film, a black-caped pouchy-eyed pilgrim shuffling along a misty road towards a cross impossible to see. I was woken up by what I thought were her cries, but it was only the chirping of my alarm clock. I had a hard time getting out of bed. I stood in the shower for a while, then shaved and prepared for work. The lump had continued to shrink, but still sent out jagged waves of pain if I moved quickly. Standing in front of the mirror to shave I saw that a bruise had formed on my ribs. I put on Henry's old football jacket, the baseball cap Martha had given me, went out to the elevator. My body felt small and shrunken, and I had that bad feeling in my stomach I always got after a fight with Judith.

As though called up by my dream, Eileen was visible through the coffee-shop door. She was facing a wall, without even a newspaper in front of her, stirring her coffee.

The wind off the lake had scoured away the clouds, leaving the sky a hollow blue. I started walking towards the bookstore. The wind on the back of my neck, my ears, tugging at the peak of my cap. The cars pouring down University Avenue. Some still had their lights on. Drivers talking into carphones. The cars themselves, sleek and shining, heading towards the stock exchange and the big corporate office towers. The sidewalk also filled. Men in suits, raincoats, with attaché cases. Women's faces layered in make-up. Others like myself, less sure. A few winos lying in the grassy median between the lanes, absorbing the sun, finishing last night's bottle or starting a new one.

As I got closer to the bookstore the suits gave way to nylon ski jackets, multi-plaid sports coats. Only a few people here were on their way to work. Everyone else was out scrounging or begging or hoping; out because they were too hungry to stay in; or, like the man who suddenly stopped in front of me, a bearded man in a grey coat with, as always, a knapsack over his left shoulder, out because there was no in. He stopped in front of me, blocking the sidewalk. While I dug into my pocket for change I looked down at his feet. This time he was wearing running shoes: one with a red rim around the sole, almost new; the other a different size, the colour of pavement, the upper and the sole bound together by thick bands of black electrician's tape, like an old-fashioned hockey stick.

"I thought you were dead," he said. His name was Neil. He used to work at the pool hall, cleaning up. "Some strange story there," Sam would say. "You ever see inside the bag he carries? This guy reads books in Russian."

"I was away."

Neil was looking over at the place he always looks when he's talking, a place off in some sideways universe so you see his face from an angle, the angle that doesn't quite hide his half-closed eyelid, the red half-moon socket of his missing eye. "Shoving it at people like that," Sam would complain. "I told him to go and get himself fixed up. I even offered to pay."

I gave him what was in my pocket and we both moved on.

When I arrived at the store Fenwick was just unlocking the door. He looked down at me for a moment as though I were a total stranger and he was wondering what I might be doing there. Then his usual affable smile appeared and I followed him inside. I was feeling tired. I sipped at the coffee he had made. There were little bubbles around the edges and I started counting them. I suddenly remembered another time I'd counted coffee bubbles like this, an exhausted morning after a night of love-making with Judith. Alone in the store I had decided to search for the name of post-sex exhaustion in the old home medical encyclopaedias and almanacs that Fenwick had on a special shelf. The condition was apparently too insignificant to be listed. However, I did find graphic descriptions of various disgusting sexual diseases and their dire effects. In one of these almanacs, perhaps written by someone with a literary background, there was a long digression on Friedrich Nietzsche, the possibility that his chaste adult life could be explained by his fear that he had contracted syphilis as a teenager. "French authors of his generation did not always share his scruples," this British writer went on to explain. He then detailed the problems of Gustave Flaubert; the pleasure-loving creator of *Madame Bovary* had apparently ruined his health and appearance with mercury cures that turned his flesh scarlet, made his eyes bulge and caused his hair to fall out. As though, like the hidden picture of Dorian Gray, Flaubert's face was the mirror of his vices. What moral lesson will be featured in the almanacs of the next century when they describe the collapse of entire immune systems, the slow desperate deaths of whole populations?

I had progressed with my coffee from staring to drinking when the telephone rang. I answered, hoping it was Judith. "May I speak to Paul Stevens, please?" Jeanine's official voice, contained and proper.

"It's me," I said.

She asked me if we could meet during my lunch hour, but only if I would promise to keep it secret from Henry. "I'm serious, Dungo."

"I know," I said. And I did know, because it had been so long since she had used that name with me, Dungo, that just hearing her speak it had driven me back to the old days when everything we said was serious, wild, life and death.

We met in a coffee shop near the bookstore.

"I think Henry's in trouble," Jeanine announced as soon as she slid into her seat.

"Sick?"

"No. Nothing like that. Though God knows why he hasn't drunk himself dead."

Jeanine, my brother's first and only love. She was carrying a purse, a big shapeless leather bag that she opened now, reached into for cigarettes. When we all lived together in the apartment across from the pool hall, Jeanine would often take one of her big shapeless bags to the market and shoplift our supper. "God knows I'm only doing this for you two," she would say.

Back home we would wait for her return. Then, like attentive students, we would sit across from her while she took her booty out of her bag, one item at a time. Henry and I had to try to guess what was going to come next. Jeanine's fingers had been slim and supple, quick as a magician's. Into the bag they would dip, out would come frozen broccoli, chocolate bars, steaks, a handful of peas; or suddenly she would be offering an eggplant to the setting sun, its dark burnished skin glowing as she held it to the light, spun it round, pressed its mysterious colours against her cheek. "Eggplant," Henry would groan. But Jeanine would only smile as she let it slide from her hand down her arm and back into her bag.

Since I'd seen her last, my image of Jeanine had retreated to the very beginning, the confident unimpressed young girl who had flipped her blond pony-tail back, then hopped onto her bicycle and ridden away into the sunset. Now her hair was darker, except where it was streaked with grey, and her eyes seemed resigned and tired.

"You're looking well."

"You too."

"Sorry I crashed out so early the other night."

"That's okay."

"I thought Henry would talk to you then."

"You know Henry. He doesn't like to ask for help."

"Yes," Jeanine smiled, "I know Henry." Later, when she told

me what Henry had done, I thought about that smile. It wasn't bitter, the way it might have been, nor was it forgiving. It was a smile, you might say, of acceptance. Henry had done what it had always seemed Henry would eventually do. Jeanine had known it, known Henry, better than anyone.

"The bank phoned me last week," Jeanine said. "They said we were late on the mortgage payment. Of course I was surprised. We paid off the mortgage years ago, when my mother died. The first thing that came into my mind was that Henry must have had a cash-flow problem at the garage. He's always mumbling about how long people take to pay their bills and you can imagine what things must have been like the last couple of years. But it seemed strange to me because we both own the house and I would have thought we would both have to sign for a mortgage. If you know what I mean. So I said I'd put the cheque in the mail, and how much did we owe them?"

She stopped and lit a new cigarette. Her face seemed suddenly lank and horsey, the way it had when she was pregnant and she would point to herself and say, "Dungo, if this face of mine gets any longer I'm going to gallop away." In all the years they'd been together Jeanine had never before said anything against Henry to me. Nothing. There had been days, that summer she was pregnant, when anger, exasperation, whatever had sent her storming off to see a friend. But she would never criticize Henry to me. Brotherhood. Solidarity. Perhaps that day in the restaurant I should have shown some solidarity. Things might have gone differently if I had just shook my head and said, "I don't mix in Henry's business."

"How much?" I asked.

"A lot, Dungo. So much that I called a real-estate company and had someone evaluate the house. It was mortgaged for more than its worth. Which told me this whole thing had been going on for a while, since before prices fell."

"You should have been a detective."

"I've had my moments." Jeanine gave that dry laugh she'd always had, the one that lets you know her whole life with Henry, staying at home with the children and being the mother to them that Henry had wanted for himself, was just something she'd done, just a game she'd been playing for Henry's sake, a game she could drop anytime.

It was lunch hour. We had both ordered western omelettes, the way we used to after Henry announced he had seen "scientific evidence" in *Reader's Digest* that western omelettes, with brown toast on the side, were the best nutritional choice in "today's restaurants".

"Dungo, I couldn't keep it to myself. When I asked him about it, Henry cried. Then he told me the whole story. It's so stupid. The garage started to get into trouble. People not paying. He complained about it to the cops who go there to get their cars fixed. No problem, they said to him. You know all that monkey business that goes on at the track. They said they would let Henry in on it. Everybody does it, Henry says. They would tell him which races were fixed and Henry would make some easy money. One of those policeman is even called Mr. Clean, because he never let himself be bribed. So Henry thought, if Mr. Clean does it, he could go along for the ride. Everything was fine, according to Henry, until Mr. Clean suddenly threatened to turn in the others unless they paid him off. So they're paying. At least Henry's paying. He paid his winnings at the track. Then he forged my signature for the house. Mortgaged the business. Everything."

"And everyone else is paying?"

"Dungo, who knows? Henry says they are."

"If they were all about to lose their houses, don't you think this Mr. Clean would, you know, have some sort of accident?"

"Henry says they're afraid. This guy is untouchable. He's

some kind of hero. No one would believe anything bad about him."

"And you?"

"I say Henry's afraid. You should see him at night. Looking out the windows as though he's being followed. He can't sleep. He's so scared."

Jeanine hadn't touched her food. I took one of her cigarettes, the way I used to when she was pregnant and I was in training and we were both having to pretend to Henry that we'd stopped smoking.

"You could get a job."

"That's not the point. They're going to squeeze him until he cracks, Dungo. And then they're going to kill him."

Good citizen Henry. His downtown garage. The little island of stability he'd spent his whole life building. The way he always kept his hair combed, his face shaven, said, "Yes sir", and "Yes ma'am", and even if it cost him always honoured his estimate. Good citizen Henry who wasn't afraid to hire ex-cons, who was tough and fearless and joked with the cops across the street who came to get their cars fixed and whose presence protected Henry's garage from the bad things that can happen. Except that now Henry was having to pay the price for his protection.

We were in the booth at the back. It was the booth the waitresses used when things were slow in the morning and if I came in alone I took it for lunch, because the morning papers were always stashed there.

Now I looked down and saw a cutline: "Headless corpse found in school parking lot." It showed a picture of a car surrounded by police.

"He's been asking everyone for money. I think he even went to see Fenwick last night. Then I thought, well, I'd never forgive myself if I just said nothing and Henry—"

"Jeanine."

"Don't worry. I'm not going to cry." She produced a smile, lit a new cigarette, pushed back her hair.

"I could try to find out about this Mr. Clean."

"That's what Henry calls him. I don't even know his real name. Probably Henry doesn't either. You know how he's always giving people names then he forgets—"

"I know."

Jeanine laughed. Things didn't seem so bad. I made her promise to call me the next morning with Mr. Clean's real name. A quick kiss on the cheek at the restaurant doorway. Then Jeanine headed towards the subway, looking like any other housewife making her way about the city, while I crossed the street and went back to the store.

A couple of weeks after that day in the restaurant, when all of the worst things yet to come in this story had already happened, I found myself holding a biography of Charles Dickens. It was one of those slack moments in the store, dusty mid-afternoon hours when I drift from shelf to shelf, book to book. I dip in here and there, sentences swirl together in my mind, make vortexes, carry me into the weird submarine world of language where everything is joined together in a blur of constantly shifting meanings that suddenly focus, clarify; there is a quick beam of light into the centre of everything but the moment you try to follow its lucid path, the light dissolves and all you are left with is the memory of having somehow grasped something you can no longer name.

The Dickens biography was bound in leather of a dark mustard colour. Inside was a frontispiece of the man himself, Charles Dickens at the age of twenty-five. Twenty-five! Exactly my age the year I came back to the city. Exactly my age the moment I was holding it in front of me, as though it was some kind of mirror gone crazy. I took the book closer to the window. The author was shown sitting at an angle to his desk, his hand holding down a sheaf of manuscripts; his piercing black eyes were looking out to future admirers like myself, his well-formed features, framed by long dark curling hair, were turned towards the light. Dressed in shining black shoes, a dark suit, a velvet waistcoat, his features composed and pensive, Dickens seemed less a real person than someone posing for a portrait in the grand manner of his day. Yet beneath it was a quote attributed to Thackeray: "Here we have the identical man Dickens." To think that at twenty-five years of age Charles Dickens was already famous, a married man in the midst of his enormous success with *The Pickwick Papers*; to think that at twenty-five he was already far beyond the reach of the Norman Swardlows and Mr. Cleans of this world, was already a man so established in his reality that his portrait might or might not be "the identical man".

Leafing through the book I found myself reading about the way he had, in his early public appearances, exhausted his voice with his enthusiastic renderings of his characters. To save himself he took voice lessons. Imagine Dickens, dressed to declaim, orating the climax of *A Tale of Two Cities* or the piteous speeches of *Oliver Twist* while, ruler in hand, some long-forgotten elocution master, himself like a Dickens character in his stained waistcoat and ill-tied ascot, kept interrupting him to improve his style. Imagine Dickens practising the exact moment to drop to his knees, to fold his strong hand over his strongly beating heart, to allow his voice to descend into hoarse piteous gasps or leap up into frightened soprano cries.

The door opened and in came Martha. She stopped when she saw me, the way people did at that time, as though they couldn't quite absorb everything that had happened; then she came forward with a look of such sympathy that I dropped the book. As we bent to pick it up our heads collided. I drew away. She reached for me, kissed me on the lips, said, "That's better." Then as we stood up she squeezed my hands, hard. The last time I remember kissing Martha.

Those days after my return to Toronto, those days during which everything happened so fast, time seemed to telescope upon itself. There was hardly a pause for sleep or reflection. Although as I look back, even the benefit of hindsight has never shown how to escape what couldn't then be escaped. It was as though that last week was just the accelerated and inevitable conclusion of forces and undercurrents that had been been gathering strength for years.

For example, that same day I had lunch with Jeanine, Swardlow came by with a strange proposition. I had just come back into the store, had not even taken off my coat, when Swardlow suddenly appeared. "Great weather," he said, as though he knew I'd been watching him through the keyhole.

"You played high-school football? You'd be amazed at how many Canadian poets pride themselves on their athletic ability. Did you see my documentary on writers who play baseball? There was a terrific poem by that Vancouver fellow who is always carrying around a matchbox full of worms—" He was talking at me, his hand on Henry's old football jacket. Swardlow's fingers were stubby, almost fat, tanned, hair on the knuckles, nails amazingly smooth and trimmed, as though he had them professionally done. The nation's literary ringmaster with his hands docilely stretched out towards the manicurist. All he needed was some of my mother's pearl nail polish.

Swardlow. His podgy fingers, his slightly swollen face with its lopsided fringe of beard, his nails trimmed in a suspicious manner.

Now Swardlow was in mid-mutation from the literary Liberace of radioland to the cultural ringmaster of the television screen. The man once known only by the oil on his mid-Atlantic vowels could now be seen, live on tape, on our national television network. "Not prime time," Swardlow was explaining, "but we're working on it. Do you know what our numbers people found out? On any given night except Saturdays, more Canadians reach for a book or magazine than for their consenting partner. In this supposedly illiterate age, print, my good man, has become more important than sex." So Swardlow, for his new emission, was making a documentary on the subject of used-book stores. Judith and I were to be, Swardlow explained, figures in this program, a cleverly presented mixture of fact and fiction, "docudrama" Swardlow called it, that would use us as "young, attractive, contemporary role models that the audience can identify with. The kind of people they can imagine in their homes. The kind of people they want themselves or their own children to be." Swardlow's eyes gobbled at mine. "You know what I mean?"

"What about Judith?" I asked.

"She's involved," he said. "Using you was her idea. I won't say I agreed with her at first, but as the assistant producer she has a certain amount of weight. And as you know, she's a young woman with a lot of talent. Too much to waste—"

Now he stepped back, gave me one of those fake appraising glances I used to use when Fenwick and I went on our expeditions. "She's right, you know. I think your look is exactly the kind people associate with used books."

It was the end of the day and I was going out the front door, Fenwick behind me ready to lock up, when Jeanine appeared before me again. She said something about being just in time. She must have been running. Her hair was tousled, her face glowing with the cold.

"Dungo, look." She had a sheaf of papers in her hand and was breathing hard. "Mr. Clean. I found out his real name and did some research. I was afraid I'd miss you —"

I led her into the doorway of a restaurant to look at her papers, and then, there he was, his picture in the newspaper, Constable Nicholas Ross.

For these and other details Jeanine had gone to the library and searched the last ten years of newspaper microfiches. Ross's name had been in the paper several times. Twice he had been pictured as part of the city police rope-pulling team, the second time as captain. On this second occasion the team's picture had also appeared and there was "Constable 'Nicko' Ross", his hair cut close to his skull, square features younger and sharper, straining at the end of the rope. The next mention of Constable Ross came in the coverage of the annual Police Association banquet. One of the newspapers simply reported that "Constable Ross" had been cited for "his courage when, driving home off-duty, he interceded in a struggle between three men and their victim, in a downtown parking lot, and managed to single-handedly arrest the three assailants." The other newspaper devoted much more space to this incident, showing a picture of "Constable Nicholas Ross" accepting the plaque and quoting the man he had helped as saying, "He saved my life. I was lying on the ground thinking I was going to die and suddenly it was like a scene out of a Superman movie. You could hear their bones crunching." In the cutline beneath this picture he was referred to as a former member of the undercover drug squad now "on special assignment".

A year later there was a report of him being in a car accident resulting from a police chase. He had been the passenger in a police car that crashed into an abutment while pursuing two hold-up suspects who had, seconds earlier, gone off the road and been killed. The report mentioned the possibility of an inquiry, but no follow-up story had made it into the papers.

So Leonard Marks had been right. Even as I was re-reading the clippings and checking the picture I was remembering

Nicko's easy confidence about everyone from Sam to the police; the questions I'd always had about where he got his drugs, how he supported Vivian; the way Henry had seemed to know so much about Judith; Nicko's curiosity about Henry. I even supplied myself with little scenes of Nicko down at Henry's garage, giving him the dope on his little brother, filling him in on Judith's habit, perhaps even repeating my imitations of Captain Bill. Or at the racetrack? Why couldn't they be doing all their talking at the track? In retrospect, the brain always rearranges itself so that even the unthinkable can be taken for granted.

ELEVEN

HENRY told me Nicko Ross had taken up lifting weights. I found him lying on his back. Around his waist he had one of those big belts weightlifters wear to keep their guts from exploding when they're lifting. Nicko was lifting. He had more than four hundred pounds suspended above him. A smooth sheen of sweat covered the carefully tanned flesh of his legs, big slabs of muscle emerging from bright red spandex shorts. Over his torso he wore a black singlet that emphasized his huge shoulders and made his neck look like an advertisement for the benefits of steroids. The veins at the sides of his neck bulged, ran up under his jaw, reappeared as scarlet claws at his temples.

I watched him from the doorway between the jogging track and weight room. Like Nicko, I was sweating. In a baggy grey sweat suit Henry had dug out of some closet, I'd been jogging slowly around the track. Every few laps I would step from the track to the adjacent weight room to look at Nicko Ross. He'd signed the weight-room ledger with a flourish, writing his name in big rounded letters. On the level below, an early-evening exercise class was jumping, skipping and stretching. The exercise class was mostly composed of young women in tights; the men were older executive types wearing too much flesh, floppy shorts and T-shirts, doing more ogling than aerobics.

In the old days, the days when I was supposedly in training, I would come up to this gym as a change from Gold's, where I was officially working out. Here I could exercise unwatched by my supposed competitors-to-be, do weights, work the speed and body bags, run a few laps; in the summer you could even go up on the roof to lie in the sun and read.

In Kingston I had done more running. At first it was a substitute for drinking, then it occurred to me that running would help drive all the residues of the various poisons I'd been ingesting in Toronto out of my system. Except that, as the months wore on, it became clear that my real addiction was to Judith. I couldn't run her out of my system but at least I could exhaust myself. So after work, summer and winter, I would pound along the lake, a peaked cap jammed down over my eyes to keep out the sun when it was sunny and the rain when it was raining.

The last time I stopped in the weight-room doorway, Nicko Ross was standing in front of the mirror admiring his rippling muscles while he did wrist curls. He had a lot of muscles to admire. In Judith's kitchen he had been big, his arms thick and powerful, but now he was wasp-waisted with bulging defined muscles in the style of Hercules magazines.

While he examined himself in the mirror, a woman from the exercise class came to join him. She had put on a hernia belt and was standing beside him, a towel around her neck, doing slow deep knee bends while she leaned forward to check her form. Nicko's taste in females had apparently evolved along with his body. Vivian Armstrong, skeletal and febrile, had been replaced by a scarlet-spandexed Miss America complete with flushed cheeks and confidently exposed cleavage.

His body, his girlfriend—what hadn't Nicko exchanged? His jeans for a uniform, Judith's kitchen for Henry's garage. My intention had been to confront him—but now I realized I wasn't yet prepared.

I dressed and hurried out to the street. I felt betrayed, as though the man who had listened to me across a kitchen table owed me something better.

The wind had changed direction. Now it was a chilly blast from the north and as I walked my wet hair froze and banged against my neck and ears. My destination, at first unfixed, became the illuminated clock of the Wing On Funeral Home. I went round the back. The first night I'd walked from the restaurant to Judith's, I had passed by, but no lights were on. Now a promising glow shone from the kitchen window out onto the landing of the fire escape. I climbed the steps and knocked on the door. A woman answered, looked at me dubiously, then said the only thing she knew about Leonard Marks, a tenant twice removed from her, was that he still received *National Geographic* magazine.

I went round to the press. There was a printer standing at the Heidelberg, watching as it churned out the sheets, but he also knew nothing of Leonard, though he remembered someone talking about a man who had worked there once then left.

When I went back to the gym the next evening, Ross wasn't there. Which didn't surprise me. Serious lifters don't work out every day. Working with weights, if you know your own limits, makes little tears in your muscles. The idea is to let them heal—the scarring makes your muscles bigger—then, forty-eight hours later, they're ready to tear again. Put the right amount of pressure on the right muscle, and you can design your own body. If you see someone doing all this at twenty-four-hour intervals you know they're either stupid or taking steroids. With steroids the muscles heal faster, you can work out more often, you can make yourself bigger, faster.

So Nicko was clean in at least one respect. After his night off he was back at the weights, sweating his way around the room. To loosen up from his weights he took a few laps around the track. He had the awkward musclebound gait most weightlifters acquire, but he moved with plenty of spring, those big quads in his thighs sending him bounding through the air. You'd want a good head start if you decided to run away from Nicko Ross.

When he'd finished his laps he came back into the weight room, took a pair of thin leather gloves from his pocket, the kind I sometimes used to use, and gave the speed bag a little workout. After he'd tortured it for a while he moved to the body bag. Each time he drove his fist into it he grunted. Then he suddenly turned sideways and delivered the bag such a powerful karate kick that the bag swung on its chain until it slammed into the ceiling.

The sound of his foot smashing into the heavy bag, then the thunk it delivered as it hit the ceiling made everyone in the room stop and look towards him. Nicko gave a little smile, then stepped back and carefully peeled the gloves from his fingers.

It is a long way from Dickens and Flaubert to the details of Nicko Ross's muscles and sweat. Although perhaps today's Madame Bovary would not find it so far. For example, here is a fact that may or may not have any meaning: I once paced out the distances between the following three locations—Martha Fenwick's former studio and site of the Eisenhower follies, Fenwick's Books and the weight room. They form the points of an almost perfect equilateral triangle, each of the sides being about one hundred metres in length. This means that on foot a champion athlete could get from one to the other in less than ten seconds. An anxious lover, a Madame Bovary in search of her gallant Mr. Clean, or even someone wearing high-heeled shoes and hurrying to a blind date would require a minute at most. Even a hung-over middle-aged Canadian bibliophile, carrying two briefcases with the collected works of Ethel Wilson, Frederick Philip Grove and a selection of Pierre Berton, could make the distance in three or four minutes.

Such is our city's intimate geometry linking love, sweat and literature.

Speaking of love, I read a strange thing the other night: Flaubert, at a dinner with the Goncourt brothers, told them he had learned how get along without women. How? When you go to bed, you sleep on your heart.

After my second night spying on Nicko Ross I went down to see Henry. You leave the city. You come back. The man who once reminded you of your brother is now mixed up with him in some way that can't yet be decoded. You begin to feel like someone trapped in an elevator whose walls are coming together.

Jeanine hadn't needed to force me to be responsible for Henry—a reminder was all it took. Now on my way to see him I felt the way I did that first fall when he'd moved out from our father's place to the rooming house. There would be the brave face on things, the cash in the pocket. But behind it all would be the same old Henry, fleeing a catastrophe he would never discuss, whose centre I would never see.

We sat in the kitchen. There was a fresh pot of coffee, a new bottle of Scotch. Henry in the mode of atonement. He was standing at the sink, pouring some water into my drink, when he finally just started talking. The style was casual, Henry-style, indirect. "Yeah. Nicko Ross, you met him up at Judith's years ago. He told me all about it." A pause for the fatally wounded organs to wrap themselves around the knife. "We were into some things together."

"For example?"

"Oh, you know, we used to go places—get away from things...." His voice trailed off. Henry's silences, always so easy to read. He meant he used to go out with Nicko to get away from Jeanine. That was an option I hadn't considered before:

Henry, the bored husband, going out with the boys to cheat on Jeanine. I wondered if Henry remembered that time we met Nicko at the track. Nicko with the suit-busting blonde. Even Martha had seemed drab in comparison. Henry grinning at the sight of Nicko Ross, pointing him out to me, winking at him. Probably even back then they were out screwing and betting together. Everything had been laid out in front of me, but I'd been so busy smelling the horse manure and enjoying the way Martha was rubbing herself against me that I'd missed the whole story.

"Why didn't you tell me he was a cop? Weren't you worried he'd arrest me?"

Henry shrugged. "Don't be silly. You and Judith and Vivian were just part of his entertainment. Anyway, I already owed Nicko then. He made me promise not to tell you."

"Great, thanks a lot."

Henry refilled his glass. "Dungo, even before you left I was having—things were tough. The house, the shop, interest rates. Every time interest rates went up it was like someone was tightening the wire around my balls."

In the end, Henry's version was much the same as Jeanine's, though with a different twist, this being that he had beaten the money squeeze by playing the horses until Nicko Ross had decided he was doing too well and started to blackmail him.

"He calls it 'protection money,'" Henry said.

"Why don't we go to the police?"

"Get serious." Henry flicked a cigarette so hard that it skittered off the table onto the floor. "I'd be lucky to get out of there alive."

"We could get a lawyer. Someone can't just squeeze you to death. Not just like that."

Henry looked at me, shaking his head back and forth the way he always did when I refused to understand what was obvious to him. "Dungo, they squeeze people to death all the time. They're big. I'm little. That's the story, right?"

"And when you can't pay?"

"I don't know." He lit one of his cigarettes, as though this was an interesting problem, a mechanical puzzle that needed to be thought over before he stuck his hands back into the greasy engine, or waited for that wire to be tightened another notch. "I guess they could either drift away, or they could decide I know too much."

"How long can you keep this up?"

"Don't know. What am I supposed to do? Knock over milk stores? They gave me one week but I figure two."

"Are they serious?"

Henry gave me one of his patented stares. "Dungo, last Tuesday night, when I got into my car and turned on the key, there was an explosion under the hood. I ran into the office. The telephone was ringing and I picked it up. 'It's that easy,' a voice said. 'Happy driving.' No one I knew.

"Until then I thought I could put them off until my luck changed. But now I've got it figured out." Henry had that little smile he sometimes wore when he had put together a surprise. "Look at my options." He stuck out one finger: "I try to take out Nicko Ross. That's ridiculous, right? For one thing the guy's a barbarian. For another, even if I did drop something on his head or shoot him, the rest of them would get me. And not only me. There'd also be the family." He stuck out a second finger. "Two: we all disappear. That was my plan. I even managed to put some money aside for a while. One night we just take off, head for the coast or something. Problem is, we're a family. Too easy to track down. These guys have friends everywhere. They'd be afraid sooner or later I'd spill my guts to someone. Even Jeanine. Which would put her in danger, too." He put a third finger out. "Three: only I disappear. Make it look like suicide. Not a bad

plan. If I kill myself, especially if the body is right there, they figure I'm so ashamed of everything that's happened I just offed
myself. That way they could be sure I hadn't told Jeanine. So
she'd be in the clear."

"Good thinking," I said. "What's number four?"

"There is no number four."

"But you've got the body problem. And then there's the life
insurance. You don't get your life insurance if they think they
blew your brains out."

We were in Henry's kitchen. Jeanine had gone to bed long
ago. "Take the life insurance first," Henry said. "The fact is Jeanine doesn't need it. Not really. She could move in with her parents. That would help save her from these guys. And you could
keep an eye on her. Take her to movies every now and then or
something to make sure she didn't go nuts with the old folks."

"Where are you going to be all this time?"

"Dead."

"Right." When Henry has a plan, you have to listen slowly,
ask the right questions, get it out of him a bit at a time. Eventually it seems that he's thought of everything. Except that in the
end it never works, which is Henry's peculiar riddle, his karma,
Meribel T. Simmons would say, and why Henry had gotten
himself into this mess in the first place. "But while you're supposed to be dead, where are you going to be hiding? What are
you going to use for money? How are you going to fake the
body? Henry, these friends of yours might not be very nice, but
they aren't idiots. You can't just go away and leave a suicide
note."

"I know."

"So?"

"Number three," Henry said. "The only number three that
works is the one where they find a body. That way they know."

"No problem. We just dig someone up, strap on your watch,

and throw him into the lake with a beeper so they find him. Got anyone in mind?"

"Me, Dungo. I'll do it at the garage. You just attach a vacuum cleaner hose to the exhaust pipe. I bought a new one the other day. One of those nice shiny flexible plastic hoses, guaranteed not to leak for at least a month. I won't feel a thing."

Henry had worked out the perfect plan. He just had to kill himself and all his problems would be solved.

TWELVE

T HIS MORNING I was out at the grave again. Lately the nights have been windy. Every morning the branches of the trees are barer, and through the bare branches the sky is grey. But the ground is still soft, and gives out that peculiar bitter autumn smell it has just before it freezes. I was thinking about the way my mother shouted "junkie" at me across the open grave. I could have pointed out to her that according to the biographies in our store the whole nineteenth century was addicted to drugs. Everyone from ships' captains to writers to princesses was taking opium, morphine, the poppy and its cousins in all their glorious forms.

But drugs and their promised lands stopped attracting me long ago. The feeling I get out at the cemetery has nothing to do with visions, literary or otherwise. On the contrary, during my strange hours at the grave I feel peaceful and relaxed. There I am free to carry on my quiet conversations with the dead, certain I am in the one place in the universe where it is no longer necessary for me to pretend.

Pretence, on the other hand, was essential for the General's Annual Costume Drunk, a pre-Hallowe'en event for the downtown Toronto literary marginalia—the anti-establishment of used-bookshop owners, scouts, faithful customers, bearded winos and druggies specializing in dusty corners of knowledge from naval history, to necromancy, to palm reading. As the General himself once said: no guest too famous to be welcome, no reader too cheap or illiterate to be offered a drink.

The night after I saw Henry was to be the General's night. I was still deciding how and where to confront Nicko when Fenwick commandeered me to go with him to the liquor store.

There we bought a few cartons of cheap wine, a couple of cases of beer and a bottle of cognac—Fenwick's annual tribute to the General. "And now, something special for the big boys," Fenwick said. At the back of the store was a rack of specialty wines. He selected two dusty bottles of Nuits-St-Georges that were almost half my age.

It was our job to arrive early, bearing alcohol. Fenwick never wore costumes. Other years Judith and I had disguised ourselves as Romeo and Juliet, the prime minister and his favourite secretary, other duets that appealed to us at the time.

"You look splendid," Fenwick boomed as we walked in the door. The General was dressed in full regalia, including an admiral's hat adorned by multicoloured feathers. The rest of the uniform, the General later informed us, was that worn by Admiral Lambert, when he was presented to the King in 1943, after the battle of Hong Kong. I later looked up this particular battle—not difficult, after all, since we bought all the books, and discovered that it was judged to be a disastrous defeat.

Since then the moths had been at work. The General, when he drew himself to his full height, looked a ghost in the making; behind the brilliant colours of the uniform emerged patches of skin and underclothing.

The General looked at me closely. "You're back," he said.

"Yes, sir."

He nodded. "Glad to see you've come out of the rain."

"Thank you, sir."

"How's your wife? Are you being good to her?" I was still working on that one when he clapped me on the shoulder and turned to Fenwick. Fenwick had opened a bottle of the Nuits-St-Georges and was pouring the wine into tumblers.

"A toast," Fenwick proposed.

"Great books and great friends," the General responded, and we raised our glasses.

The General started up a tape of *Sergeant Pepper's Lonely Hearts Club Band*. While he and Fenwick drank, I walked about the store. I found myself in front of six identical copies of the second volume of Winston Churchill's history of the Second World War: *Their Finest Hour*. Were Winston Churchill alive and in Toronto he would probably stalk used-book stores, making sure such injustices did not endure. Like Meribel T. Simmons. This afternoon she had distressed me by actually insisting on buying one of her own books, saying that "a friend" had requested it for her birthday. I had given her a discount, then felt sad as I watched her walking down the street carrying her own poems.

Further down the row I came to a whole section of books about the military history of the Ukraine. A few were in English or German, most were in various Slavic scripts unintelligible to me. But I knew all about these books. Their previous custodian was a butcher whose shop was near Fenwick's bookstore. He had tried to sell them to us after the death of his brother, a historian. Fenwick, who hated to refuse anyone outright, had sent me to the brother's house to evaluate the books. The house was in a suburb of the city where I'd never been and I arrived much later than predicted. Fenwick had not warned me, or perhaps he had not known, that the historian had died less than forty-eight hours before. The butcher, his wife, the brother's wife were all introduced to me. Along with various other relatives they had been drinking heavily; a dozen bottles of fruit liqueurs stood half-consumed on a coffee table, and a soccer game was playing on the television set.

I excused myself for being late. "We've got all day," said the butcher. Then he led me into the study, which contained the books. The former historian was also there, in a glass-covered coffin. The butcher put his drink on the coffin. "Go ahead," he said. I followed suit. The study was not large, but against every wall were massive shelves crammed with books.

I was wearing the tweed jacket I used for these occasions, but it was too heavy and I was sweating. The butcher was also sweating. The dead historian was dressed in a light blue suit. I took out my black notebook, opened it, then realized I should wipe my wet palms against my pants or I would stain the pages. At the same time the butcher raised his handkerchief to wipe his own brow. We caught each other's eye in the midst of trying to dry ourselves off.

"Hot," I said.

"That man was a devil."

The dead man's eyes were closed. Like many historians who had fled the Communist invasions, he had been outspoken in his condemnation of the Soviet threat. His black hair was attractively streaked with grey. He looked the image of his pictures in the newspaper, a few years before, when he had written a series of columns on the Soviet plan to invade Western Europe.

The butcher shrugged his shoulders and left. The bereaved wife came in and explained the collection to me, while I took notes.

When she finished, the historian's wife closed her eyes and threw back her head, as if offering her throat. I felt she was inviting me, the army of commerce, to pillage her city. When I didn't respond she opened her eyes, looked at me impatiently, left the room. I came out among the mourners and made my awkward excuses. The warm welcome that had greeted me was now replaced by a congealed silence. Even though I knew they were watching from the window I took off my jacket as soon as I got outside. My shirt was sticking to my back and chest. The mourners were lined up at the window, like so many potted plants determined to stay rooted in place until I disappeared.

Music again filled the store. There were guests in every aisle, some dressed in military regalia to honour the General, others in different costumes impossible to decipher, some not costumed at all, but simply passers-by attracted by the noise. There was beer, there was wine, there were people leaping onto the General's desk and making speeches that were drowned out by music and catcalls. The General switched from wine to various forms of distilled alcohol. His skin began to glow. He put on his sword, a huge curved sabre encased in a jewel-encrusted scabbard. An hour before, he'd appeared ready to fall dead at my feet; now he was able to whip his sabre from its scabbard and slice through the air like a Richard the Lion-Hearted mowing down the Saracens.

I began to drink. My jacket came off. The musty air of the store had given way to the smell of sweat, cigarettes, alcohol. I had taken possession of a bottle, a half-litre of cognac that refused to leave my hand. The General was dancing with a princess whose tennis shoes bore an amazing resemblance to those worn by Meribel T. Simmons. I began to feel tired of the voices of strangers. Norman Swardlow was standing beside me. He had painted his face, which was a slight improvement. Swardlow was leaning forward, and his eyes were peering sincerely into the eyeslits of someone wearing a green-and-brown caterpillar suit. "Literary history will prove me right," he said.

"Bullshit," I provided.

Swardlow paused. "Bullshit?" He looked at me. "Stevens, for God's sake, why have you dressed as yourself?"

Someone had turned the music up so loud I wasn't sure if I

had heard Swardlow say these words, or just imagined them. "Your head looks like a speed bag," I said to Swardlow. It *did* look like a speed bag: round, evenly covered with short dark hair, temptingly mounted on his neck.

"Don't hit him," said the caterpillar.

A dancing couple flung themselves down our aisle, knocking us all over. When we got up, the caterpillar had one arm around me, her other hand had found the bottle, miraculously unspilled, and was holding it first to her mouth, then to mine, as we ourselves danced away.

We were in a corner. The caterpillar was Martha Fenwick. She had pushed back her cloth paws and her hands were holding mine.

"Mister Mystery," Martha said. "What have you been doing?"

"Stupid things."

"How stupid?"

"You wouldn't believe."

She put the bottle on the shelf and began kneading my hands, the way she used to when I was so wound up about Henry I couldn't do anything but sit in her studio and tremble. Then she would take my hands and rub them until my fingers forgot what they were or where they belonged.

"Dr. Paul and Mr. Dungo."

The music was loud, but the General could be heard roaring, "*Carthago delenda est.*" Martha pushed back her mask, her hair tumbled out. In this light, this non-light, she looked like the Martha I had never met, the Martha who must have existed long before she became Martha Fenwick. I slid one of my hands under the fall of her hair to touch the back of her neck, the way I used to. She twisted her head, her lips touched my wrist. I was feeling so sad. I wanted it to be years ago. I wanted to be with her in her studio. I wanted to be with her again, years ago, my hand on the back of her neck and her lips on my wrist and me not thinking of her as Martha Fenwick, the way I used to, Martha Fenwick someone else's wife on vacation with me; I wanted to be with her again, years ago, this woman's lips on my wrist and the ghostly light of the Chinese funeral home clock making our skin shine like raw silk. I wanted to accept what she had offered me.

"I was wrong" was all I could say. Martha was leaning against me. I felt as though my youth had turned into one of Meribel's unwanted poems.

I finished the bottle, edged up the aisle, around a corner. Fenwick was sitting in the General's chair. He saw me and his eyes swivelled towards mine. For the first time I noticed he had long dark eyelashes. Those big doggy eyes. I was drunk. Fenwick rolled his eyes towards me and they didn't look like doggy eyes any more, they looked like big round crocodile eyes. Fenwick was a crocodile: big eyes, long eyelashes. You would only see his teeth once. I slid by him, opened the bathroom door. It was empty. I went inside and closed the door behind me.

Darkness.

I put the lid down on the toilet, sat down. Now I could see light from the street coming through the window. I pushed it open. Cool air, noises of cars from the street. There was a knock at the bathroom door.

"Go away," I said.

The door opened.

"Busy," I said.

"I'll show you a trick," Judith said. She pushed back her cowl, her mask. Then, before I could say anything, she opened the window wider. "Out here."

We climbed through the window. We were in what must have once been a back yard, was now just a pile of rubble. "This way." She led me farther back, to a fire escape. It twisted up into the night, arrived at a barred platform. There was a ladder. "Go ahead," Judith said. I climbed the ladder. When Judith came to the top she pulled the ladder up after her.

We were on a flat gravelled roof in the middle of downtown. Rising around us from every side were voices, the sounds of traffic, the smells of restaurant cooking. Judith drew me back into the shadows. Against a windowless brick wall was a mattress.

"So," Judith said. "Here we are. Tell me everything."

I couldn't remember what everything was.

"I'm sorry," Judith said. "I still love you. Is that so bad?"

I was lying down on the mattress, the buttons digging into my back. Judith was lying beside me. I remembered the way we used to lie, the way I would listen to the counterpoint of our breathing.

A few stars glowed faintly. Our legs had gotten mixed up. I breathed slowly, let the new air slip down to the bottom of my lungs.

White fireworks exploded across my eyelids. Then Judith's fingernails traced little rivers down my cheeks, under my chin, canals across my chest and belly. "What are you thinking?" she whispered but I couldn't answer. I was sliding into the darkness, some strange prayer of darkness, the rumble of metal wheels on iron tracks, my blood smoking hot inside me nowhere to go—

"Close your eyes and open your mouth," Judith said. The way she used to.

And if I close my eyes now, the way I did that night, I can still feel the cool weight of Judith's body settling into mine. The silky feel of her skin, the strange way she would suddenly be seized with cold at the most unexpected moments and her skin, her lips, her nipples, all grow taut and pebbled, the shy still centres of her eyes finally opening to mine.

I close my eyes, I am there again. Judith's hands pushing open my shirt. Her teeth playing vampire at my throat. Me flooding into her while we cling to each other and horns from a nearby traffic jam celebrate our union.

Afterwards it was down the ladder again, out the door of the rotting wooden fence and onto the street. Arms enlaced, damp with each other, we made the slow pilgrimage across town to the Honeymoon Suite. The details of that night are written so deeply into my nerves that the slightest familiar odour or chance noise can revive them. Why so much this one night? Perhaps my long absence. The music and traffic that masked the sounds of sirens criss-crossing the city. Our mutual surprise and relief that time seemed to have wrinkled the universe, skipped a beat, returned us to that very place we had never before quite been able to inhabit.

All night we played honeymoon in the Honeymoon Suite. By morning it was too late to go back. But yes, I inspected her body for tracks. I sucked the insides of her elbows, traced my tongue along the backs of her knees, checked her eyelids, between her toes, every little hiding place a needle might want to find a home. She was clean, smooth, entirely unremarkable except for a certain look to the small pouches that had formed beneath her eyes, a sniffle she said was allergic but I attributed to a few cocaine relapses.

By sun-up we were starving. We had double omelettes in the hotel coffee shop. "Nicko Ross," I said. Judith was dabbing jam on her toast, drinking coffee, smoking her morning cigarettes. Under the table our legs were twined together and our heads leaned close because during this breakfast we had to keep touching each other, kissing, sliding our hands beneath each other's sleeves to reassure ourselves we were still together again.

Judith's lips moved silently, undecided. Then the air got a bit cold, the way it had felt that morning a week earlier when I'd been lying at the base of the beech tree in Judith's front yard. I remembered the time I had stood with Nicko Ross in midst of traffic, looked in a car and wished Judith and I were in that car, driving away. That's what we should have done. We should have driven away while we still had time and destinations we could believe in. Instead we'd ended up in the hotel kitchen, Vivian's eyes giving me the brush job.

Then Judith told me what I already knew about Nicko, that he had been playing with her and Vivian while he was supposedly "undercover". Under Vivian's covers until he got her arrested, "for her own good".

While she was telling me all this Judith looked away from me, off at an angle, the way she angled away when we first knew each other, before we were surrounded by immortality. Though our feet and legs were still entwined, unable to let go after being separated for so long. I didn't have to ask myself which end of my body was giving the orders. I put out my hand and turned Judith's face towards mine. It might have seemed like a gesture of pity or compassion—maybe Judith took it that way. I never asked. Her lower lip had a little quiver it didn't used to, and there was something in her eyes I couldn't read. "I don't want to be without you," I said. Unconditional surrender.

THIRTEEN

LAST NIGHT I went to Le Troubador with some clients and our favourite poet, Meribel T. Simmons. It is a long time since I have been there and I must admit I chose it for reasons purely nostalgic—it seems I spend more and more time these days seeking out the old places, trying to understand all those events for which there is no explanation.

We found the restaurant much as it used to be. The plaster angels still keep watch over the chequered tablecloths, but the actual cloth is thicker than I remember, and the napkins are also of cloth instead of paper. Another addition is a separate wine list, one of those fancy menus with a leather cover that promises so much until you open it.

The clients are a couple who have only recently started coming to the store. When they first walked into the bookstore their fingers were laced together and so my first thought was that they must be married to other people. I was wrong, it was a case not of adultery but bigamy: they are married both to each other and to their geographically separated careers.

His name is Peter Ferris; he teaches English at UCLA and one of his specialties is Canadian literature. That first afternoon he bought several hundred dollars' worth of first editions: Fenwick's old favourite, F. P. Grove. I told him the story of Grove's ex-mistress running around the streets of Greenwich Village and Ferris turned to me and replied, in a very Boston accent: "I always think it's such a shame that Canadians regard their own authors as extensions of America."

His spouse, Alice Langkrup from the University of Alberta, turned out to be an expert in this subject. Yesterday she even brought me a literary review featuring her article on "Frederick Philip Grove's Vision of the Woman as Prostitute".

At this moment, in came Meribel, her plastic shopping bags bulging. After depositing them on the floor and squeezing some blood back into her fingers, she took up her usual post at the poetry shelf. She has a new book, her collected poems, and the review copies have already started to drift into the store.

Alice Langkrup, one of those dark heavy English Department types who wear numerous layers of clothes along with a couple of tons of silver bangles, turned to stare at our Meribel. Then she exclaimed: "Peter—that's *her!*"

"*No.*" But he twisted to get a look. Then they both started walking towards her on tiptoe, as though she were a butterfly that might be scared off.

Meribel, her mouth open in terror, retreated.

"*Meribel T. Simmons!*" they exclaimed in chorus. "We thought you were *dead.*"

Meribel looked down at her feet, her hands, the copy of her own book she was holding. "No," she said weakly, as though willing to be convinced otherwise. "I'm not dead. I'm—"

"Then we must—you must—"

Which is how I came to invite them to dinner at the Golden Hole, just as though Meribel were quite regularly taken there to meet her admirers, and how it was arranged that Meribel would make her first reading tour so that she could be introduced to her western public.

The morning after the General's party, Judith and I had our reconciliation breakfast, then went back upstairs and fell asleep. An hour later the alarm woke me up. I stood in the shower for a few minutes, then started on my way to the store. In the years I have worked at Fenwick's, I have never been late or missed a day without advance warning.

I was reading the newspaper and standing at the door when Fenwick unlocked it. Arriving at work on time often meant standing outside until Fenwick arrived, which could be five or ten minutes, even half an hour. Fenwick unlocked the front from the inside, having let himself in the back, and he was so certain of my punctuality that a cup of coffee was usually waiting at my counter. In winter, when the store was just heating up in the morning, the steam from the coffee could be seen rising in a big cloud, and I would have the cozy feeling that I was getting onto a tugboat with Fenwick, one on which we would ride the choppy seas of uncertain commerce, doing our best to tow the remnants of the world's literature into a safe harbour.

In the days since my reappearance at the store he had hardly spoken to me—he was cataloguing some pre-war magazines and I had the impression he was coming to work hours before the store opened. But this time, as I came in, he stood over at one side of the store, leaning on the stool the way he liked to, a position in which he looked like a large rock tilted at an impossible angle.

"You're well?" he asked. As though we were talking on the telephone and I weren't right in front of him, obviously unafflicted.

"I'm well."

"Martha was worried about you the other night."

"I'm fine, really. Maybe a bit hung over from the party."

"Henry was by here the other day."

Fenwick said this softly. He was leaning forward, his lips

pursed, his eyebrows knit together—the way he looked at certain customers who never paid their bills.

"He asked me for money," Fenwick said. "I refused. But if you want, I could loan it to you."

He was looking right at me. We had never discussed money. When I started working I didn't know how much I would make until the first time Fenwick paid me. It was in cash, in a small brown envelope. Every few months he would give me a raise. Even now, for example, I had no idea how much would be in the first envelope after my return. "How much did he want?" I finally managed.

Fenwick started to move his mouth, then took a pad and wrote down a number. He tore off the sheet and handed it to me.

The sight of the number—eighty thousand dollars—an amount of money totally beyond me, made Henry's situation seem more hopeless than ever.

"I'm prepared to loan it to you," Fenwick said.

"I could never pay it back."

"There's no hurry—"

"Please. I can't accept."

Fenwick slowly straightened himself. He was obviously relieved. Yet I was already wanting to change my mind. But Fenwick's face had gone so clear, so normal, I didn't have the courage to say I wanted to think more about his offer. In fact, far from feeling courageous, I felt as though I was going to collapse. I had spent years trying to escape Henry, trying to make my own life, and now here I was, dragged back down, trapped.

After work, I went down to Diamond Billiards. For a moment I stood outside, looking up at the apartment I used to share with Henry and Jeanine. In those days, when we were short on money, Jeanine could make more by shoplifting than I could hustling pool. Now the burden was on me. The whole afternoon

I'd imagined myself at Henry's funeral. Then driving out to Jeanine's parents on weekends, visiting Jeanine and the boys. It would always be October, like now. Late October. The wind would be cold, the ground would be frozen, we would feel like shit. "I feel like shit, Dungo," Jeanine would say to me. We'd cry over Henry and my throat would feel the way it feels right now.

When you start imagining that your own brother is dead, it's time to reposition yourself. Which is what I always liked about playing pool. The balls on the table. You walk around it, taking your time. Nothing exists but those balls and they aren't moving. They're lying on green felt, glistening with light. Beneath them, rock-solid slate. They are still, you are moving. They are a puzzle with a million solutions. When you are finished playing everything else has receded into the distance. Another problem to be laid out, scrutinized from every angle, poked judiciously with a long stick until bit by bit it disappears and nothing is left but the smooth green felt.

As I walked through the door Sam's arms stretched out in their phantom embrace, then slowly fell. He reached under the counter and pulled out a package of cigarettes. I took one from the pack and then, without talking, put it into my mouth and waited, the way Sam's cronies always did. "Closest you're going to get," Sam said, holding out a lighter featuring a naked lady spurting flame from a scarlet nipple. "See, I still got attractions. What were you doing staying away so long?"

The only tables in use were those farthest away. In one corner was a group of six teenagers. Jeans, T-shirts, four-letter words. The play was casual—most of the action was in the smoking of cigarettes and drinking pop. The other table was more the kind of clientele I'd been used to when I first came here: white, early middle age, playing for money but not much. There were three of them. One was better than the others. You could see by the way he balanced before a shot, the perfect stillness in his arm and shoulder followed by a smooth, unhurried stroke. When he was on his feet some of the Chinese kids would stop to watch him. He was running five or six balls every time. When he got down to the colours he just shrugged apologetically, then cleaned the table. The other two reached into their pockets.

"Think you could take him?"

"No," I said.

"You're right. The guy's a shark. Just comes around here to make some small change. Evenings, week nights, he plays downtown. Pretends he's a regular. Weekends he plays tournaments. I saw him once out at The Golden Mile. Thought he was going to shit his pants when he recognized me."

"He's good."

"You bet he's good. Some mornings he comes to practise. That's how dead this place is. You can come here and practise and no one's going to see you. After that time I caught him at The Golden Mile he came by the next day, carrying a little leather cue case under his arm. He has another one he uses here at night." Sam waved at the rack where the serious players kept their own cues locked into place.

"So he's standing there, his cue case under his arm, like I'm supposed to sniff it and die. I put the balls on the counter. He takes them back to the corner, the same table he's at now. Sets them up and starts shooting. A few minutes later a broad walks in, never been here before, goes straight to his table. After a while I drift down. He's putting on a little show for her. After about an hour she leaves. Then he packs up the balls, the way he always does, brings them up to the counter. 'So?' he says.

"'So?' I say.

"Then he gives me this little grin. Here's this guy, must be one of the best snooker players in the city, and he's blushing like a twelve-year-old because his biggest thrill in life is taking small change off fish. I find out later that when he plays in tournaments he loses it. Like some guy who looks like a movie star but when he gets the broad home his dick goes dead."

Sam shook his head and gave that little laugh he always had, the laugh that said everyone but him was crazy and maybe he was too. "Nowadays they're all dealers anyway."

"Them?" I asked, nodding towards the table of teenagers.

"All of them. You know how I knew people had started dealing here? When they started going to the bathroom together. You think that's supposed to seem normal? Two guys going to the bathroom together? Coming out, rubbing their noses like they just got some sort of allergic attack. Or patting their pockets or duckwalking or God knows what."

We were leaning against the counter, Sam and I. Leaning against a counter, watching people come and go, you get a particular view. As my father used to say about certain men: "He's just a shopkeeper." The way Sam had become with his pool hall. The way I had become at Fenwick's. Watching people in the store with their petty little battles of heart, pride, wallet. Knowing certain ones must have glued their wallets into their pants to make sure they could never buy anything. Watching others trying to outguess you, get away with something. Their hands, their coats, their bags. The way some just walked up to something they wanted to steal and took it, whereas others circled around their prey, like a hawk circling a meadow. Not knowing I was watching in the same way I would watch a hawk, fascinated, knowing what was going to happen, but more eager to see the details close up than to stop them from stealing a book I had bought for a few cents. Sometimes I was so intent on the thieves I would hardly notice the others, the ones like Judith, who picked up a book and held it so gently, so full of the promises that book had made to them they hardly dared open it in public.

Shopkeepers, Sam and I. In this city everyone is either a shopkeeper, a dealer or a fish.

Both tables finished at the same time. I made way for the trays of balls. Sam punched in their cards, told them their totals. As they left I noticed the hustler eyeing me furtively, a future mark he might eventually need.

While Sam was putting the money in the cash I took one of the trays of balls, started walking towards the back. I racked up the reds, placed the colours, took a couple of cues and rolled them on the adjacent table. That was one of the first things Henry had taught me. How to choose a straight cue by rolling it on the table. If it rolled smooth, it was straight. If it bobbled, it was curved. Of course the best thing is to have your own cue, the kind that comes apart. The shorter pieces aren't as likely to warp; you keep the tip fresh and perfectly trimmed.

I found the kind of cue I liked, nineteen ounces, which is a little bit heavy, but with a narrow tip. The narrow tip lets you give the ball spin, if you can control it. And I like the extra weight. It keeps you from trying to muscle the cue, slows you down, makes you follow behind.

So there I was, thinking thoughts I couldn't remember from one moment to the next, leaning low enough into each stroke that I could feel the varnished wood sliding along the underside of my chin, listening for the click of the balls, the tiny whispers of spin against the felt, the soft solid thunk of ceramic bouncing off the hard rubber rails. The first balls made a hollow sound as they fell into the empty leather pockets. It was late October. The radiators were clunking. A dry powdery smell rose from the felt, mixed with cigarette smoke, unemptied ashtrays, half-finished cups of coffee and bottles of Coke.

"He's scum," Sam said.

"Who?"

"Henry."

I pretended I hadn't heard. There was a ball I wanted to make. A red bank that would leave me an easy black, a red to follow, then a pink in the side. I breathed out slowly, looked at the way you could see the pool-hall ceiling reflected on the ball. The red went in, the white spun just as I'd planned, two inches behind the black.

I walked around the table, avoiding Sam.

"I mean that you've got no idea what's going on. None. *Nullissimo.*"

"I'm just getting back into practice."

"I'll say," Sam said.

"Okay. Speak."

"He's small-time. He's a shit. What more can I say?"

"What brings this on?"

"He was around this afternoon with his sob story."

"And?"

"You know how it is, Dungo. Some days the bullshit thermometer gets blown right off the wall."

Then Sam turned around and walked away. I bent over the table, butchered what was left of the game, stumbled through another. I put the balls and the chalk back on the tray, then took it to the counter. Other customers had come in, Sam was showing off his new cigarette lighter. But after I'd paid he followed me to the door, out onto the street. "I never liked him, but I admired his guts. You know what I mean?"

It was nine o'clock now—the sidewalks were filling up. Across from us a streetcar had stopped. The passengers' faces were illuminated against the windows, and I found myself staring at them, as though I expected to find myself, hunched over a newspaper, riding home.

Sam's hand came down on my shoulder. He turned me around to face him. In the bright red glow of his sign his face looked other-worldly, fishy. His nose had grown longer, thinner; it was pushing into the night, and the skin drawn across its bridge, his cheeks, his jaw, all flowed down into his neck as though he were swimming in the light. His grip tightened, his fingers dug into my bones. "You can count on me." Then he turned me sideways, took a couple of steps with me in the direction I always went, let go.

I see myself continuing up the street. It is dark and a cold wind blows paper cups and newspapers along the sidewalks. I am still wearing Henry's old coat. I am remembering the night he brought it home: purple and gold, shining satin, his first school letter sewn over his heart. He displayed it proudly, then the telephone rang and he put down his jacket down while he ran to answer. I tried it on. Henry was still bigger than I was then. The waist of the jacket came halfway down my thighs, the sleeves pooled at my wrists. I pulled up the sleeves to look at the cuffs. They were knitted wool cuffs, like the cuffs of a little boy's jacket, smooth and warm.

Those cuffs no longer cling warmly to the skin; they are stiff with grease, frayed. I still have that jacket. The lining is torn, the sweatmarks on the collar are permanently ingrained, there is a hitch in the zipper that makes it stick near the neck.

At the first corner I stopped for the traffic light. There was a bank there. As always, a couple of winos had installed themselves for the night in the shelter of its doorway. One of them had a newspaper and was reading it by the yellow glow of the cash dispenser.

Across the street was the apartment I used to share with Henry and Jeanine. Henry must have gone to the pool hall hundreds, even thousands of times. And now Sam was calling him a bum. Even though Henry had been a regular. Drunk his shitty coffee. Listened to Sam and his friends talking about their "broads".

Easy for Sam to say Henry was a bum. Sam had given up smiling, except when he wanted to. Instead he had cigarette lighters with tits. And if people didn't like it, they could find somewhere else to sell their dope. "You see that guy over there?" Sam asked me once. Another time, years ago, when after a bad afternoon with Martha I'd drifted back to the pool hall for some old-fashioned bad coffee and to listen to Sam's friends boast about their secretaries' bums. "He's got an attitude problem. You know what I mean?"

Sam had been pointing to someone who looked not unlike Henry. A short pale-skinned angry-looking man who was arguing about nothing with two other men who didn't seem to care. And I had known right away that Sam had been talking to me about Henry.

Certain things. At first you don't want to think about them because they are too painful. After my father died, for example. I wouldn't have said I was so attached to him. Until she left, it was my mother who ran the family. My father was way out in orbit, hardly there, a shopkeeper who worked twelve hours a day six days a week, a short stubby man who looked down at his feet in the mornings, drank a few whiskies every night so he would get enough sleep to last until the next day. Well. You don't in a sentence or a paragraph tell who your father was. And anyway, as Henry said, "He died great", meaning with a beautiful woman leaning over him, pressing her mouth to his.

The point is, talking about what you do or don't think about, while my father was still alive I didn't think about him. But afterwards, I couldn't hear a siren without picturing the way, after thirty years of standing behind a counter, he'd just collapsed.

The truth is that Sam and Henry and Fenwick were probably more father to me than my own father was. But now Henry was in trouble, and Sam and Fenwick seemed strangely immune to it. Seemed ready, almost eager, to watch him go down.

There is an Italian café with loud music where Judith and I sometimes used to spend the evening. It has a few pool tables in the back. Judith liked to be there; she would listen to rock and roll or that crazy Italian movie music they used to play, drink espresso coffee she doctored with bourbon from her purse and perch on a stool while I did silly tricks for her. Not that I was so good, but the tables were old; every time you touched the ball it would find a valley and start homing in for the pocket.

I went into the front, stood at the marble bar. Someone new was at the espresso machine. "Hey," he said, looking at me as though I had just arrived from Mars.

When I had finished my coffee I went back to the pool room. At a table in the middle, showily lining up his shot with much chalking of the cue, pacing about to examine his position, peering here and there to calculate exactly where everything might be left as a result of the magnificent blow he was about to strike, was none other than my brother, Henry. He did not look like a man desperate for money. His blond hair slicked back, his cheeks bright with the glow of good wine and brandy, Henry was wearing a sparkling white shirt, one of those painted silk ties you see in uptown boutiques where professors' wives shop for their husbands, fashionable wool pants. You would have thought he was not the desperate owner of a bankrupt garage but one of those well-off lawyers who sometimes get bored with their imported rugs and their houses with alarm systems and come to this part of the city to sniff the exotic odours of poverty and immigrants from far-off countries.

Beside Henry, his own shirtsleeves rolled up, the cue like a toothpick in his massive paw, none other than Mr. Clean, Nicko Ross. I stepped behind a pillar, backed slowly into the darkness of the bar. Then went round the outside so I could watch them through a window. Also watching were two women, leaning against the wall, in sleeveless dresses, laughing at whatever Nicko was saying. One was Nicko's friend from the gym, the other I didn't recognize. Henry made a couple of balls, then missed an easy combination. Nicko bent to the task. When the game was over, it was Henry reaching into his pocket. Good old Henry, still the hustler, losing early so he could raise the stakes and win later on. Although he couldn't resist winking at the ladies. And no doubt, somewhere inside, Henry still believed that he was going to get the best of Nicko. But, having played with Nicko, I knew Henry didn't have a chance. Henry was like Napoleon in Russia; the deeper he went, the more committed he was; the higher the snow and the dead piled around him, the more convinced he was that at the very last moment he would turn everything around and emerge victorious.

I walked a couple of blocks, called Jeanine from a phone-booth. When she answered her voice sounded young and fresh. You would have thought she was a teenager waiting to be asked on her first date. "Is everything all right?"

"Everything's fine. Is Henry around?"

"He's out with Nicko Ross. He said I should tell you that he had a plan, a number four, that you'd know what he meant."

"Great."

There was a silence and I began to feel guilty. Maybe I was wrong to doubt Henry. Maybe Henry did have a plan, after all. "I'm sorry," I finally said.

"Don't be sorry."

I was in one of those old-fashioned telephone booths, a glass-walled cupboard. Some enthusiast had ripped the door off. The walls were covered with graffiti. A streetcar rattled by and I couldn't hear if Jeanine was still talking.

"I better go," I said.

"You want Henry to call you when he comes in?"

"I'll talk to him tomorrow. See you soon."

I walked back towards the café. Through the side window I could see Henry and Nicko were still playing. I paced about, undecided, then returned to the telephone booth and called Jeanine again. Again her voice sounded hopeful and fresh. "I'll come over to wait for Henry there."

"He said he might be late."

"I'll sleep on the couch or something."

That's where I was, on the couch with my old sleeping bag for a blanket, when Henry came bouncing up the steps. By the time he got in the door I was sitting up. It was seven in the morning, the room was filled with a grey light, but Henry came skipping towards me as though it were high noon in the meadow of childhood. "Hey, Dungo, did Jeanine tell you? It's number four. I mean, little brother, that I'm out. Home free. Safe. Everything is cool."

He grabbed my shoulders. He smelled of whisky, tobacco, a thick streak of cheap perfume. He was rubbing his hands together. "I can't believe I pulled it off."

Henry started towards the kitchen and I followed him.

"So it's finished."

"Absolutely."

"No more money? Back to the life of the solid citizen, employer, husband and father of two sons?"

"Exact, little brother. Back to life. Shit, Dungo, I haven't felt this good since the day I left school."

The kettle was boiling. I splashed water on my face to cut away the fog.

"One more payment, Dungo. That's all I need and I'm out. We're definitely in the number-four situation. Just like you said."

"One more payment?"

Henry had the Scotch down from the cupboard above the stove, was spinning the cap off with his thumb. "A monster payment, little brother. He's not letting me go free."

"And where are you going to get the money?"

"It's waiting for us. It's been there all the time."

Henry was looking at me in a certain way, his head cocked

and grinning. He had the bottle of Scotch in one hand, a glass in the other. Then he poured and handed the glass to me. "You're going to need this."

He told me his plan. "What do you think?"

"I don't know," I said. What did I think of Henry's plan? It was like all his other plans.

Later that morning I called Nicko Ross at the station. "This is Paul Stevens," I said.

"Paul Stevens. I know you from somewhere?" Then a laugh. "How you keeping, Paul? I heard you were back in town. So, what's up? You got a crime to report?"

We arranged to meet that evening at the weight room of the gym. When I came in Nicko was examining his muscles in the mirror. "Good to see you," he said. Not before he shook my hand. Nothing sadistic, just a little squeeze. "I thought you'd be gone for good. Figured you couldn't take the city any more."

In the old days he would have leaned in to hear my answer. Now he just turned and started on one of the machines.

"So I guess you got to know Henry," I said.

"That's right. But if you want to talk about Henry, you have to wait until I finish here. Why don't you try running a few laps? A guy who looks just like you was running the other night."

Then he made me wait while he went around the machines and did his routine.

When he was finished he nodded for me to follow him down to the changing room. "In here," he said, leading me to the shower. After he'd soaped his muscles for a while he went into the sauna. When he'd finally thrown enough water on the rocks that my lungs were burning and everyone else was driven out, Nicko turned to me. "Okay," he said. "You want to talk, talk."

"My brother—" I started.

"That jerk," Nicko said. "I should have pounded him out

months ago." He had one towel around his waist, another around his shoulders. Now he took it off, dipped it in the water and squeezed the water over his head. "You know, Paul, I used to think you were the one with problems. I would talk to Henry about you, try to get him to take his big-brother responsibilities. You know what I mean? But I had it wrong, Paul. You weren't the fuck-up you were pretending to be. The problem was Henry. We all like Henry, you know that? Everyone likes Henry. But then he started taking advantage. He got into trouble. I loaned him some money. Now he owes me."

"How much?"

Nicko shook his head. "Not so much. A lot. Depends on how you see it."

"And if—"

"Look, Henry's brother. Unless you got a microphone up your ass, this conversation is between you and me. You know what I mean? I'll tell you two things. One is that I'm going to let you walk out of here. Nothing to worry about. The second is I have a certain belief which is that every person should mind their own business. So my advice to you is to stand up and leave the premises. I don't like you spying on me. I don't want to see your face again."

I'll admit, there was part of me that wanted to laugh. *I don't want to see your face again.* Where had the old Nicko Ross gone? The carefree version with arms full of groceries promising his Saturday-night special? But then Nicko was standing up, standing close to me, standing as though ready to make his wish come true by simply obliterating what he didn't want to see.

I pulled the towel more tightly around my waist. "Okay," I said. "But I didn't come here to spy. I came for Henry. We want to pay."

"We?"

"I'm helping him on this."

"You can't pay what your brother owes."

"How much would it take to clear him?"

With one step Nicko Ross closed the space between us, put his arm across my chest and pressed me so hard against the cedar panelling I could feel my vertebrae trying to make holes in the wood. "I told you once, Henry's brother, mind your own business. Henry knows all the numbers." He pushed harder. I had to fight for breath.

"You got me," I said.

"I've got you by the balls."

"You know what Henry always told me to do when someone has me by the balls?"

"No," Nicko said. "Tell me, little brother, what did Henry tell you to do when someone has you by the balls."

"Piss on him."

The sauna door opened. Nicko released me and I went out. Nicko followed me to the changing room, talking in a voice I could hardly hear. "You really want to help your brother? You tell him people got to perform." He put his big hand on my shoulder and turned me around to face him. Mr. Clean was clean. The sauna had scoured his skin, his eyes shone, his hair glowed. "We should go shoot pool sometime, the way we used to. I liked that, buddy." With that final *buddy* he gave my shoulder an extra squeeze, just enough to leave fingerprints for a week, then turned and walked towards the "Executive Club" door.

Judith was waiting for me in the Honeymoon Suite. She had brought over a bottle of wine, a pile of books and magazines. "Like the old days," she'd said, meaning those weekends when we'd shut ourselves up and I'd drink and read and watch over her while she lay on the floor and planed through the cosmos until suddenly she would leap to her feet, shower, demand that I take her to the movies.

But without drugs she had taken on substance, desire. When I told her about my reunion with Nicko Ross she came across to where I was standing, pulled my shirt-tails from my waist and began massaging my back. Soon I was lying face down on the bed. Judith was pouring wine on me, then licking it off. "You're so thin now," she whispered. "But it's good to be thin. The thinner you are, the more dips you have, the more wine your body holds, the more you get licked."

FOURTEEN

I DON'T LIKE the fate of others to be pushed into my hands. To volunteer—yes, that can be rewarding. During my time in Kingston, for example, after my own brief fling with the muse, I decided to do something for Meribel T. Simmons. Using the name Ellen White, and labelling myself a "feminist graduate student", I first wrote glowing reviews of Meribel's latest book, then actually tried a couple of learned articles on her work, using as models articles I dug up in an Australian literary magazine. When Meribel's professorial admirers later cited these articles in their own appreciations, I felt as though for once in my life I had actually made a tiny contribution to someone else's welfare. But the burden of doing for someone else what I wish he would have done for himself—

I began by telephoning my mother. Though I hadn't spoken to her for over two years she seemed unsurprised to hear from me.

She still lived in Pikeville, north of the city. When I asked if I could come to see her the next day, she gave me directions to her house as though I were a stranger about to deliver a television set.

My job, according to Henry, was to extract from her that sum of money which would save him from people who put things under his hood, from Nicko Ross, from the consequences of whatever sins he had committed. Mostly, of course, the sin of being born Henry. The money, Henry had explained, would come from the insurance fund our father had left to our mother. My father's idea had been to leave his full insurance to her on the understanding she would use what she needed to support herself and save the rest to pass on to us. So Henry said. Of course he'd made his will before my mother left. Why didn't he change it? Perhaps he simply forgot. More likely he left it as a kind of hostage for her return. He was always saying things like "when your mother comes back", even after she had moved in with Captain Bill and he was sending us there for the summers.

I arrived at my mother's house early in the afternoon. She lived on a sidestreet made up of small brick bungalows like her own. On one side of the double driveway was parked a motor launch on a trailer. In the centre of their lawn—as in the centre of every other lawn on her street—was a maple tree. The leaves had all fallen; the trees looked bare and defenceless.

My mother must have been waiting for me. I saw the living-room curtains move as I parked, then the door opened as I got out of the car. The woman stepping out to meet me was plumpish, white haired, smiling. She looked like an advertisement for the benefits of retiring young.

I had done most of my growing after she left home, even after we stopped coming up for the summers, so I was always surprised to find myself looking down at her. We stood in front of each other. Since we had both turned into our current versions of ourselves, we had seen each other so seldom we didn't seem to have any habits. I wondered if I should shake her hand, the way I sometimes did with certain regular customers. She made no move to kiss me. I could imagine her standing this way, puzzled, over my crib as I cried. "You must be cold," I finally said.

"You get used to it." Then she smiled at me and I saw that

since my last visit she'd had her teeth redone. They'd been large, not quite uniform, milky. Now they were smooth and even, smaller than they had been, and when she smiled the tip of her tongue showed. Suddenly there was this small pink triangle where her teeth used to be.

"Nice boat."

"We won the lottery. Didn't Henry tell you?"

"You're rich?"

"Not rich, Paul. It was just the Kiwanis bridge-club lottery. Now we spend all our money on gas."

Inside we sat across from each other at the kitchen table. Tea things and a plate of ginger snaps, my old favourite, had already been set out. Seeing the ginger snaps I reached for them automatically, the way I always had as a child, and this time when my mother smiled I could no longer imagine how I was going to tell her about Henry, his quick fixes, the muscular and sweaty Nicko Ross.

My mother poured us both tea, added milk.

"I suppose Henry told you Bill's been in and out of the hospital this last year."

Of course he hadn't.

"What's wrong?"

"Something to do with his back or his sciatic nerve. It means he can't move his leg properly. Crazy thing—every time he tries driving the taxi across the lake he falls over. And he can't carry anything."

My mother looked down at her tea. She was a woman who was starting to get old. Her husband was in the hospital. Wouldn't be able to work again.

"Do you have enough money?"

"We're okay. Bill says we can always sell the boat." Then she cocked her head and gave a more familiar smile, the one Henry had learned from her. "He's tough. He'll be okay."

This woman who had been my mother. She had changed her teeth, her hair, her husband—but then she reached for a ginger snap and there was something about the way her arm moved, so slow and deliberate, the way it used to move when she was unhappily married to my father and baked to console herself.

As we drank our first cups of tea, then our second, I kept waiting for a chance to broach the subject of the inheritance. If she brought up money again, for example, I could ask if Bill had insurance. Or I could inquire again after her financial situation.

Near the end of the second cup of tea there was a long silence. I excused myself to use the washroom. Bill had panelled it in dark wood, like a ship's bathroom. I looked at myself in the mirror. This was the mirror where I had first tried to shave. For lack of anything else I'd ended up trimming my sideburns up into my temples. At the top of both cheekbones I'd cut myself, and had been so afraid of the bleeding I used bandages. Now I imagined going back in to face my mother, little bandages on my face to show something was wrong.

We started talking about Henry. My mother asked how business was. I said that Henry was having a hard time. My mother nodded. This was my chance. I felt as though Henry was in one corner of the room—"Go for it Dungo, you've been jabbing away for three rounds. Give her the Sunday punch." And in the front row, Jeanine, face turned trustingly upwards, waiting for me to deliver.

I leaned forward. But even while the background music was heating to a frenzy, I could feel my mother's attention slipping. I couldn't seem to find the exact formula that would lead me to the key phrase: "insurance policy".

"There is something you could do," I finally started. My voice broke and stopped. As when I was a little boy about to say something to her, I'd gotten so excited that I'd forgotten to breathe.

"I promised to go to the hospital this afternoon," my mother broke in.

"I'll drive you."

We went out to the car. I backed slowly down the driveway, past the lottery prize, letting the silence settle in so I could return to Henry.

"Crazy thing," my mother said, "but what I miss most is the bridge club. Bill and I used to play duplicate every Tuesday and Friday—now he can't go and I can't bear to go without him."

She motioned me to turn right. Suddenly we were there, in the parking lot. I turned to her. "Sometimes I really wonder if Henry is going to make it. The other day he told me he desperately needs an angel to invest in his business."

My mother appeared not to hear this. She opened her door, got out of the car. I came around to stand beside her. The centre of the hospital was made out of bricks, but there were two new wings in concrete blocks. My mother pointed to the closest one.

"He's in there. You won't want to go in. They've got him on some kind of sedative to relax the muscles in his back and Bill doesn't like people to see him when he's in his pyjamas." She smiled, showing the tip of her tongue. "Really, he's like a little kid."

She closed her eyes and offered her face to be kissed. I was still waiting for her to respond to what I'd said. Her lips tasted the way they used to, sugary with tea and cookies. Then she started off down the sidewalk. When she got to the hospital door she turned and waved, as though she knew I would be standing and watching, as though she had waited decades for this particular opportunity and didn't intend to miss it.

"Wait," I called. My mother hesitated. I went running across the parking lot, stopped breathless in front of her. She was holding the door open and looking at me inquiringly as though I was a stranger about to ask directions in a foreign tongue.

"How were you going to get home from the hospital?"

"I—"

"Let me drive you."

My mother's eyelids lowered. "That would be nice, Paul."

My mother started walking down the hall. I followed. We passed a gift shop, then came to a bank of elevators. My mother looked at her watch. "Two hours?"

The elevator doors opened. They closed. I was left with the reflection of myself in the shining metal. Blurred but still standing, ready to retreat to my corner with the knowledge that I had at least survived to fight another round.

There was still light in the sky but the sun was at a sharper angle here than in the city, and the wind from the lake was cold enough that I had to put my hands in my pockets. Some of the cars had turned their headlights on. I suddenly shivered and went in the first door, a tavern Henry and I sometimes went to that second summer.

Dim lights. Smoky fug. I moved through to the back, a leather booth far from the speakers. On stage, a small light was rotating, sending fluorescent green and red flashes through the gloom. A waitress leaned over me, said she'd try when I asked her for a coffee. I leaned into the leather. The music changed to country but the lights kept flashing. I closed my eyes. Country music, flashing lights, and then I was thinking of that summer night I'd been standing in the woods, spitting blood and watching headlights flashing by us, blinking as the cars travelled past the trees. Until finally Jeanine ran out to stop one.

"You okay?"

"Thanks," I said. The waitress was standing over me with coffee, a wooden bowl of peanuts. There was something familiar about the way her cheek curved in the light, the way she held her head as she peered at me. But at certain times you start thinking that everyone seems familiar, everything a repetition of what's gone before.

When I left the tavern, it was already dark. From the drugstore across the street plastic Hallowe'en decorations shone: there were orange pumpkins with flashing red eyes and mouths, skeletons that sent a bloody glow into the darkness, a witch with fluorescent yellow teeth riding on a black broom with long orange bristles.

I bought a newspaper, then went back to the hospital to meet my mother. She was in the lobby talking to a woman who seemed vaguely familiar from our summers in Pikeville. My mother introduced her, then said she'd also come with me, if I didn't mind, since they would be eating at my mother's before returning to the hospital that evening.

I drove them home. "What am I supposed to do?" I kept demanding of an imaginary Henry. "Ask for her insurance policy in front of a stranger?"

I stopped at my mother's house, not even going into the driveway.

"Thanks," my mother said. When her friend was out of the car my mother stuck her head back in: "You sure you won't join us for supper?"

I wished Henry could see this. The way our mother had set up this whole scene. The way she had no desire to speak to me further, to be confronted by my presence, let alone any demand I might make. I wished Henry could see that I had come out for the next round—rested, ready, eager to deliver the Sunday punch. But how can you fight against someone who's decided to go home instead?

"I wanted to talk to you about that angel," I said.

My mother's eyes swung to mine. Her mouth opened and her tongue poked out. Very slowly and clearly she said, "No thanks." Then she smiled.

"I guess I'll be going," I said. But she had already started towards the house.

I drove off slowly. As I turned the corner I shouted, "Give my regards to Bill, the poor old fucker," but of course there was no one to hear me but myself and I couldn't think of a single reason I should have called Bill a poor old fucker save that he was married to my mother.

I was driving south. The traffic was thick and slow. Headlights in my mirrors, in my eyes. I turned on the heat. Fenwick's car was big and powerful. I stepped on the gas, turned the radio up loud, moved into the passing lane.

Just as I came into Toronto I saw a service station with a lit telephone booth in the corner of the lot. I went in and called my mother collect.

"It's Paul," I said.

"I know. What's wrong?"

"Henry. He really does need the money. He needs it for the garage. I thought maybe the insurance policy…"

I paused for a moment, unsure how to continue.

"How much?" my mother asked.

I thought of the sum Fenwick had written down to show me. Unfortunately it was impossible to pass a piece of paper through the telephone and, anyway, it was too much for me to say. "Fifty thousand dollars," I tried.

"Is that right? That's what he needs to save the business?"

"Yes."

"You know, Paul, when you started on that line about Henry's garage, I knew what you were here for. Why else? How many years is it since you've called? Sent a letter or a birthday card, even a postcard? I am your mother, Paul. I haven't been perfect but I wasn't so bad. You remember when Henry killed that girl at the beach party? I had to borrow a lot of money to make sure Henry didn't end up in jail. There were lawyers. There was the family. Half that insurance money went to pay off the loan. The other half was supposed to be for you, but I gave it to Henry last year, when he told me the same story about the garage. That's it, Paul. I'm sorry. I'm cleaned out." By the time she finished she was crying. Then, before I could say anything, she hung up.

When I got back I left the car in the garage, then walked round to the front of the store. It was nine o'clock. A Monday night, but there was plenty of action on the street. The restaurant windows were full, heads bent over carafes of cheap wine. Taxis were double-parked in front of the tavern. On the sidewalk a man everyone called "the drummer"—I hadn't seen him since I came back—was bundled up in a ski jacket and toque, pounding out his rhythm on a full set of drums while passers-by stood around and clapped. A leather-jacketed skinhead pulled a bottle from beneath his pocket. He had hoops in both ears, a purple-dyed Mohawk fringe running from his forehead to his neck. He took a drink, rubbed his lips against his sleeve, then suddenly lit a match and held it to his mouth.

Flames leapt out of his mouth and throat. Someone yelled, "Encore", and he lifted the bottle again. But I didn't see what happened next because I had crossed the street and was walking quickly, trying to follow Nicko Ross who was by now almost a block ahead of me. One of Nicko Ross's big hands was spread out on the back of Judith's coat as he guided her along the sidewalk. Further proof of my own density, if needed: for the first time I connected the size of Nicko's fingers with the big smudge-marks I had once noticed on Judith's brandy snifters.

FIFTEEN

As soon as I got back to my room at the hotel I dialled her number. The line was busy. It was midnight. My stomach was in knots.

Judith. Henry was right. I couldn't shake her, couldn't keep away from her. I got dressed, put on Henry's old football jacket and the baseball cap Martha had given me. Outside the wind had picked up. I began walking quickly.

For more than a year I had tried to get Judith out of my system. But now I was back where I had started, standing outside Judith's apartment, looking up at her dark windows, ready to howl.

The rain was dripping from the remaining leaves of the beech tree. The grass I'd slept on the other night was now soaking wet. I kept looking about as if someone might pounce on me. I walked around the block. When I returned a light had been turned on at the back of the apartment. What might have been a shadow moved across the drawn living-room curtains. I felt in my pocket for the key. I held it in my hand as I walked around the block again. When I got back to her apartment all the lights were off again. I kept walking, dropped the key into a mailbox at the corner. The rain came down harder. I pulled the baseball cap farther forward. Only a few cars were on the streets—their lights threw long yellow reflections onto the wet pavement.

Closing time. People streaming onto the street, taxis clustering at tavern doors. I am moving along the sidewalk, almost in a trance. A group stumbles out from one of the taverns I used to go to. I'm caught up in their midst as they push out from the sidewalk into a waiting streetcar. Then I'm inside and the bright lights are shining on me, the soaked cuffs of my pants, my brother's too-small purple-and-gold satin jacket complete with athletic crests sewn onto the back and shoulders. The others keep talking. They have the kind of faces I often see in the bookstore: young, smooth, mobile and passive at the same time, the unmarked skin waiting to be stamped. The way my face used to be. They are laughing, slightly drunk, leaning eagerly towards each other, their eyes gleaming with the hilarity of it all as they reach out to touch each other, crowd close together. If I am watching them wistfully, staring almost indecently, they don't notice or care.

After two more stops I can't stand it any more. I ring the bell to get off, then stumble onto the wet street. The streetcar rumbles off into the darkness. Suddenly I've lost the thread. I look around. A few streetlamps shine on dark buildings still glistening from the rain. I feel cold and defeated. I keep looking at the buildings. There is something dark and sinister about the way their walls rise from the pavement.

"Excuse me." Another passenger from the streetcar. "Excuse me," he says again. He's carrying an umbrella and briefcase, wearing a fedora and a trenchcoat that is unbuttoned to show a triangle of white shirt.

"I'm sorry—"

"Paul Stevens," Leonard says. His deep voice cracks and he laughs. He takes my arm. "I knew it must be you." In the distance the rattle of a streetcar. The light changes. Rain on my face, in my eyes, the dark slippery pavement of the street. Leonard's got my arm and we're on our way, moving down the street, walking fast. He's telling me how one day he got sick of printer's ink and the class struggle and traded them for a job as a bicycle courier for a stockbroker. Then started doing his own buying and selling until he had enough money for a fancy suit and a job interview.

We stop in a doorway and he's explaining that now he's so deeply in debt that last week he had to sell his television set for money to get his shirts back from the dry-cleaners. We go around the corner and he says, "This is perfect." We climb an outdoor stairway to an apartment. No lights are visible. Leonard knocks and the door opens.

"A friend," Leonard says.

"Does he have a light?" This is a woman's voice, but deep, as though she was forcing it down to imitate Leonard's. Another woman giggles. I reach into the pocket of Henry's jacket, my fingers close around a package of matches. We're all a little huddle in the night kitchen. The flame shows their faces and I smell the wine on their breaths as I hold out the match. There's a tiny crackling as seeds explode. Then a whisper, "And if he's a cop?" "It's okay," Leonard says. "He's not. Ask him." "He's not," I say, taking my turn. Water is running down my neck as the smoke hits home. *Hey, little brother, what are you doing? You promised me, remember?* A car passes, tires tunnelling through the water, city sound tailing into a sudden gust of wind, spatter of rain against us. "What are we waiting for?" The door behind us closes.

"This way." The deep-voiced one leads me. She is holding my hand; her palm is so much smaller than her voice, and she keeps my hand as we sit on pillows in the room whose only light comes from a small electrified picture of a boat, a red-and-yellow yacht painted on glass and hung in a corner to peek through the leaves of a tropical plant. I'm hearing the blues, the same dippy melancholy tunes that have been going through my head ever since I got back to the city, and as the smoke hovers in my mouth, then wills itself into my lungs again I think how strange it is that I've been hearing this music in advance, hearing it the way I used to hear sirens, hearing it as though it's been in the air the whole time and I've been spending all this time homing in on it, not knowing I was, every step leading me closer so finally I would be here, with Leonard, kneeling between these two giggling women, rocking slowly back and forth, feeling the burn in my veins while the music I've been homing to runs through my bones. Now I see the piano, the woman who is playing it. She is swaying to the same rhythm as I am, her fingers dancing in the blackness, one hand reaching out for the joint Leonard is offering. The woman with the small fingers and the deep voice starts humming, just the perfect pitch to make the walls tremble; the floor feels as though it is suspended in nothingness, her fingers still holding tight to mine but I can't feel her skin any more; her flesh and mine have disappeared; it's just bone to bone, a hollow bony bridge her voice is crossing into me. I'm kneeling, my bowed head reaches the floor, the bone of my forehead against the hard wooden bones of this hard city place; the hard wooden bones of the city are mourning to the music and then I hear my own voice trying to detach itself from somewhere deep inside, my own puzzled voice trying to reach out through my bones, through the hard aching bones of the city.

I'm lying on the floor, face in my arms, crying. "What a drag," says the one who thought I was a cop, but the other replies, "No," and her small fingers are massaging my back and neck. I feel like such an idiot, and I can't imagine how I will ever get out of this thick feeling, this thick situation, this place the music has been leading me all this time, surely not just to lie on my face and make a fool of myself.

I struggle to my knees. Shake my head. Stand up. Piano notes are racing through the dark room. The doubtful one is talking, talking fast, turning the music into background for her incredible patter, freight trains of words. Three of us are standing. The doubtful one is on an incredible talking jag about the restructuring of brains or the whole world will collapse by the end of the century. Leonard is nodding enthusiastically. We are lost in a labyrinth of syntax but our smoke-crazed brains are holding the whole thing up. We are Atlas. Her words are melting together, I've lost track of everything, her voice is a dentist's drill boring deep into somewhere I want it out of. Then I'm on my way down again, down towards the floor, falling in a perfect faint that can't be interrupted, a nineteenth-century swoon. But when my body hits the floor I don't go unconscious—the exact opposite: the collision of my bones with the wood is like a bubble bursting and suddenly I am completely lucid, more lucid than I ever have been in my life, so lucid I can feel myself bouncing up again, like an acrobat, and even as they are leaning over me I've already regained my feet and am brushing off my clothes, deaf to everything except a certain total clarity that sends me walking towards the door, then into the clear rainy air of the night that I breathe in so deeply I can feel the drops of water on my tongue.

I go down the stairs. I turn the corner. I jump. Then I'm off, running through the sidestreets, houses with open windows, voices, music, long stretches of sleeping darkness.

SIXTEEN

T HE LIMOUSINES and taxis were lined up outside the hotel, but the lobby was empty. At the desk the night clerk gave me the key and two message slips. The elevator was open and waiting. There was something about the way the elevator sometimes stood there, its door open, pale light shining into the lobby. Like a tired mouth waiting for something to swallow.

I went inside, pressed the button for six. The doors slowly closed. I looked at the messages: both said simply, "Call Jeanine Stevens." Tonight was to have been the big climax: my triumphant return from our mother's, insurance money in hand. The plan had been that if I got home in time we'd have some sort of celebration.

The elevator featured an old-fashioned dial with a needle pointing to the number of the floor. At 4 it wavered, at 5 it stopped. The doors didn't open. A perfect place to end a futile day: stuck inside the Savoy Hotel elevator with a few crushed cigarette butts and two yellow message slips. I hit the button and kicked the doors at the same time. They started to open. I kicked them again and squeezed through. The doors were still banging together when Eileen came out into the corridor. She waved at me. Same room, same hall. "Hey, stranger," she said. When I came close she put her arms around me and kissed me on both cheeks. "I heard you were back. Hiding?"

"Working."

"Me too," she said. "Guess we're on different shifts."

She closed the door behind me. She was dressed, the cover had been pulled loosely over the bed, there were a couple of bottles on the dresser and an overflowing ashtray.

"You want a drink?"

I shook my head.

"Quit?"

"For a while. Just to see if I could."

"I know what you mean," she said. Then held out a pack of cigarettes. "At least you'll smoke. You always bummed my cigarettes."

"Thanks." I leaned forward to accept. "You're looking good."

"I feel like shit."

"Still working for the same guy?"

"He's in jail. I'm on my own."

I had another cigarette and went upstairs. My telephone was ringing as I opened the door. I wondered if Judith had seen me. Had seen the look on my face as I turned away from her. When the telephoned stopped, I unplugged it. Two a.m. and except for me, the Honeymoon Suite was empty and bare. I turned off the lights, undressed and got into bed. When I closed my eyes I saw rows of headlights sweeping towards me. As I slid into sleep I rolled into the pillow and it was almost as though Judith was beside me, and we were the way we used to be, so intoxicated with our youth and each other, drugged guardian angels listening to the city, watching over it in our dreams.

I was almost asleep. I was still falling asleep or I was crawling back towards consciousness. Then suddenly I was running to the window, looking down at the street to an ambulance whose blue light was sweeping in wide circles, siren wailing. The back doors of the ambulance were open, and while I watched a stretcher was wheeled into it. The light spun faster, the siren wailed louder, the ambulance sped away.

I dressed and rushed down to Eileen's room. But before I could knock I heard her muffled birdlike cries.

I went back to my room, lay down and closed my eyes. Imagined the hotel half a century ago, more, back in that prehistoric era when its windows were clean and its rooms filled with commercial travellers: men with heavy leather suitcases full of samples, men wearing thick woollen suits and suspenders over their starched shirts. But of course the Savoy Hotel would still have been itself. A purer, newer, version of itself. Its brick exterior a brighter grainier red, its place on the street not yet undermined by the surrounding oppression of giant office towers. But at heart, the same. For with their dark heavy suitcases, their journeys back and forth to the train station, the commercial travellers also would have been prey to the temptations of the night. There would have been all-night card games, taxis arriving with bootleg liquor, lonely wifeless travellers searching for an Eileen.

I had often thought of this hotel in its golden years. The solid men who marched out to their appointments in the mornings and back from their dinners of roast beef and potatoes in the evenings had been the Fenwicks of this world, strong capable types who knew when to close their eyes and on what exact fractions their profit margin depended.

The person who had been taken out of this hotel on a stretcher was more likely a Henry. A desperate gambler who'd come to make up his debts by playing in one of the all-night poker games that took place on the lower floors. A wayward husband blowing his blood vessels with the help of a few poppers.

It was six o'clock in the morning. The rumble of traffic was starting in the city and I could hear the bells from the big Catholic church around the corner. I checked to make sure the alarm was on, then was settling back to sleep when I heard the knocking at my door.

"Dungo. Dungo, are you there?"

I put on my pants and opened the door to let Henry in.

His fancy suit was wrinkled, his sparkling white shirt had lost its silk tie and looked as though he'd taken it swimming. The worst was his face. His face was hardly Henry any more. It had lost the glue that usually held it together. He looked wild, stricken, out of control.

"Dungo, I've been looking for you all night—"

"What's wrong?"

Henry let his head slump over to one side. "The money."

"I didn't get it."

Then Henry's face really did start to explode, a look of such total terror that I felt I was going to be torn apart. I told the only lie I could: "Not right away, I mean—Henry. It takes a few days."

"Christ, Dungo, never do that to me again."

"Sorry."

"I mean, Dungo, you know what you're doing to me. I've been waiting to hear from you—"

Henry's face had begun to reorganize itself. Not exactly into the Henry I knew, but into a slightly different version of Henry, an alternate Henry, a thicker-faced sullen Henry trying to hide his fear. The face of Henry that Nicko Ross must have been seeing. "How many days?"

"I don't know. There are details to work out. Could be as long as a week."

"I knew she'd come through."

He sank back into the armchair, pushed his hand through his hair, the way he used to, and when he looked at me again his face was easy and confident, the old Henry.

"You got a drink or something?"

I shook my head.

"Doesn't matter." He took out a cigarette. "I could kiss her. You too, little brother. Tell me everything. What did she say when you asked her for it?"

"She didn't want to talk about it."

"But then she agreed?"

I nodded.

"They're loaded. Look at those white Mercurys Captain Bill always drove. And the lottery—Christ, did I tell you they won some kind of lottery? They're probably worth millions. What did she do, just write you a cheque?"

"She didn't write me a cheque, Henry. She doesn't have that kind of money just like that. It's going to take a few days to arrange things. Everything will be ready in a week."

"A week?"

"That's the best I can do."

"I promised tomorrow." His face was beginning to fall apart again. "I'll call her up and see if—"

"Henry. You have to promise me not to call her. She was really angry. If you talk to her the whole thing's off."

"I can't even thank her?"

"Not a word. She was really upset."

"What did you tell her?"

"I told her your business was in trouble. That you needed an angel."

A little while later, Henry left. I washed and shaved, then went down to the coffee shop. A picture of the hotel was on the front page of the morning paper. Someone had been killed by a speeding car when he stepped off the sidewalk. The picture showed the hotel, the victim lying on the pavement under a blanket, the ambulance arriving. I was just about to leave the hotel for work when the desk clerk waved to me and handed me a thick letter. Standing in the lobby, I opened the envelope and started reading.

Dear Paul,

One of my professors once said to me, "I am a man of books, not letters." That is my situation, and one excuse for my having taken so long to write you this letter. Another excuse, one you may find less easy to forgive, is the reason that makes it necessary.

I have begun this letter thousands of times in my mind, and all of those beginnings were much more elegant than this stumbling one.

The fact is, Paul, I am a nineteenth-century man caught in a twentieth-century situation. Martha likes to stroke my whiskers and say how much I resemble my grandfather. In this she is wrong. My grandfather was born in 1862. A stonemason and an engineer, he built the kind of houses from which I have often rescued a few cartons of books. He would never have done anything like I do. He built from the ground up, aiming solidly and confidently towards the future. I am the future towards which he built, but instead of carrying on in that direction I have aimed myself towards the past. I have even failed to reproduce myself. The only son of an only son, I am often in the position of contemplating that with me our seed, as my grandfather called it, has gone barren and will soon be extinct.

But although Martha and I are without children, it is undoubtedly true that in a strange but understandable way the store has become our child. It is our joint creation, and I can only hope that it has given as much joy to the community it serves as that community has given to me.

In the same way, and here I enter that territory that has made this letter so difficult for me to write, you and Judith have been—I would not presume to say substitutes for children—but human beings towards whom I have felt some of those feelings a father feels.

I must also admit other feelings. When you first fell in love with Judith I considered you, with your troubled family history, to be particularly vulnerable. This was a subject I often brought up with Martha.

At this time, I should tell you, I was under treatment by a psychotherapist. I won't bore you with the details—I was suffering from a kind of depression that you needn't know about until you reach my age. The point is that because of this therapy—or perhaps this is only another excuse for another fault—my perceptions and emotions were particularly vivid.

I began to realize my real objection to your relationship with Judith was not that you might be endangered, but my jealousy. I, too, wanted to be young, attractive, involved with a beautiful and exciting young woman? Why not? Who would not prefer to have their life ahead rather than behind?

Just as I was understanding these feelings, you left Toronto.

Judith was devastated, almost inconsolable. Perhaps because of her vulnerable state we became friends. She told me the whole story of your relationship, of the role Nicko Ross and his girlfriend had played in your lives, of her own tragic involvement with drugs.

I began to see things differently. Speaking to Detective Ross I learned that almost the whole time you had worked here, you also had been under the influence of drugs. He detailed to me the lengths he had gone to attempt to save the two of you—and others—from the worst consequences of your habits. With you gone and Ross returned to regular police work, I became convinced that only I could save Judith from herself. I tried to win her over and gain her confidence. Then I arranged for her to see an excellent doctor. Every day she improved was a victory. It was several months before I realized that while telling myself I was helping Judith, I had actually fallen in love with her.

I confess all of this to explain what happened, and also, I will admit, because I don't believe my own recovery can be completed until I admit to others all the harm I have done them, and try to redress the damage.

By the time you returned to Toronto after your absence, I believed myself to have resolved my feelings about Judith, and to be able to continue with her in the normal employer-employee relationship. But the afternoon of your return, her delight in seeing you, your manifest eagerness to see her, led me back into my own dilemma. At the same time, I was aware, as never before, that you were a man of deep feeling, especially towards Judith. This made me more jealous than I had ever been. My jealousy persuaded me that I must act to save Judith from you, from being dragged back into the morass from which I had rescued her.

Once again I must ask you to excuse me, but each of us is occasionally condemned to expose our own fantastic universe to another.

On the night of your return to Toronto, I thought Judith had left the city for a research trip with Norman Swardlow. This was something I had been instrumental in arranging— surely by now I've said enough to explain my own unhappy motivations.

Of course I knew that after dinner you would attempt to get in touch with Judith. I decided this was the opportunity for me, once and for all, to break your liaison. Using a key Detective Ross had once given me, back in the days when we were concerned for Judith's safety, I went from our dinner to her apartment. My plan was to answer the telephone when you called and then, in this surprising situation, to inform you of her new alliance with Norman Swardlow—although I should now admit that I have no real details about the nature of their relationship. I felt only such a dramatic intervention could make you understand that your affair with Judith was over. Detective Ross had already persuaded me that should you ever return, drastic measures would be required to protect both of you from the weakness you brought out in each other. Imagine the scene from my point of view: you dialling Judith's number, ready for some sort of romantic confrontation, and hearing instead my voice at the other end of the line. The shock! The implications! The opportunity for me to say many of the things I've now finally written in this coward's way out. It would have been good for both of us.

But when the telephone began to ring, I lost my nerve. I decided to wait until you phoned again. Then I fell asleep. When I heard the door open I thought it must be Judith, inexplicably back. But when you began creeping around, I deduced the intruder must be some sort of drug dealer. Therefore, when the opportunity presented itself, I did what was necessary. Only when I carried the body outside did I realize it was you whom I had assaulted. You can imagine my guilt and shame when I saw how you showed up the next morning at the store.

For what I have done I can offer no excuse save the usual mixture of goodwill and malice. Forgive me for having to tell you this way. Yet I felt I must offer this explanation for what happened at Judith's apartment two weeks ago so that my actions, at least, will not have been an impediment to your and Judith's happiness, a happiness for which you now have my true support. I sincerely apologize for my doubts and mistakes. My best hopes—these last years I have learned to believe in hope—are with you. God bless—

James Fenwick

SEVENTEEN

M Y FIRST MORNING back in the city, walking up from the train station, the air had been filled with the bittersweet fragrance of leaves about to fall, the bittersweet golden light they made. Now the fragrance and the colour were gone, all that remained were a few last stubborn leaves still clinging to branches sheltered from the cold wind.

When I got to the store Judith was waiting outside, drinking coffee from a foam cup and reading the paper. We had long ago promised each other we would never live together, never allow our relationship to become one of husband and wife, one of habit. Committing ourselves to this non-commitment we'd been proud of ourselves, as though by doing so we'd escaped the major error of human existence and guaranteed ourselves eternal youth.

She looked up at me, smiled. "We have to talk tonight," she said. "Dinner?" I stood beside her. On the train I had promised myself I wouldn't go back to the store, wouldn't start up with Judith again. But I had gone back to the store. Needing her, offering myself. And with a single touch of her hand she had taken possession of me once more.

"How's the hostage drama?" That was what Judith had taken to calling Henry's saga.

"Fuck you," I said.

"Pardon?"

"I said, fuck you. Or to be exact, fuck you and your fucking Nicko Ross, your fucking James Fenwick, your fucking Norman Swardlow."

"Paul."

I shifted away from her.

"Paul, look at me."

On the patch of sidewalk at which I was staring was a bit of tinfoil, crumpled up, a few cigarette butts, various stains.

"Paul." She had come right in front of me, was holding her hand to my face again.

"Careful, you'll spill your coffee."

"All right," Judith said. "I'll spill it." She threw the cup, half full, out into the street. She was pressing herself against me, had her face in my neck. "Paul, I love you. Don't be an idiot. You've got everything wrong. I'm trying to help you, don't you understand?" Then she was kissing me. People were walking by, staring. "Paul, stop doing this to me." She was trembling and my neck was getting wet. She was crying. Then she looked up. Her eyes dark and bruised. Her lips full. She was looking at me, searching my face as though it was an opaque window behind which everything had to be seen in half-light, divined. I felt like that window. Opaque. Brittle. Begging to be shattered.

"Poor Paul," she said. "You don't know anything, do you?"

I heard Fenwick's keys rattle as he started to unlock the door.

"Nicko told me Henry's going to pay."

"He did?"

"And after that, it's all over."

"And how did you and Nicko get to be such buddies again?"

"Paul, don't be an idiot. I can't believe you would be jealous of Nicko. You know what an asshole he is."

"Thanks for telling me."

"Paul."

The bookstore door was open. Fenwick had already retreated into the back but Judith and I were still standing on the street. I turned away and started walking quickly.

The sky was dirty grey, the air cold. North of the city they were expecting snow, my mother had said. I wondered if she knew the truth about Henry. But my mother had long ago learned not to question. She had learned that you become responsible for everything you know. That's what had happened to me: I had found out about Henry's problem, now it was mine.

Sam was holding court with his cronies. They were telling each other their usual jokes and laughing. When he saw me Sam motioned me to join the crowd. I stood beside him for a moment, accepted his cigarette, the light from the flaming tit. Then, a few seconds later, without my even having to ask, Sam put his arm around my shoulder and led me outside. The street was jammed. Taxis, cars, buses, streetcars, trucks bulging with produce for the market.

"So?"

"So. You remember you said I could count on you?"

"How much do you need?"

I named a number. Sam took his arm off my shoulder and poked his face forwards, his long beaky nose like an arrow. "You crazy?"

"No."

Sam shook his head. "You still working at that bookstore?"

I nodded. "I can pay you back. It might take a few years. Henry would help."

"Look," Sam said. "What are you afraid of? You're afraid they're going to do something bad to him, right?"

"Right."

"You got this as some kind of horror scene where they carve up your brother and his family, right?"

Sam had put his arm around my shoulder again and was walking me down the street, away from his pool hall. "I know what your brother's mixed up in, Nicko Ross, all that shit. You think this is the first time? You think I haven't bailed him out before?" We had stopped in front of a car wash. As always, there was a Help Wanted sign in the window. "But this is ridiculous, my friend. This is beyond your means. It's beyond mine. You understand what I mean? And if I give you the money? Henry will be back for twice as much six months from now."

A black-and-yellow cab was coming out of the wash, its colours gleaming wet. The owner was standing and watching, a big paunchy pale-faced man with his hands in his pockets and a satisfied look on his face, as though he were just finishing a meal.

He turned and saw us, smiled at Sam. Sam pulled him over. "Hey."

"How you doing?"

"Got a question for you," Sam said. "Ever hear of Nicko Ross?"

"Give me a break."

"What would you do if you owed him?"

"Get out of town, Sam. You want a ride?"

Sam turned me around and started up the street again. "Get the picture?" A few steps later he stopped again. "Look, I know Henry's story. It's a crock. He's got to face up to what he's done. It won't be nice but it won't be so bad. After that he either goes straight or he fucks up. You know what I mean?" Sam used his free arm to wave at the panorama of our glorious skyline. "Nicko Ross isn't so bad. He's given a hand to a lot of people, take it from me. People you wouldn't believe. He even tried to do something for your brother. It's not just him, you know. Henry owes lots of people. Nicko's standing between. You think it's easy to be a cop here? You make judgement calls, right? You take sides."

We got back to the pool hall. Sam had his arm around my

shoulders the whole time. The way, I was thinking, he would on the day of my brother's funeral.

"Well?"

"I'm his brother," I said. "I take his side."

"Why doesn't he?"

"What?"

"Take his own side. Do something for himself. You want to know why? He can't. He's too much of a fuckup. And if someone's too fucked up to help himself, you can't do it for him."

"A little downtown wisdom from a guy who plays it safe."

"A little downtown wisdom," said Sam, "from a guy who's seen you crawl out from under your brother's ass and wants to see you keep what you've won."

"Thanks."

"I'll give you half. An hour's notice and you can have it in cash. Unmarked bills. Brown paper bag. The whole thing. Just like a dealer. Big man."

I was the person who had to do something for Henry because if I didn't he would take a drive to nowhere. I owed it to Henry. When our mother left and then our father died, Henry had been there for me. I had gotten away from Henry but I was still the person he had made me: Dungo Merde, the scared little brother backing away from that left jab until there was no more room to back away.

Now I was ready to move forward. But it seemed to me, after seeing Judith with Nicko Ross, after Fenwick's letter, after talking to Sam, that the terrain had shifted. At least my view of it. The problem was no longer a certain amount of money to be paid to a certain Nicko Ross. The problem was Nicko Ross himself. Sam. Judith. Fenwick. That whole part of the city that had gradually decided Henry was just a bum, someone who could be taken, someone to be bled until the time had come to discard him.

I didn't like what they had done to me. Nor did I like what they were doing to Henry. *My* brother. As though, in the end, we were nothing more than what we had been a few years ago, the Stevens brothers, two hapless teenage punks whose father, a cuckold and a drunk, had one morning keeled over in his jewellery store—except it turned out he had already sold it.

The big show at the bookstore. What was I supposed to think? That Judith had tried Nicko Ross and, despite his big muscles, found him wanting? That she had been interviewing him for an exciting television documentary that would advance her career? That he had been chasing after her without her knowledge or consent? That she had been trying to help with Henry?

To think I'd suspected poor Norman Swardlow when Fenwick was sitting in the back room, polishing his excuses, and the mighty Nicko Ross was pumping iron only a few blocks away.

Fenwick's letter in my pocket. I stopped at a coffee shop, went in and read it again. "Perhaps because of her vulnerable state we became friends…her own tragic involvement with drugs…I had actually fallen in love with her… These last years I have learned to believe in hope." Fenwick. Of all people I had never expected Fenwick to betray me.

When I came in the store was empty. Judith was standing behind the counter, leafing through a magazine.

Judith came out, stood in front of me, put her hand on my chest. "How are you doing with the money?"

"Not good."

"I have a plan."

"Tell me."

"Tonight, at the hotel."

I nodded. The hotel, of course. Ross, along with everyone else, had his set of keys to her apartment. And knowing Judith, her need to leave herself an open door, she would not have told him about the hotel: the Honeymoon Suite, Henry's little brother—we were her escape hatch. Her bank. Her palace of pleasure. Calculating Judith. Except that, like Henry, Judith was out of her league.

"The hotel," I said, then started on my way to the back room where Fenwick was waiting.

I have already said how much comfort I used to find in Fenwick's big doggy face, the thick old-fashioned sideburns that covered most of his cheeks, the sympathetic way his big brown doggy eyes had of lingering on you long after you'd finished speaking, so you felt he was not only listening to those words you'd managed to string together, but sounding something deeper, some part of your soul that outside of his presence you were too modest, too shy, too timid to acknowledge.

He leaned back in his chair, looking at me. "You got the letter."

I nodded.

"Good," Fenwick said. He was silent, he sighed, the silence resumed. This would be, everything indicated, a silence I could break in my fashion. He had spoken in his letter, now it was my turn. On the pine worktable was a package of Martha's cigarettes. I helped myself, then looked out the small barred window to the alley.

"Don't worry about it," I said. "I slept with Martha for years before I ever came here. She thought I was the reincarnation of General Eisenhower or something."

I turned to Fenwick. He was looking slightly puzzled. I could see him wondering why I had reacted in such an absurd way. There was a placid look on his face that I needed to disturb. "She had a studio in the building facing the Wing On Funeral Home. Number 826. She Scotch-taped a cut-out rose on her mailbox. In her room was a wicker chair you bought her for her birthday, a camp cot, a kettle that shot water across the stove when it boiled.

Her favourite writer was Flaubert. I did it all to save her from herself. Her tragic involvement with drugs."

Blood filled Fenwick's face. I had his attention. "You're joking," he said in a strangled voice. But his face had gone scarlet and I knew he believed me.

Martha came in the door. She looked at us, back and forth. Fenwick, his throat working, pointed at me. I pulled the letter from my pocket, handed it to Martha, then walked out into the alley, slamming the door behind me.

When I left Fenwick's that afternoon, I wanted to find Nicko Ross. Locating Nicko was not so hard. That is the essence of Nicko Ross: easy to find, difficult to avoid. For example, I saw Nicko Ross today. I went down to D Station on the pretext of arguing a parking ticket. There he was. Can you believe it? Our Nicko, back from the hard time of his ten-year exile from Toronto and sitting in his old office, looking pretty good. I may have turned bitter and prematurely middle-aged, but Nicko— the big banger—is smoother and shinier than ever. He's let his hair grow longer and he shines it up with grease the way New York cops do in the movies. He's still got those coat-stretching shoulders, but his belly has taken on a few thousand extra lunches. When I saw him he was leaning back in his chair, laughing into the telephone. Big white teeth. Mr. Clean.

It has even occurred to me that we have begun the long slow process of stalking each other again, tracking each other down. Of course the first time I didn't realize what was happening. He made the first moves before I even knew he existed. Hard to come back from a knockout in the first round.

This time, from the moment he came into the store, I began making my plans. I've even started working out again. There's a Korean gym in the west end Ross wouldn't know about. I skip rope, sweat away on the rowing machine, pound the body bag. I leave my gym bag in the trunk with the gardening tools. They look perfect, side by side.

That day, the day I gave Fenwick's letter to Martha, Nicko Ross wasn't at the station. I went back to the hotel to sleep for a while, then went to where I was sure to find him, in the weight room. Ross had positioned himself in front of the mirror. I was standing in the doorway, still wearing my streetclothes.

"You again?" He pushed me out of the weight room and onto the track. Below us an exercise class was going through the motions to a loud *Star Wars*–style soundtrack.

"I want to make an arrangement."

"I told you, little brother, this is none of your business." He raised his forearm casually, pushed me into the wall.

"Judith said you told her Henry was paying the money, that everything was—"

"You just don't understand, do you?" Then Nicko brought his fist up into my gut with one of those short little uppercuts Henry used to point out to me in the boxing highlights. I fell to my knees, gasping. By the time I got to my feet, Nicko Ross was back in the weight room, hoisting dumb-bells and watching me in the mirror. Spaceship music boomed through the gym. A circling runner looked at me curiously as I made my way out.

Judith was waiting at the hotel. When I opened the door, she was sitting in the armchair, a drink in one hand, a book in the other.

"Paul."

"Hi!" Eileen's voice came out of the bathroom. She was sitting cross-legged on the toilet seat, carefully painting her toenails.

"We have a plan," Judith said.

Of course she had arranged Eileen for protection. If Eileen had not been there I don't know what I would have done.

"Look," Judith said, "Martha told me everything that happened at the store. Paul, you're crazy. You've got everything wrong. Fenwick made a few crazy moves. So what? Are you some kind of saint?"

"What about Nicko Ross?"

"Look, we might think Nicko is an asshole, but Nicko likes us. In his way. He's just trying to scare you off. He doesn't want you between him and Henry."

"And what does Nicko have against Henry?"

Judith shook her head. "Henry and Nicko were into their little games together. Big guys in the big city. They liked to play and party. Henry got owing a lot of money. He also got to know Nicko's girlfriend. She thought Henry was pretty cute. They starting going to hotels together. Someone saw them and told Nicko. Nicko didn't like it. One morning down at Henry's garage he gave him the message. Henry sucker-punched him and Nicko went down in front of his friends."

"Let me get this straight. My brother went to bed with a cop's girlfriend, got caught, then hit the cop when he wasn't looking just to show what a big guy he is.

"And now, because of an afternoon in a hotel and Henry's idiocy, this cop threatens to kill my brother, my brother is terrified, his wife is terrified, and I am crawling on my hands and knees around the city trying to borrow money for a debt that can't be paid?"

"That's it."

"This is crazy. This is a joke. This is some kind of stupid farce."

"That's right," Judith said, "this is some kind of stupid farce. Now you're starting to understand. So let's take it one step further. Let's do something to Nicko." She pulled a leather suitcase onto the bed and took out a video camera. "Remember what Swardlow said? We are the faces of the future. We are the faces people trust." She pointed the camera at me and pressed the button. A whirring noise filled the room.

While Eileen painted her toenails, Judith gave me the basic instructions on how to operate Norman Swardlow's favourite toy. When she made her proposition I accepted it—because I had no choice, because I had nothing left to lose, because it made Eileen giggle, because everything had gone out of control and now my job was to ride the wave and look after Henry the best I could.

EIGHTEEN

The sun has gone down behind the office towers. It is a clear night, the kind of late fall night when frost first grips the edges of the city. For the moment there's still plenty of light in the sky, especially up on the sixth floor, where we are. Across the street, all but the late workers have gone home. From our room, unlit, we can see a man with his feet on the desk, white shirt undone, talking on the phone and looking lazily out at the skyline.

On the street the white stretch limousines are already in place, the pimps on the sidewalks smoking cigarettes, waiting for the action to begin.

Henry is restlessly pacing the room. "Can't even fucking smoke," as he says. The tape recorder is in the closet along with the portable drill Henry used to make a hole for the wire we've run from the closet, under the carpet to the bed. Tonight is to be the revenge of technology. The idea is that the beginnings of the encounter will be taped and that as the crucial moment approaches, Henry and I will be taking pictures. Then we will burst out of the closet. At this point I'll be wielding our big weapon, Norman Swardlow's video camera, whirring like a plague of locusts. Nicko Ross, caught with his pants down, will be so surprised, terrified, embarrassed at the thought of these

images getting out, that farce will overcome muscle and he will
agree to abandon his war against Henry.

That's the plan.

"I'm going out for a smoke," Henry says. "Let me know if
anything happens."

He closes the door behind him and I hear him walking
towards the stairwell. I'm thinking if it weren't for Jeanine he
might have turned into one of those pimps, and his life would
have been a lot simpler. Why do I think about Henry this way? I
ask myself, not for the first time. But it bothers me that I'm
judging him the same way as everyone else. "I'm on his side," I'd
said to Sam, but now I wonder if it's true. I look at my watch. It's
just after seven. They'll be in the restaurant now. We've come
here early because we figure Nicko won't want to drink too
much. I can hear my heart beating in the empty room. Jeanine
will be at home, feeding the boys. One day she and Henry will
look back on this night, laugh. Henry will set his toy soldier
cigarettes up on the table, three of them in the centre to repre-
sent Nicko, Judith and Eileen, two of them in the corner. That
will be us. The cigarettes in the corner. In the closet, if Henry has
his way.

The telephone rings. This is the prearranged signal. I fumble
the receiver. "It's me," Eileen says.

"You coming now?"

Eileen's sharp laugh. "You kidding? I'm just in the ladies.
Your friend is out there getting wrecked. Plus he's got the hots
for Judith. She's spending half her time with his hand clamped
between her knees."

"Great."

"I'm trying to figure out how to interest him, you know? Like
my guy says. Show some tit or breathe firewater."

"Good luck," I say. This report of Nicko feeling up Judith dis-
turbs me. "It's really great of you to be doing this," I say to Eileen.

"Don't thank me yet."

"Well, hang in there," I say, though I wish I could think of some whole alternative course of action.

"You too." Then: "Gotta go before he starts banging Judith or something."

Henry is letting himself back in as I hang up. Seeing me near the phone he bolts for the closet, holds the door open for me.

"False alarm," I say.

"Right."

"They're still eating dinner."

"Right."

Henry goes into the closet and comes out with something I'd entirely forgotten about, the old velvet Seagram's bag in which our father used to keep his nickle-plated revolver. One Sunday when he'd taken us with him to help clean the jewellery store, Henry had discovered it, pulling it out of the drawer beside the cash register. The bag was dark purple, Seagram's stitched in gold writing across the front.

And my father, seeing him, had carefully withdrawn an old-fashioned lady's revolver, nickel plated, studded with jewels, a bright little handful you might imagine in the palm of some Yukon lady gold-digger or an elegant Victorian dame taking a lonely late-night taxi ride in London.

"You going to threaten Nicko Ross with that?"

Even when we were children, with our own father's hand wrapped around it, we had been unable to take this weapon seriously.

"It was all I had," Henry said apologetically. He looked down at the gun, pushed his hand through his hair, and then when he looked up at me I saw something else I hadn't seen for a long time, the defeated face Henry sometimes had when he came home from school with his report cards. *Henry doesn't seem to pay attention. Henry should be doing better. We are trying to give*

Henry more individual help. Then my mother would give him that half-smile she had, the one reserved especially for Henry, her eldest son, the one that released Henry from his crimes. Crimes ranging from undone homework to a neighbour's window shot out with a pellet gun to turning his Ford into an accordion that night of the beach party, drunk, out on some concession road whose name he didn't even know.

Henry's vaguely shameful look, his eyes swinging back up towards mine. He put the gun in my hands. As though, in passing me this useless relic of my father's, he finally realized he had made me responsible for this entire affair. If the gun didn't work, if anything went wrong—so be it. His eyes would stay clear, his blond hair thick and tufted, his smile filled with certainty and hope. His house might be repossessed, his business destroyed, his life reduced to a shambles, but Henry would just shrug his shoulders and they would move to an apartment over an electronics shop, Jeanine would get a job, Jeremy would deliver papers, Henry would find a place that needed a man who knew how to smile, shake a hand, be polite to the customers.

Perhaps this isn't fair. Perhaps Henry really did care what happened to himself and those around him. But writing these words, I feel an anger that has not lessened, only grown more bitter, with time. But I also see now something I missed then. Henry, my older brother Henry; Henry with his boyish lick of hair and his ready smile. Henry even at his worst was still the Henry I admired, the Henry who had sand in his voice, tough gritty Henry.

I put the revolver back in the bag. Now that the responsibility was mine, Judith's plan seemed entirely ridiculous. If we were going to do it my way, there needed to be some quick changes or this absurd comedy would explode in our faces. First we were getting out of the Honeymoon Suite. Then we would go down to the lobby where we would intercept Judith, Eileen and Nicko

Ross. Cameras, some sort of scuffle in public, perhaps that would be enough to dissuade him. If not, given that Henry didn't seem to care what happened any more, we would get him out of town and hide him.

"Let's go," I said to Henry, and started to pull him towards the door. Then there was the sound of the key in the lock and we both ran into the closet.

Later Eileen explained to me that while she had been calling from the bathroom, Nicko had become so amorous he had decided to skip up to the hotel and "have dessert there". He'd hustled them out to the street and into a taxi. Well, he *had* wanted her for a long time, as Judith said.

"What a dump" were Nicko's first words.

"I know," Judith said. She had that smile she'd been wearing the night I was in this same place, watching her and Norman Swardlow.

"How can you stand it?"

"My father used to own it. I feel at home here."

Nicko was walking around, running his finger along the top of the desk and dresser to check for dust. To prevent him looking in the closet we had locked the door. The plan—when it was the plan we had somehow believed in—had included the idea that Nicko, if he checked the door and found it locked, would just think it led to an adjoining room.

"Your daddy's hotel? That's a good line. Anyone but a cop would probably believe it. The piece of scum who owns this place—if he knew I was here—"

Now he threw his overcoat and suit jacket onto the armchair. The muscles that had bulged in the gym seemed even larger beneath his white shirt. He was rubbing his hands together. From Henry, crouched behind me, I could smell the drinks he'd been sneaking while he was supposedly having a smoke.

Eileen turned on the radio. I recognized the station. It was the one she always used, syrupy slow dance music. "Let's have a drink," she said.

"A drink," Judith echoed. "Perfect."

She disappeared from sight to get glasses from the bathroom. Nicko had his back to them, was looking out the window. Henry tapped me on the shoulder, whispered, "Camera", and pushed it into my hand. Great, I thought, now we're playing doctor and I'm the one who's supposed to be doing the operation. I put the lens against the keyhole the way I'd practised. It gave me a perfect view of the bed, but no one was on it. I swung it slightly to one side. Nicko was still standing at the window, looking out. I took the picture. A barely audible click. I couldn't start the video recorder yet, it would make too much noise. Nicko Ross's white shirt and muscular butt were now immortalized. If it were a capital crime to be fully dressed looking out a hotel window, Nicko was dead.

"Let's dance," Judith said. She was back into sight with a glass for Nicko. It didn't look as if she'd wasted too much water on the Scotch, in his glass or hers either. He held out one arm, my Judith fitted against him, the music was slow. They started inching about the room. Nicko danced slowly, carefully, as though he had taken lessons.

"How do you like it?"

"Great," Judith said.

"We could have done this years ago."

"I like it better with Eileen here."

"Yeah, me too," Eileen said, and put her arms around Nicko's shoulders and clung to his back.

"Hey," he protested, but then put one arm back to squeeze her closer. The lens scraped against the keyhole. To me the sound was excruciatingly loud. Like fingernails scraping across a blackboard. Even now I can feel the way the back of my throat caught and I was so frightened I thought I would throw up.

Henry heard it too. "Gun," he whispered, pushing the velvet bag across the floor at me.

Eileen had her hands inside Nicko's shirt. He must have liked that because he turned back to smile at her. This time the click seemed louder. But Judith was undoing his tie. "Thanks," he said. Then suddenly his hands made a little motion and Judith's shirt tore open, buttons popping against the closet door. You could see the welts on her arm and shoulder.

"Don't be rough."

"You know me," he said. "Sometimes I'm just a little bit rough."

I hoped Henry had turned on the tape recorder. Sweat was running down my arms, pooling at the insides of my elbows, my belt.

"Me too," Judith replied. Then she added: "Fair's fair," and started pulling open Nicko's shirt while Eileen tugged it off from behind.

"If that's the way—" And he raised his hand to slap her. But Judith has come inside, is pushing up against his chest, and then, just as his arms start to surround her, Eileen pulls him back onto the bed, and while she sits on his chest Judith starts to tug off his trousers.

I'm on the second camera, clicking away, Judith finally has his trousers off and Eileen is sitting on top of him, starting her nocturnal chorus. I still haven't got a single shot of him naked. "You too," Nicko says, grabbing at Judith and pulling her onto the bed. "You said rough, did you?"

And that's when I pick up the video camera, unlock the door, leap out with the camera against my face while Judith and Eileen follow their part of the plan, rolling away to give me a clear shot of Nicko Ross, born-again Mr. Clean, naked in a hotel room with women not his wife. Well, almost naked. I jumped out too soon and, in fact, Nicko was still wearing his briefs. Also, it later turned out, I made a mistake loading the video camera so the evidence was blank. Of course I didn't know this at the time. "Got you," I say.

This is the moment Nicko Ross is supposed to panic, his house of cards collapse. Instead, he's off the bed like a thunderbolt. I barely have time to get the camera away from my face as his fingers reach my throat. I manage to dodge his knee to my groin, but can feel my windpipe starting to close. Then I hear a little pop, his grip loosens, I return the knee and push him away as Henry shoots a second time.

"Jesus Christ," says Nicko. I don't know where the first bullet hit him. The second has just grazed his side, leaving a small channel that now begins to fill with blood. He looks down at it, unbelieving, as though he's received a nasty bite. Then he steps towards Henry who drops the gun, comes out of the crouch jabbing, his fists bouncing like a child's off Nicko's face and chest. "Idiot." Nicko grabs Henry and throws him so hard into the wall that I hear the studs squeak.

"Fucking pervert," he says. He wipes the back of his hand across his face, then leans over to pick up his coat. Henry's face is screwed up, his eyes hardly visible with the effort he's making. He's trying to struggle to his feet, the game little guy determined to come back. But he's in the wrong movie. Mr. Clean isn't Mr. Clean after all. He's Nicko Ross and, as he says, he's a little bit rough. Now Nicko's got what he wanted from his coat. His hand swells, a big lump of dark metal glowing in the light. Judith shrinks back, her hands across her breasts. Eileen has started to cry.

"Fucking perverts," Nicko says again. Henry is exploding out of the crouch, towards Nicko. Nicko's face is calm, the flesh jelled in concentration. His lips are parted, the white tips of his teeth show, the way they did when he first touched Eileen. Then, still holding his gun, he grunts and lashes out with his foot. As he does he twists his body. Just like in the weight room, his leg extension is absolutely perfect, his heel a deadly twisting missile with all of Nicko Ross's weight behind it. Henry's head plays the part of the body bag. It snaps back, smashing into the door frame with a loud crunch of breaking bones.

Now Nicko is moving his fist back and forth, like a fan keeping the rest of us back. We shrink towards the walls as he dresses himself with his free hand. Henry is lying stone-still on the floor, on his back, his broken head twisted sideways, blood pouring onto the carpet.

Nicko, his clothes on, is at the door. "Fucking perverts," he announces one last time, then he slams the door behind him and we hear him running down the hall. Judith is kneeling beside Henry. Eileen is sobbing on the bed. I telephone an ambulance and open the window because I can no longer stand the smell of my brother's blood.

The police come and take their notes. Then we drive with them down to Henry's house. Jeanine is waiting for us in the living room. In the morning Judith says I should be the one to tell Fenwick and Martha. While she stays with Jeanine, I go to the bookstore. Martha is waiting for me inside and unlocks the door when I arrive. "It's in the news," she says.

She hands me the papers and I read all about it. Minimum details, almost no names given; just the name of the hotel and, of course, Henry's name. Jeanine's. The children. "Drug lord killed," the headline says. Why am I surprised? Like everything you read in the newspapers, nothing could be further from the truth.

Then I look up again at Martha. She takes off her sunglasses and I see that she's been crying. I say to Martha that I am sorry about what happened yesterday with the letter. "Everything comes down at once," she says.

I notice that the Closed sign is still facing the street and that

Martha has put the locks back in place. Then the door from the back room opens and Fenwick emerges. He is wearing his reading glasses, he is unshaven, his face looks rumpled and distraught. He stops a few feet away from me. One of the tables of new books he introduced during my absence is between us. "How are you?"

"Not so good."

Suddenly Fenwick has circled the table, put his arms around me, and the pain in my throat is so sharp— When I finally stand back I have managed my first tears. For a long time the three of us just look at each other. So much has changed. Then Fenwick asks, "What's Judith doing?"

"She's at Henry's house, with Jeanine and Jeremy."

"And your mother?"

"I called her this morning. I told her I'd come and pick her up this afternoon."

"You can use the wagon," Fenwick said.

I had another cup of coffee. Martha went out and got us all sandwiches. I ate. I kept saying that I should go get my mother. Finally Fenwick offered to go in my place.

"I don't know," I said. But I could no longer imagine driving. I just wanted to sit.

There were the kinds of silly complications that happen at such moments. I forgot the names of the highways as I was making the map and had to ask my mother directions when I called to tell her Fenwick was coming.

There were other phonecalls, an appointment to be made with the funeral home, another appointment for making an official statement to the police. I went out into the back alley with Fenwick while he opened the garage and prepared to leave.

We shook hands. Henry's death. The thick knot of betrayal finally loosened. "See you," he said. Then he gave me one of those sly, shy smiles.

NINETEEN

THIS TIME OF EVENING, this time of year. Outside my window the yellow leaves of a mountain ash tremble in the breeze. Below, a jumble of garbage cans, cars, our neighbour's cat taking its late-afternoon nap on the fire escape.

You will say I have grown sentimental. Sentimental, yes, and old. Maybe that is why I joke about the heartbreak of autumn. Maybe that is why I stop beneath this or that maple tree, leaves fiery in twilight, content to breathe the cool northern air sliding into the liquid light.

Yesterday, Wednesday, Meribel T. Simmons came into the store. The Wednesday afternoons were Martha's idea. From four until closing time we set out dishes of cookies and a couple of bottles of sherry in the back room. Those who know where to go wander back and help themselves to the refreshments. Sometimes volunteers bring extra bottles. On these occasions closing time is slow to arrive.

Then we all go to a restaurant down the street, a last surviving palace to revolutionary Hungarian cuisine that serves us heaping platters of breaded veal, home-fried potatoes cooked in army grease, big steins of draft beer.

Each time it is my duty to insist that Meribel come as my guest. "After all," I say, "with what we're making from your books, the least I can do is offer you a drink." She alone is allowed to deviate from the menu. In the interests of preserving herself as a national treasure of poetry, she has to substitute salad for the potatoes, and to accompany her food with bottles of the beer made by the company that sponsors the prize she won last year for her latest book: *Meribel T. Simmons: The Collected Poems.* A big prize, we thought, even if visitors from out of town sometimes think she is dead.

Yesterday, Meribel took her customary place as the cultural jewel of our Wednesday-afternoon celebrations. Her new status does not prevent her from stock-checking. *Meribel T. Simmons: The Collected Poems* seldom appears in the poetry section, although most of our city's literary critics brought in their review copies, some of them personally inscribed by Meribel at the launch party that took place at our store.

"People are really hanging on to those books," she told me yesterday.

"I should imagine so." For example, unknown to Meribel, I have many of them stockpiled in our apartment.

"You think it means they haven't read them? I never bring you a book before I've read it."

"You never know."

"It's amazing the others keep selling. You'd think people would realize that instead of buying them in bits and pieces, they could get the new book and have them all."

"The public is a strange, sleepy beast. But once roused—"

The fact is that since the prize her books *have* been selling. At least in a slow trickle. But fame has its riptide. Seeing her picture in the paper must have inspired those who did have her books to search them out on their shelves. And having found them, bring them to me.

Yesterday, as I was standing with Meribel and she was glancing at her watch to see if it was four o'clock yet, a customer came in with a carton of books. She had no sooner placed it on the counter and opened it than Meribel had her nose inside. She plucked out a copy of *Little Men*. This book, my favourite, is made up of poems dedicated to intimate descriptions of those very lovers to whom her various previous books were inscribed.

"Look at this," Meribel said, turning the book over so we could see the youthful photograph of her on the back jacket. She was wearing a low-cut dress that seemed to be the main point of the picture.

"Sex addict," said the customer.

"You should try it," Meribel said. Meribel, with her prize and now her reading tour, can no longer be squelched.

Later I said to Meribel: "You shouldn't have been so hard on that customer. The next time she gets one of your books, she'll probably deface it."

"People like that," Meribel said. "You have to understand them."

For me, such understanding is impossible.

I am a cynic in some things, but can never really believe one person would intentionally harm another. And so the hearts of others are inscrutable to me. To me they seem no more than stones, despite the words of doctors and poets.

And yet here I am soft-hearted myself. Looking into the autumn twilight, reliving the anniversary of Henry's death. Soon Judith will come home. As always, when she arrives, we will sit in our living room, the curtains open, having a drink and listening to the last of the rush-hour traffic.

Eventually we will grow hungry. Some evenings I cook, but mostly we go out to dinner. There are a few restaurants we know, places we go with friends who, like ourselves, are without children. To them, to the people who see us strolling along the street, Judith and I must seem familiar and comfortable.

After a few drinks Judith always slips her arm through my own. The younger staff at the store, clerks the same age I was when I came, look up to us. We seem solid where they are frail. We have crossed the bridge from youth to middle age and now it must seem to them that we were always this way, well-off, sure of ourselves, predictable and secure.

Behind the counter hangs a picture: Judith, Martha and I standing outside the store on the occasion of its fifteenth anniversary.

Fenwick, of course, was not there. The morning he set out to pick up my mother, he never arrived. Instead, he arranged for a taxi to deliver her to Henry's house. Later that evening he telephoned Martha to say he had decided to go away for a while "to think things over". During the following weeks he would occasionally call the store, speaking to Judith, Martha or myself with great concern and courtesy. A few months later Martha went to visit him in Vancouver, where he was working with an antiquarian dealer befriended years before.

Before she returned she called to ask Judith and me to meet her at the airport. We drove out in the new car Martha had bought for the store, a sporty little import useless for carrying books and which Martha kept in the garage where the wagon used to be. We were expecting the worst. But when Martha emerged from behind the frosted glass doors she turned towards us, smiled, tossed back her hair—for the first time in years she looked like the Martha I used to know, the Martha I'd wanted back, the professor's wife who'd saved me from the bad coffee at the General's bookstore.

We climbed in the car. It was a spring evening, full of the smell of new grass and budding leaves. "The restaurant," she ordered.

When we were installed at our usual seats, plaster angels looking down on us, Martha told us her plan. Against a small payment, Fenwick had given her his half of the bookstore. The next week she would have the ownership re-made, to be shared equally among herself, Judith and me. When Judith and I started raising questions, Martha ordered another bottle of wine.

When we left the restaurant, we were drunk. In the old days, Fenwick and Martha would have swept away in a taxi and Judith and I would have gone to the Honeymoon Suite. Somewhere in the city Henry and Nicko would have been hustling each other.

Now Fenwick was in Vancouver, Henry was dead and, for his part in the fiasco, Nicko had been transferred to another police force. We stood uncertainly in front of the restaurant, as though all of us were thinking about this strange depopulation. "Come to my place," Martha commanded. Since Henry's death, the three of us had hardly talked—just carried on automatically, not daring to look ahead.

In the old days, the occasional time we had gone to the Fenwicks' house, it had been in the image of the bookstore—dark, dusty, the living room filled with antiquarian volumes stored in bookcases with smoked-glass doors to keep the pages from deteriorating in the light.

Now we discovered Martha had been busy. The bookcases were gone and the walls painted white. The windows had bright new curtains and you could sit on the chairs without causing dust storms.

By the time the sun rose a new harmonious order had been established. Martha, as always, had made everything possible.

It is now years since I have spoken to Fenwick. The last occasion was when he opened a bookstore on a small tourist island, off the coast. Since then he has moved to New Mexico, started another store and is said to be healthy and prosperous. I often imagine myself going to visit him. It will be winter. I will arrive in a car, park outside the store. The sky will be blue, and when I walk into the store Fenwick will look up at me in welcome, his fingers hooked into his belt, his hair thinner and grey, his side-burns and moustache a fine-spun silver illuminated by the desert light.

The screen glows. The fan whirs.

I am wearing Henry's old jacket, as I always do for these memoirs, confessions, whatever. His old athletic crests are in place. In one pocket is an empty cigarette pack. Another has a half-used book of matches. Sometimes I put on one of his hats. I am wearing the clothes of the dead man. I am remembering Henry, in my way. Riding one of those time-lines that must have exploded out from him the moment that he died. Later, when I finish this, I'll take off Henry's jacket and put on my own coat. Most weeknights Nicko Ross still ends up at that Italian café where I saw him playing pool with Henry years ago. He parks his black Pontiac in the back. He has a few drinks and a few laughs. Then, before midnight, he comes out to his car again. We have an appointment but he doesn't know it.

In my coat is something from Leonard. Leonard gave up stock-broking years ago. Now he runs a little restaurant where his wife makes salads and other kinds of healthy food for lunch and early dinner. Some evenings Leonard gives yoga lessons and learned discourses on his favourite mystical texts. He wears his hair in a pony-tail again. The other evenings he goes to AA meetings.

When I told Leonard that Nicko Ross was back in town, his reaction was to offer me a gun. Not a toy, like my father's, but a heavy pistol that tugs awkwardly at the pocket of my coat.

In the end I got my chance for revenge. Nicko Ross and I stood facing each other in the dark.

"Do your worst," Nicko Ross said. He grinned. Dragging down my pocket was the gun Leonard had given me. My hand was already around it. Nothing to stop me pointing it at Nicko Ross and pulling the trigger.

"Go ahead. You got me out here. You must have wanted something."

Despite the cold, his overcoat was open. He had his hands on his hips and his white shirt bellied out into the night.

I tried to imagine Henry's ghost here in the darkness watching us. Henry's ghost leaping onto Nicko Ross's back and shouting *fuckface* as he pummelled him to the ground.

"So?" Nicko reached out and grabbed my coat. Then something amazing happened. As though Henry's ghost did have one last trick to play. When I went to brush Nicko away, he somehow lost his footing and stumbled. He fell into a parked car but couldn't keep himself from going down. I could almost hear Henry's wild laugh. The way he'd laughed that night he hid in the front seat while I searched for him in the water. The way he laughed after football games when he, the tiny unstoppable dynamo, had squirted from the arms of his lumbering pursuers.

Nicko Ross was lying helplessly in the mud. For this occasion I'd put on the heavy shoes I wear for working on Henry's grave in the fall and spring. Now those shoes were only the length of a kick away from Nicko's face and head.

"Shit," Nicko said. Then: "Now's your chance. You got me."

"You're right," I said, my hand still on the gun. But I knew I wasn't going to use it.

"What are you waiting for? You know your brother was an asshole and would have got himself killed anyway, but you've spent the last ten years blaming me."

I stepped back. Nicko struggled to his feet. He brushed the mud from his coat and pants. Then he came up to me and put his hand to my coat again. This time I didn't move. This time he didn't stumble. We breathed at each other in the dark, then Nicko dropped his hand and turned towards the café.

When he was out of my sight, I started home. A few teenagers in their costumes were still roaming the streets, and even now as I type, I can hear the last echos of Hallowe'en, garbage cans being kicked into the street, shouts of laughter.

What Henry was and is to me, I still do not know. Meanwhile I am willing to believe anything. I am even willing to believe that the night which is coming is only an ordinary night, a night like other nights, a night to be followed by days like other days. A day during which the entire universe could hinge on a cough, a sigh, a book opened at a random page, the first person who walks through the door.